CRIME IN LEPERS' HOLLOW

AN INSPECTOR LITTLEJOHN MYSTERY

GEORGE BELLAIRS

AGORA BOOKS

ABOUT THE AUTHOR

George Bellairs was the pseudonym of Harold Blundell (1902-1982). He was, by day, a Manchester bank manager with close connections to the University of Manchester. He is often referred to as the English Simenon, as his detective stories combine wicked crimes and classic police procedurals, set in quaint villages.

He was born in Lancashire and married Gladys Mabel Roberts in 1930. He was a devoted Francophile and travelled there frequently, writing for English newspapers and magazines and weaving French towns into his fiction.

Bellairs' first mystery, Littlejohn on Leave (1941), introduced his series detective, Detective Inspector Thomas Littlejohn. Full of scandal and intrigue, the series peeks inside small towns in the mid twentieth century and Littlejohn is injected with humour, intelligence and compassion.

He died on the Isle of Man in April 1982 just before his eightieth birthday.

ALSO BY GEORGE BELLAIRS

Littlejohn on Leave
The Four Unfaithful Servants
Death of a Busybody
The Dead Shall be Raised
Turmoil in Zion
The Murder of a Quack
He'd Rather be Dead
Calamity at Harwood
Death in the Night Watches
The Crime at Halfpenny Bridge
The Case of the Scared Rabbits
Death on the Last Train
The Case of the Seven Whistlers
The Case of the Famished Parson
Outrage on Gallows Hill
The Case of the Demented Spiv
Death Brings in the New Year
Dead March for Penelope Blow
Death in Dark Glasses
Crime in Lepers' Hollow
A Knife for Harry Dodd
Half-Mast for the Deemster
The Cursing Stones Murder
Death in Room Five
Death Treads Softly

Death Drops the Pilot

Death in High Provence

Death Sends for the Doctor

Corpse at the Carnival

Murder Makes Mistakes

Bones in the Wilderness

Toll the Bell for Murder

Corpses in Enderby

Death in the Fearful Night

Death in Despair

Death of a Tin God

The Body in the Dumb River

Death Before Breakfast

The Tormentors

Death in the Wasteland

Surfeit of Suspects

Death of a Shadow

Death Spins the Wheel

Intruder in the Dark

Strangers Among the Dead

Death in Desolation

Single Ticket to Death

Fatal Alibi

Murder Gone Mad

Tycoon's Deathbed

The Night They Killed Joss Varran

Pomeroy, Deceased

Murder Adrift

Devious Murder

Fear Round About

Close All Roads to Sospel

The Downhill Ride of Leeman Popple

An Old Man Dies

Crime in Lepers' Hollow

GEORGE BELLAIRS

This edition published in 2019 by Agora Books

First published in 1952 in Great Britain by John Gifford

Agora Books is a division of Peters Fraser + Dunlop Ltd

55 New Oxford Street, London WC1A 1BS

To the sweet memory of Goofy, our bobtail sheepdog

I will not think those good brown eyes
Have spent their light of truth so soon;
But in some canine Paradise
Your wraith, I know, rebukes the moon,
And quarters every plain and hill,
Seeking its master... As for me,
This prayer at least the gods fulfil:
That when I pass the flood, and see
Old Charon by the Stygian coast
Take toll of all the shades that land,
Your little, faithful, barking ghost
May leap to lick my phantom hand.

— *ST. JOHN LUCAS*

(By courteous permission of Constable & Co)

"For the common people, when they hear that some frightful thing has befallen such a one in such a place, are of opinion that that place is haunted with some foul fiend or evil spirit; when, alas! it is for the fruit of their own doing that such things do befall them there."

— JOHN BUNYAN

1

DEATH AT CHRISTMAS

On the moors above Tilsey, several gentlemen from the town had gathered for Colonel Bulshaw's Christmas shoot. There were still a few days to go before the Feast itself, but the gathering always bore that title. Grouse do not come amiss in the larder after a surfeit of turkey, and game was plentiful that year. Beaters were busy putting up the birds, the sportsmen strode banging away with their guns over the thick heather and bilberry, and Colonel Bulshaw himself, too portly to walk far, was being driven about in a jeep, greatly to the good of his liver. He blazed away with his guns and his tongue and blamed his driver for his bad shots.

On the extreme edge of the ragged file of hunters, Nicholas Crake, Recorder of Tilsey, was pursuing an erratic course. He looked far from well; and no wonder. Overwork, family worries, and, to crown all, a day on the moors in pouring rain were telling on his constitution. He was a medium-built, sturdy man, with a clean-shaven, legal face, large Roman nose and square determined chin. He wore a raincoat, leggings and a tweed cap and, in spite of the weather, had loosened his coat and pushed back his headgear, for his breath was coming with difficulty and he felt to have a temperature. By his side walked Murphy, his loader, dressed like a scarecrow and wet to the skin. Murphy never sought protection against the elements and seemed none the worse for it. Crake brought down two birds with a single shot and then handed his gun to Murphy.

"I think I'll pack up," he said.

Murphy opened the breach of the 12-bore and ejected the spent cartridge. Then he looked at Crake.

"You don't look so good, sir… What about a nip o' brandy?"

He paused and looked again at his companion. Crake's eyes were glassy and bore in them no signs of recognition or even intelligence.

"The court is adjourned for lunch…"

Murphy sniggered dutifully, thinking the judge was just having his little joke.

"We 'ad lunch two hours since, sir…"

"Adjourn…"

And with that, Crake collapsed in the heather.

Murphy's eyes popped. He passed his grubby hand over his face and wiped away the rain. Then he looked along the line of shooters and singled out the tall, bulky form of Dr Bastable, heavily treading the turf and bringing down a bird with every shot.

"Just a minute, yer honour… Jest a minute," said Murphy politely to the prostrate form, and he set off and ran for help, bounding over the undergrowth like a gaunt jack-in-the-box.

"Somethin's up with Judge Crake," he said when he reached Bastable. He dodged the wet barrels of the doctor's gun.

"Eh?"

The rain streamed down the doctor's livid, chubby face and off the tip of his rounded chin. He was clothed from head to foot in oilskins and looked like the coxswain of a lifeboat.

"Judge Crake…'e's fell unconscious…"

Bastable floundered along by Murphy's side to where the body was lying. On the way, he fished out from beneath his strange garments a stethoscope and a thermometer in a shiny case. It looked as if he expected a professional consultation wherever he went and wasn't going to be caught without his outfit. He knelt with difficulty beside the prostrate judge.

"Get him home at once. Where's his car?" he said, as he laboriously elevated himself to his feet.

Crake suddenly opened one eye, like a child cheating at a game of hide-and-seek.

"Take me to my sister's," he wheezed, and collapsed back on the heather.

Murphy and the doctor eyed one another owlishly. Considering the wife he'd got, it wasn't surprising that Crake preferred to trust himself to his sister in an emergency. Murphy shambled across the moor back to where Crake's brother-in-law, Arthur Kent, was banging away at birds, oblivious of the drama going on not far away behind the curtain of stinging rain. On hearing the news, Kent, long, thin, nervy and morose, crossed the heather with quick strides and joined Bastable.

An hour later, Crake was in bed in his sister's spare room at St Mark's, the Kents' home. He was down with pneumonia. There was a glowing fire in the grate and his sister was attending to him with steady, capable hands. She was a small, fair woman of forty, or thereabouts, and had been a local beauty in her heyday. Now she had a slightly faded look. Her hair was touched with grey, there were shadows under her blue eyes and her generous mouth wore a sardonic twist. Living with Kent for twenty years had damped her spirits and embittered her. The faults were on both sides. Her affection for her brother, Nicholas, had always driven Kent to take second place in her life and he resented it. On the other hand, Kent, a successful lawyer in Tilsey, was temperamentally as dry as a stick and as cold as ice. How this incompatible pair ever came to wed was a local mystery.

Outside, the rain still pelted down from a leaden sky. The

wind seized the tall trees which ringed the house and tortured them like a giant trying to shake off the water as it fell. Crake was asleep, breathing harshly and muttering now and then to himself. Beatrice Kent kissed her brother's damp forehead, clenched her hands until the nails bit into their palms and stood looking through the window on the scene of desolation around. Downstairs, Kent was seeing off the doctor.

"He'll be all right… Pneumonia… Careful nursing, yer know…"

Bastable breathed a blast of parting whisky in Kent's face, crouched under a large coloured golf umbrella and dived through the rain to his car. He held it in low gear as he coaxed it down the waterlogged lane which led from St Mark's to the main road. The water in the ruts swished noisily from the wheels in great wet fans which washed the hedges. As Bastable turned into the highway a small sports car, driven at great speed, shot past him into the side-road. He had to swerve to avoid it.

"The bitch!" he muttered round his cigarette and broke into paroxysms of smoker's cough.

It was Dulcie Crake, careering to take charge of her husband. She didn't even ring the bell of St Mark's. She drove her car at top speed through the gateway and down the drive, stopped it with a squeal of tortured brakes, flung open the front door and rushed inside. There was nobody in the hall.

"Anyone about?" shouted Dulcie in a voice which sounded hurt that no reception had been prepared for her.

She was a handsome, tall, well-built woman. Had she been fair instead of dark, she would have resembled a Wagnerian goddess. But she was half Spanish. Her father, British consul in a city of Spain — in days gone by the family liked to describe him as a diplomat! — had married the daughter of an impoverished grandee. Dulcie had inherited her mother's features; fine high-bridged nose with flaring nostrils; broad, low forehead; blue-black hair; gleaming, regular teeth; and delicate olive complexion.

Histrionic and overdone though it was, the nurse's uniform Dulcie wore set off her personal beauty, unspoiled in her early forties. She had done some voluntary work in a hospital during the war, and, intent on supervising at her husband's bedside, she had dressed the part. She always did; it was often inappropriate, but it always suited her appearance.

"I'm in here. Nick's in the spare room. He asked to be brought here..."

Kent answered her from his chair in the dining room. He was lolling there, finishing his whisky. He rose slowly and came into the hall. When the pair of them met, the atmosphere changed and grew charged with tense emotion.

"H'm... Dressed like a proper little nurse... Really, Dulcie, you're the ruddy limit..."

"Arthur!"

She drew herself close to him, as if expecting him to take her in his arms.

"Stop it! Beatrice is about...and Nick's sick. There's a time and place for everything. Besides, I told you..."

The door on the landing above opened and Beatrice stood there looking at the pair of them over the balusters. She drew her breath sharply. Whether it was Dulcie's dress or her closeness to her husband, nobody knew. She descended quickly.

"Why did they bring Nick here?" asked Dulcie by way of greeting. She hated Beatrice, resenting the bond which held her and Nick so closely.

"He asked for it..."

Dulcie mounted the stairs and rustled into the spare room, mentally chalking up another point against Nicholas and Beatrice. Below, Beatrice faced her husband.

"Really! I saw the pair of you. Arthur... And Nick gravely ill in the house. To say nothing of me..."

Kent made as if to take hold of his wife.

"She's nothing to me, Bee. I told you before. She doesn't mean a thing to me. She's that way with any man she comes across. How Nick puts up with it..."

"I don't want to discuss it any more... I saw you both and that's enough..."

"Can't we...can't you and I...?"

"I have the hot bottles to fill..."

"I'll help..."

He was eager to justify himself and followed her, like a lapdog, into the kitchen.

"We've gone over it all before. It's no use, Arthur..."

She filled a kettle and switched on the current.

Kent made as if to plead again, then shrugged his shoulders and left the room.

Beatrice Kent looked wearily round the kitchen as she waited for the water. Margery, the maid, had gone to her sister's with presents for the children's Christmas. There was holly draped over the picture of Queen Victoria which hung on the wall and a bunch of mistletoe rotated over the outer door, an invitation from Margery to the milkman, on whom she had designs. Beatrice remembered that she had forgotten to buy-in the Christmas decorations. She had no heart for it. The Christmas spirit between her and Arthur was spurious and put on to deceive Margery and the Thompsons, with whom they usually had dinner at The Bull, in Tilsey, on Christmas Day. They wore paper caps and flung streamers about like the rest, but her own heart was in the past, with Nicholas at their old home at Christmas gone by.

The kettle began to bubble, and she finished her task. Dulcie was removing a clinical thermometer from Nick's mouth when his sister entered.

"Dr Bastable's done all that, Dulcie. His temperature's a hundred and three..."

"Bastable's a drunken fool! That's why I came to look after things. Nursing's vital in pneumonia. If Nick doesn't improve, I shall call in Archer..."

Beatrice noticed the acid, purring tones of her sister-in-law. Her anger rose.

"And why has Nick suddenly become so important to you, Dulcie? You've neglected him and made him miserable for years with your silly affairs. If you hadn't worried him so, he'd never have fallen a victim to this..."

"I don't care what you think. Nick's very dear to me. He's the father of my children. You won't understand such a bond, Beatrice, will you?"

Beatrice bit her lip.

"...Which reminds me; I ought to get the children home. They *would* be away for Christmas, just when I need them most. Alec's in Paris and Nita's in London with the Mackenzies... I'll have to phone some telegrams to them when I've fixed up Nick. By the way, I shall want a bed made up here in the room. I won't leave him till the crisis is over..."

Beatrice smiled. It was like a third-rate melodrama. The errant wife repenting at the bedside of the sick husband. "Yes; there's a camp bed in the attic..."

"A camp bed? I couldn't..."

"That's all we've got. Unless you want a bed making up on the floor..."

"Very well. But you might be a bit more sympathetic at a time like this. I've always wanted to be your friend, Beatrice..."

"Treat Nick better then, if you want my regard..."

Dusk had fallen, and Beatrice put on the lights and drew the curtains. The rain was abating under the strength of the wind which caught and bellied the material.

"I've fastened the casement. The little window at the top will provide enough air. Have you had any food, Dulcie?"

Dulcie pouted and tried to look like a martyr.

"I never gave it a thought and I'm not hungry."

"Don't be silly! I'll send you up a tray when Margery gets in.

She's due any time. Unless you want to have a meal with me and Arthur..."

She said it diffidently. When Arthur and Dulcie got together, she felt quite out of the picture. They'd thought she never noticed anything, but she'd long been aware that her husband was completely fascinated by his sister-in-law. Whenever she saw them together, she watched Arthur following Dulcie with his eyes, gobbling her up with them, eager to please her and flatter her. And Dulcie parading her charms, impudently and shamelessly, like a nasty, purring she-cat. Then, Arthur had cooled off. No wonder! He was fundamentally respectable, and he had a well-established position in the town. A churchwarden and prominent freemason. It wouldn't do for his name to be mixed up with that of another woman, especially his sister-in-law. Arthur had retreated. But not, it seemed to Beatrice, before something intimate, maybe a furtive, unstable affair, had gone on between him and Dulcie. Beatrice had sensed it in Dulcie's conduct. That feline, possessive way she had at one time developed when Arthur showed himself. Now, Arthur was trying rather pathetically to extricate himself, unsuccessfully attempting to wheedle his way back into Beatrice's affections, avoiding Dulcie and thereby seemingly adding fuel to her flame.

"I'd rather stay with Nick. He'll need me if he wakes..."

The barbed shaft fell without making the least impression on Beatrice. She knew just how she and Nick stood. They had become estranged when they married. Nick never thought much of Arthur, whose parsimony and narrowness he despised. He'd never been good enough for Bee. And Nick's brief infatuation and whirlwind wooing and wedding of Dulcie had left her stupefied. In fact, when Arthur proposed shortly after Nick's wedding, Beatrice had said Yes almost without thinking what it implied. Anything to get away from the home so forlorn and cold after Nick had gone. Now, Dulcie and Arthur between them had forged the old bond between brother and sister stronger than ever.

Dulcie was eyeing Beatrice curiously. She was wondering what Arthur ever found in her. A mouse! A small-town girl. All right, of course, for Nick, the pipe-and-slipper man, the dog-lover, the simple-Simon. But Arthur... Educated, sophisticated, ambitious, travelled and hiding a passionate nature behind his legal mask... How could Beatrice...?

"I'll send up the tray then..."

Nick's temperature was down, and he was sleeping quietly at bedtime. Bastable's medicine was acting already and the patient had responded well to treatment. Beatrice was almost ready to scream with nerves. Bad enough to have her only brother sick on her hands without Dulcie fussing. They'd made up the bed and then all Dulcie's fantastic preparations for the night had to be faced. About a dozen telephone calls to start with. Everybody had to know that Nick was ill, and his wife stricken and watching by his bedside. Then, of course, Dulcie had brought no things for the night. And she could never rest in the borrowed attire which Beatrice offered her. Nothing would do but that Arthur should go to the Crake home and bring them. At first, Dulcie had suggested going with Arthur in the car. Arthur had then trumped up the excuse that he'd another call to make. He could pick them up, but it would be awkward for Dulcie waiting whilst he did his business. Arthur, who only a week or two since had been making any excuse to get Dulcie to himself, was now backing down! It ended by more telephoning to the Crake maid to pack a bag with dozens of things including a mass of cosmetics and medicaments.

Finally, they settled Nick comfortably and left Dulcie getting ready for bed. She had selected four books to read on her vigil; she said she wouldn't sleep, of course. It was midnight before the house was settled and all Dulcie's fussing ended. The Crake children: Alec, aged twenty-five, pursuing doubtful and prolonged studies with a view to becoming an architect when he was ready, and Nita, nice little Nita, just turned twenty-one, her father's girl, training as a nurse in a London hospital. Nita was coming post-haste on the midnight; Alec had sounded peevish at the idea of leaving Paris behind at Christmas. Of course, Dulcie had telephoned all the way to Paris and her beloved Alec!

As his affair with Dulcie had developed, Arthur had shown an increasing inclination to sleep by himself. Beatrice had raised no objection, but now that he was making overtures to get back to his old bed, she resisted it. He could stay where he was in the second-best room. His precise, fussy way of dressing and undressing, his parading about with tooth brushes and bottles of gargle, his morning exercises, his alternating bouts of sulking and amorousness, his noisy yawning when he woke in the morning and the way he pounded his pillow before sleep had long got on her nerves. She did not propose to suffer them anymore. Tonight, he had renewed his request on the excuse that they might be needed in the night for Nick. She quietly declined and retired, locking her door. She had no particular wish to hurt Arthur, but she was prepared henceforth to guard her privacy. He had not hesitated to hurt her in his behaviour with Dulcie.

Beatrice did not get to sleep until nearly four. The house was quite silent. Once she rose and, peeping through the window, looked across at the room on the wing where Nick and Dulcie were. A light showed dimly through the curtains. That would be about two o'clock. After that, whilst quite cosy in bed, she could not cut out of her imagination a phantasmagoria of scenes in her early days with Nick. She enjoyed them as though they were actually taking place. Then, returning to present affairs she pondered the mess she and Nick had made of their lives by their stupid marriages. She fell asleep hoping that somewhere, sometime, she and her brother would be together again to end their days in peace.

She did not seem to have been asleep long when the disturbance awakened her. In the half-world between sleep and waking, she could not make out what it was all about. Then, slowly, the noise assumed shape and became a tune, albeit a disordered and distorted one. And the words gradually sorted themselves out and grew plainer.

For it is of a Christmas time that we wander far and near,
Pray God bless you and send you a Happy New Year...

It was Trumper's Waits, a time-honoured institution in the locality. Tom Trumper was seventy, if a day, but for three nights before Christmas he led a group of carol singers into the dark to sing at all the big houses in the district and he annually collected thereby nearly two hundred pounds for Tilsey Infirmary.

Her first thought was that it would disturb Nick. She jumped from bed, flung on a gown, and hurried down to the front door. Tom Trumper was already on the mat waiting to bring in his party for refreshments. He was very upset and sympathetic when he heard the news.

"Is that you, Tom?"

"Yes, Miss Kent..."

"I'm terribly sorry, Tom, but would you mind asking them not to go on singing. Mr Crake, my brother, is here, very ill, and you might disturb him. I do appreciate your coming...but...you *do* understand, Tom...?"

"Sure, I do, Miss Kent..."

Since he'd lost a good customer once, in his grocery shop, by endowing her with "Mrs" when she was a sworn old maid, Tom had always called grown women "Miss". He quietly spoke to his troupe and they slowly melted away in the dark, coughing apologetically, and some of them walking awesomely on tiptoes out of respect for the nearly dead.

As she closed the door, Beatrice Kent marvelled at the endurance and faithful persistence of Tom Trumper and Co. The night was dark, and a cutting east wind was now blowing, which, if the bad weather of the previous day returned, would mean a copious fall of snow. The casements chattered, and the draught beat down the chimneys. Kent's spaniel, sleeping by the stove in the kitchen, rose, sniffed his way to the hall, greeted his mistress with a friendly, cold nose, and then apologetically retired to his warm corner.

The house was uncomfortably still. Kent was, of course, sleeping at the back of the house and probably had not been disturbed by the carol singers. And once she got going, nothing short of an earthquake would break the sleep of Margery in her attic. There, with a photograph of the almost naked milkman, cut from the local paper when he won a prize at a swimming gala, standing guard on the bedside table, with his cup in his hand and his medals on his swimming costume, she smiled all night as she dreamed of a little home and a milk-round of her own. But Dulcie...what of her? Surely, Tom Trumper's bass right under her window must have roused her if not Nick as well. Beatrice had half expected her to be down first to silence the singers. As it was, all was quiet. A slit of light shone under the door of the guest room, but not a sound could be heard.

Beatrice paused and listened. Nothing but heavy breathing; too heavy for peace of mind. She turned the knob and looked in. Both beds looked remarkably tidy, as if they had been recently made straight, and Nick was in one and Dulcie in the other. Both were asleep or seemed to be. Dulcie's black hair made a startling mass against the white pillows. One arm lay out on the eiderdown and Beatrice could not help a thought of involuntary admiration at the beauty of its shape and tints. The same with the face, lying right side up on the pillow. The delicately chiselled nostrils and the perfect modelling of the jawbones. How happy might Nick have been if only Dulcie had been capable of controlling her hot blood and roving desires...

Such thoughts came in a flash, and, even as they passed through her mind, Beatrice was aware that all was not well with Nick. There was a curious rattle in his breathing, and, as she drew near his bed, she knew that the sleep was not that of health but of acute illness; it almost amounted to unconsciousness.

Hastily she turned down the clothes and pressed her hand to her brother's heart. She could not hear or feel the beat for the vibrations of the chest and she sought the pulse of his damp wrist. It was weak and low. No need either, to use a thermometer to take the temperature. It was high; very high. Nick had taken a turn for the worse!

"What are you doing?"

Dulcie's voice bore no signs of sleepiness. It was quick and harsh, as though she had caught Beatrice in some underhand or secret act.

"Get up and get the doctor at once. Nick's worse..."

"How silly! He was better when I looked at him last... What time is it?"

"Nearly five. When did you last attend to him?"

"Four..."

"But surely, he wasn't right then? All this hasn't come on in an hour."

"I tell you..."

"Stop arguing! Get the doctor."

Dulcie made movements towards her clinical thermometer, but Beatrice had had enough. She took it from the table and slipped it in her pocket. She faced her sister-in-law bellicosely.

"No more amateur doctoring. Get Bastable," she said. She wanted Dulcie out of the room, and, as her sister-in-law left and descended to the telephone in the hall, Beatrice covered Nick and glanced quickly round. The fire was still glowing nicely, but the room seemed chilly. She hurried to the window. The casement was fastened as she had left it, with the small one open for ventilation. The glass of the panes was clear, and Beatrice could see the lights of the main London road from the town in the valley below, glowing yellow with their sodium filaments. She felt something was wrong yet could not lay her finger on it. Then it dawned on her!

The window in her own room was exactly similar and when, on cold or wet nights, she closed the casement and opened the small window at the top, the rest of the panes steamed over and became opaque with beads of moisture. When you opened the window, they dried up again…

"What are you looking for?"

Dulcie had returned. Beatrice turned on her like a wild cat.

"What were you doing with the window wide open and Nick needing a warm room? On a night like this, too!"

"I left the windows exactly as you fixed them when you left us…"

"Liar!"

Beatrice was overwrought and beside herself. She could have killed Dulcie for what she'd done to Nick.

"Liar! If anything happens to Nick after this, I'll kill you…"

"Now, now, now… What's all this?"

It was Arthur, sleepily standing in the doorway in his dressing gown. In spite of his waning interest in Dulcie, he couldn't keep his eyes from her as she stood there, flushed and towering over the enraged Beatrice, her dressing gown open at the neck displaying the lace of her nightgown and the smooth, even-coloured olive of her throat and breasts.

"Nick is worse… Dulcie opened the windows and then fell asleep leaving the temperature to fall. If he dies, it's her fault…"

"Be quiet, the pair of you. This is no way to carry on in the sickroom. Have you sent for Bastable? What's up with Nick?"

"He's in a sort of coma and his temperature's all up again…"

"It's all her jealousy! Ever since I married Nick, she's done her damnedest to break it up… Now she's trying to say I want him to die… It's all part of her scheme to separate us. But she shan't, she shan't…"

Dulcie's voice rose to a shriek and then she started to laugh. Shrill, wild laughter, unceasing.

Beatrice slapped her face hard and that ended it. She sat down and cried.

Bastable blamed both women when he arrived. He criticised their methods of watching and nursing and refused to listen to their accusations of one another.

"I've got to get oxygen now. He's too ill to move to the hospital or else I'd have him there out of the way of the pair of you. Ring up the hospital, Arthur, and ask them to send up a cylinder right away... And then get your car and go to my place and ask my missus to give you my other handbag. I'll need all the stuff I've got if I'm going to save him."

On Christmas Eve, a small party of waits — local schoolboys out to cash-in on the festive spirit — began to sing under the window of Nick Crake.

God rest you, merry gentlemen, let nothing you dismay...

They let them go on singing, because Nick Crake *was* resting... his long rest. All day Bastable fought for him, but he failed to respond. It was as though he didn't care about it. He gave up the ghost just before the waits arrived, and their carol was his requiem.

2

THE DANCING WIDOW

Beyle House, for generations the home of the Crake family, stands a mile outside Tilsey in four acres of wooded grounds. Alexander Crake, who built it, was a horticulturist of some repute and surrounded it with fine trees which were well tended whilst the family money lasted. In recent times, however, the political levelling trend and the shortage of labour to keep the place in order have given the property a shabby, neglected air. The trees are ragged, the bushes and grass beneath them overgrown, the once graceful yews, fuchsias and box, which topiary art converted into peacocks, cones, and even dancing ladies, are now running riot. Rhododendrons still bloom, but the bushes are the size of haystacks and as coarse. The little ornamental fishponds are choked with weeds and the dead leaves of many autumns, and the rustic arbours and the rose beds have tumbled down in decay.

As if repenting now and then the merciless destruction of her ruthless moods nature has, here and there, gently touched the ruin and decorated the sharp and tragic outlines of corruption with a wild beauty. In spring, the lawns and woods are carpeted by masses of bluebells, daffodils, and primroses. Violets peep through rank grass and from overgrown banks, the convolvulus thrusts its white trumpets from neglected hedges, and flaming gorse and ragwort hide the cobbles of the forsaken stable yard. Wild lilies float on the ponds which attract crowds of frogs to populate them in their season with millions of tadpoles and to make the air melancholy with their ecstatic croaking. In summer, a rose bush, gone wild from neglect, becomes a mass of sweet white blossoms and fills the air with its old, unspoiled fragrance.

By day, no song birds lighten the sombre ruin by their singing. Rooks and ravens chatter and hatch plots in the tree-tops, and, after dark, the hooting and screeching of many owls adds to the gloom.

Beyle House itself, built in a hollow and approached by a neglected gravel drive through rusty wrought-iron gates of old and exquisite craftsmanship, was once a pleasant place to see from the top of the hill, nestling comfortably in its leafy amphitheatre. Its two pepper pot towers, each with its gilded weathercock, rise to tree-top level and its steep gables and slender chimneys made it look, in its prime, like a castle of old romance. Now overgrown by untended ivy, which invades even the slates of the roof, it has the appearance of a setting for a gothic tragedy.

The judge's body had been decently laid in his room and his children were eating a meal in silence in the long dining room. There was a large fire of logs in the Adam fireplace and family portraits watched the food on the table as though hungry from their long vigils. Juanita, the younger of the two, resembled her mother in dark features and colouring and in the fine chiselling of her face, but was otherwise her father's child. She had his short, strong body, firm limbs, home-loving temperament and kindly humour. She was stricken by his death and her fine eyes were red-ringed from grief and tears. She played with the food which did not attract her. Her brother, bent over his plate, eating slowly, now and then raised his eyes furtively without moving his head. He was tall, slim and dark, too. Women found him attractive. His high-bridged nose, flashing eyes, sleek black hair, sharp chin and the fashion he assumed of wearing "sideboards" after the manner of the gallants of Spain gave him, in his proud moments, the look of a first-class bull-fighter; otherwise, he might have been a gigolo, a lounge-lizard, wasting his time on other people's money. He was his mother's favourite and depended during the period of his dubious and protracted professional studies on her bounty.

"Where's mother?"

He was always asking for his mother. As fast as he spent his money, he pursued her for more. He had been cynically unmoved by crazy scenes in the presence of the dead. He had been too busy wondering if it would upset his mode of life. He might need to earn a living now the judge had gone. They had little money beyond his father's salary as Recorder. Uncle Bernard, who lived with them, kept himself by selling, one by one, and, with many lamentations, his large collection of gold and silver coins, a legacy from his own father, who had been a numismatist in his day. Perhaps his mother, enriched by the dead man's heavy and sacrificial life insurance, would start again the career of squandering by which she had scattered all her late husband's available capital whilst it lasted and brought ruin to Beyle.

"Where's mother?"

"With uncle. They're trying on their mourning clothes..."

Nita's voice was colourless and heavy. There was no humour in it, although, unconsciously, she registered the thought that her father would have been amused, in his dry fashion, at the thought of his wife and her dotty brother rehearsing their parts for the funeral. Nita felt utterly alone; a stranger in a strange house. Without her father about the place, the spirit had gone. The rooms were cold and dank, the passages dark and terrible, the warren of empty rooms upstairs neglected, rot-infested and damp, and the very air full of menace and impending doom. It seemed as if somewhere a secret was held, locked either in the cold breast of Nicholas Crake or in the wild heart of her mother.

"I'm going out. I can't stand this any longer. It's like a mausoleum..."

Alec rose, screwed up his napkin and flung it violently on the table. It struck his coffee cup, tipped it over, and spread a black stain over the white cloth. Neither of them seemed to notice it.

"You're not going to the airport tonight, are you, Alec?"

There was a bar at the Tilsey airport at which the young bloods and exhibitionists of the town gathered to boast, flaunt their cleverness and talk nonsense every night.

"No... Just a run round for a breath of air..."

Nita knew he was lying. He would come home half tipsy after the place had closed...maybe hours after, if he could find a girl to drive around with him and submit to his caresses in his car...or rather, his mother's car. He would drive drunkenly back, risking his own and other people's necks, beat on the door and disturb the whole place till someone let him in, and then upset the rooms by lighting fires or scattering food about. Alec was a born liar. He rarely lost his temper at interference or questions about his conduct. He defended himself glibly with his ready-made lies, taking a pride in the revenge of deception. It was now so bad that you never knew when he spoke the truth.

Old Elspeth, the only remaining servant, who only put up with the family now out of fidelity to the Crakes, Nicholas and Nita, entered. She was nearly seventy and would never get another job, but the Old Folks' Home would have been preferable to Beyle had not Nita existed. Elspeth was a stooping, spare old woman with white hair gathered in a bun on top of her head. She always wore black. Her hands were large and masculine from arthritis, and given a tall hat, a gown and a broomstick, she would have passed for a classical witch. She claimed the gift of second-sight.

Elspeth started to clear the table without saying a word. She was enjoying her triumph. She had, in her visions, seen her master dead and her mourning for the event was cancelled somewhat by her self-congratulation on the accuracy of her prognostications.

They had laughed at her soothsaying. She was waiting for them to mention it now and beg her pardon. Instead, they were so immersed in their own devices that they forgot even her presence. She clicked her teeth at the sight of the mess of coffee on the tablecloth. Her great knotted hands moved over the dishes like false ones, their locked joints giving them an inhuman look. She sighed from time to time, her grey eyes, never still, glancing malevolently at Alec.

"She's dancin' again..."

Elspeth said it as if to herself. Her voice was flat and tired.

The young man shrugged his shoulders. He didn't care what his mother did. He wasn't interested in her behaviour which, like his own, had always been queer and without consideration for anybody else. She had never restrained herself; not even before her children. In Alec's younger days, she had even taken him, as an alibi, to various rendezvous with her lovers. He had been sent to play, foisted on servants, left at the cinema, even lodged like a parcel of left-luggage with her friends whilst she had kept her assignations. He had grown impervious to anything his mother did. Now he regarded her and her treatment of him in the past as excuses for his own strange conduct and misdemeanours. She had always taken his part when his father remonstrated. She would always defend him before the world...

Nita, closely bound to Nicholas almost from birth, had adored him. In unspoken ways, she had sensed his sorrow, his patient suffering, his infinite and tragic kindness. He had married, impulsively, a woman who had brought him nothing but unhappiness. The honour of his family and profession soon came to mean nothing to Dulcie Crake. Tired of her husband's solid, faithful nature, she had sought shameful adventure all over the countryside. Only the respect and affection in which the Crake family were held, and in which Nicholas and his daughter shared, made his position tenable.

Nita wondered if her father had wanted to get well in his last illness... Now, she thought, she would say goodbye for ever to Beyle and let it fall to further ruin without a thought...

"She's dancin' again..."

The girl felt the hot blood rise in her throat till she almost suffocated. This dancing was some kind of ritual, some secret between Dulcie and her crazy brother, just as humour and laughter had for so long been a secret between her and her father. Sometimes the strange pair would not indulge in their capers for months on end. Then, like an epidemic of mania, it would seize them, and they would lock themselves in Uncle Bernard's room and he would play on his piano, exquisite, wild music, tarantellas and mazurkas, for hours on end until, exhausted, Dulcie would collapse into a deep sleep and lie on the couch like one in a trance.

In her childhood, these fantastic orgies had terrified Nita. There was something nightmarish, diabolical, obscene about them. She remembered how, curious and fascinated, she had peeped through the keyhole and seen her mother, hair dishevelled, feet bare, whirling round and round, scantily dressed, clutching an invisible partner in an orgasm of sensual pleasure with Uncle Bernard playing softly and beautifully, his wild, dark eyes fixed on his sister as she moved...

Now, even in the presence of death, Dulcie Crake was dancing! It was like resorting to drugs or alcohol in a crisis. It was indecent...an affront to the dead! Nita rose and with quick steps ran upstairs to her uncle's quarters.

The last rays of a wintry sunset shone through the stained-glass window on the turn of the stairs and reflected the coloured uneven pattern of rubies, yellows and blues, on the opposite wall. The rain had ceased, and mist floated in the Beyle valley, rising from the stream and its overgrown banks in an unearthly vapour which from the road made the towers and steep-pitched roofs of the house seem to float on clouds like the castle of a wizard. Her uncle's room was at the end of the corridor, a large and sombre place in which he slept and took his meals. It was cluttered with masses of old books, the walls were covered with them from floor to ceiling: music, medicine, alchemy, black arts, strange religions, outlandish practices. In one corner, a large, four-poster bed stood, gaunt, without hangings; in the bay window, the splendid grand piano which, according to his moods, he hammered in wild abandon or gently caressed with exquisite grace. Sometimes he continued far into the night; he even got up in the small hours and played to himself if the whim broke his sleep. His small dressing room and the bathroom they had fitted for him years ago, when he came for a holiday and stayed for good, were littered with the apparatus of his scientific experiments, test tubes, retorts, furnaces, ovens, glass fashioned in fantastic shapes, bottles, essences, powders and liquors. Sometimes he caught rats and mice in the old outbuildings for his strange researches in alchemy and surgery. Now and then he made trips into the woods and fields around to gather plants, barks and fungi, and even stones, for his work. During such absences, Nita had often explored his rooms. The linen room key, unknown to Uncle Bernard, fitted the lock. Finally, finding two caged rats with their tails cut off to bloody stumps and madly trying to escape, she had fled, shrieking from the place, forgotten to lock the door behind her and lived for days in fear and trembling lest the alchemist should discover her intrusion by his magic arts. Uncle Bernard never announced the results of his researches; he seemed to relish keeping his secrets locked in his breast.

And now he was playing a Spanish dance again, and, without peeping through the keyhole, Nita knew what her mother was doing. With her father still dead in the house! She beat on the strong, locked door with both fists. Hysteria rose in her throat like a globe of ice.

"Stop it! Stop it! It's disgraceful..."

The music continued as though nothing had happened. She flung herself on the panels again but still without avail. Panting from her exertions and sobbing with anger, she ran to the end of the landing, thrust her hand round the door of the linen room and took the key. Back again, she inserted it in the lock of her uncle's room. At first, the key on the other side resisted her efforts, but by juggling and forcing she thrust it out and heard it drop on the floor. The occupants inside must have heard it too for the music stopped. Before they could act, Nita had opened the door.

Her uncle was just rising from the piano. She had never seen him look so diabolical. He was tall and emaciated at the best of times. His thin face and sunken cheeks bore several days' growth of beard. His high nose, like the beak of a bird of prey, and his dark brown-shot eyes gave him a perfect Mephistophelian cast. His hair was still jet black for out of some strange pride he anointed it with a colour-preserving pomade of his own make. His eyebrows and long, slender drooping moustache were quite white, however. He always dressed in black with a waisted out-of-date frock-coat like a Continental virtuoso of the early nineteenth century. His tall, starched collar kept his neck stiff and erect and, as he looked angrily at the intruder, seemed almost to be pushing his head backwards. He pointed a long slender forefinger at Nita as though casting a spell upon her. In his dishevelled state, he looked like Don Quixote himself after a battle with fantastic assailants.

"Get out! Get out! For the love of God, get out!"

Nita was not looking. Her eyes were fixed on her mother who had sunk exhausted on the long couch behind the piano. She was either at the end of an epileptic seizure or had fallen into a peaceful sleep. Her cheeks were delicately flushed, her face serene, and she moved her limbs voluptuously now and then as though enjoying the luxury of a feather bed instead of an old sofa. Her feet were bare and her dark, silky hair hung loose about her face.

Before she could stir a step further, her Uncle Bernard had Nita by the shoulders and propelled her swiftly to the door, flung her in the passage, locked her out, and hurried back to his sister. Nita felt to have no strength left. Vainly she sought in her mind one solitary person on whom she could rely implicitly in her trouble. Her brother would laugh at her. Her aunt hated her mother so much that emotion always impaired her judgment when she had Dulcie to deal with. There was a young doctor at the hospital who loved her; he had told her so many times and he asked her to marry him nearly three times a day. But she didn't feel that way about him and it didn't seem fair… Utter silence in her uncle's room! Such a silence that it seemed to grow upon her like a great weight. Her knees gave way and she sank on the carpet. Feet shuffled upstairs, and there was Elspeth. A weak old thing but a comfort at such a time. Nita took the tired outstretched hands and clung to them.

"There'll be more deaths in this house before the next moon," intoned the old woman in the dull voice she used when seized by her "do's" of second-sight.

In Uncle Bernard's room, the piano started again. It was not a dance this time but the second movement of Beethoven's *Emperor* concerto which Uncle Bernard had forgotten years ago on the concert platform and ruined his musical career. As he reached the bars which had once evaded him, Bernard played them with confidence. Then he pounded the keyboard in harsh discord and burst into yells of demoniacal laughter.

3
THE BRIDE WORE BLACK

On the day of the funeral, Dulcie and her brother rose early and conducted themselves sedately as though they were the sanest people in the world. She was clad in full black, a dress of exquisite design, executed by a first-class maker. She was going to take full advantage of the limelight on that day, like a bride on her wedding. Even the hat which supported the heavy black veil was a model.

Uncle Bernard wore black from head to foot. He had in his room large chests of clothes, past relics of his family, out-of-date ceremonial raiment of days gone by in many kinds of foreign styles. The usual stovepipe collar was held together by a large black bow; he wore a three-quarter frock-coat, black trousers and black elastic-sided shoes. In his hand he carried an ancient top hat and, as the day was chilly, was wearing, although it was warm in the room and there were still two hours to go, a heavy top-coat with a collar of astrakhan. He kept pulling his watch from his fob-pocket and looking at it. Two great seals clanked and clicked as he did so. He looked annoyed at the slow passing of time. He was going to give his sister his arm at the funeral. She had refused to have Alec do it because he declined to wear mourning. Instead, he was waiting impatiently, dressed in a grey suit and red tie. The three of them were like actors standing in the wings ready for their turn in the show; whilst Nita and Elspeth were left to make all the arrangements and do all the work. Nita wore a simple black costume. In the past, it had not been the practice of the Crake women to attend funerals. Dulcie, however, was not going to miss this chance of playing a part, so Nita had decided to go as well to see that things went decently.

The body had gone to the undertaker's parlour. There the cortège was to assemble and enter into procession to the church. The vicar, the Rev Joshua Roebuck, was already with the widow making sure that nothing in the arrangements had been missed. Nita had strongly objected to his having anything to do with the funeral. Her father had never liked him, and she knew he would have preferred the court chaplain, a sterling young parson who would have conducted the affair in a seemly fashion and without fuss. But Roebuck belonged to Dulcie's clique. He had called and engaged himself for the occasion as soon as the death was known.

"Leave it all to me, dear lady," he was saying to Dulcie.

They had invited him to breakfast; so, early had he arrived, and, although he had finished a large meal before he left the vicarage, he had drawn up to the table and started again. He was busy at the sideboard filling up his plate for a second time.

"Leave it all to me… In your grief, dear lady, you must not be harassed. I will take full charge…" He balanced a kidney on his fork, turned his fat beaming face to the widow and bowed slightly, like a counter-jumper assuring a customer of absolute satisfaction. He looked quite in keeping, a bird of the same feather as Dulcie and Bernard. A small, spindle-shanked man with an enormous gluttonous barrel of a belly which he made no effort to hide. His red-moon face was always perspiring as though toasted before a fire, his button-nose was livid from wine and digestive corruption, and his fleshy mouth was moist and ever-moving in full function ready to gobble anything that came within reach. He shovelled his bacon and kidneys eagerly between his thick lips with hasty gestures like a dog who fears its dish will be removed by malicious hands.

"I didn't want the band, but they insist. Besides, Sir Ronald is vice-president and we must satisfy his whims. He wishes it..." Mr Roebuck spoke with his mouth full and paused to wash down his food with a copious draught of coffee. He then mopped his lips and started again.

"The band!"

Uncle Bernard halted in the act of drawing on his black kid gloves for the tenth time.

"I cannot bear it. Every discord is agony to me..."

The town boasted a prize band and Nicholas Crake had been its president. In his young days, he had played the trombone himself and until his death had done all he could to encourage local talent. In this he was assisted by his friend and vice-president, Sir Ronald Goosenargh, and, patronised by these two potentates, the band had been of festival strength. However much the local pundits had hated bands and their music, they had, with two such influential men in the lead, pretended to give their support. Thus, the Tilsey Town Brass Band had a large following. They were going to church to play their dead president to his last rest.

"I'm afraid we have no choice..."

Mr Roebuck squirmed and leered. Sir Ronald helped to make up the stipend of the church, and his wish was law. To tell the truth, Goosenargh had a sense of humour. When he heard of the pomp and circumstance which was going to see the judge to his grave, he insisted on the band. He smiled to himself as he did so because Nick would have enjoyed it too. That was why Nick had included the request in his will!

"Then I shall stuff my ears with cotton-wool whilst they play," said Uncle Bernard. He put on his hat for the third time and pulled out his watch again.

"Isn't it time yet...?"

The church filled quickly and long before the funeral service. The local gentry, the MP, the Mayor and Corporation, the bench and the bar, the police and the fire brigade were present in their numbers. Special portions of the church had been allotted to each faculty by that master of ceremonies, the Rev Joshua Roebuck. The choir were there as well, with Tom Trumper, principal bass for untold years, glowing in their midst yet with his usual beefy smile missing. Something was worrying Tom. He had done a lot of whispering about it too over the days since the judge's death. Already the thin wind of his gossip was developing into a gale of disapproval levelled against the widow of Nicholas Crake who had not yet arrived with the body.

The church bell tolled dismally and the Mayor, who had developed a cough and cold, snuffled miserably and sucked his cough lozenges. His chain of office, worn for the occasion, felt to weigh a ton. Mr Huxtable, for that was his name, dolefully wondered how long it would be before they gathered to speed *him* on his last journey. Certainly, the way he felt at present, it wouldn't be long. The Town Clerk, sitting beside him, a long, thin, chilly lawyer named Legge, had been up late the previous night playing bridge and was only with difficulty keeping awake. He nodded off now and then only to be wakened by the Mayor's hacking cough ringing in his ears. It's an ill wind... Nobody spoke. They all looked petrified, their faces masks of what they assumed to be reverence and regret. The building was cold for they were short of coke and the corporation fuel officer, seated in the nave, received black looks for withholding supplies. There were approximately four hundred people in the congregation and they seemed to draw together like animals, to heat one another against the cold. At the back of the privileged sitters stood the humbler fry, about a hundred of them, huddled together. These were composed of those who had really loved and respected Nicholas Crake, publicans, sinners, lesser public officials and workmen, widows whom he had helped, jailbirds he had treated with mercy, outcasts he had befriended...

A child in arms started with the unmistakable paroxysms of whooping-cough and from the mass of heads in the body of the church rose the faces of three doctors, angry and questioning, like hounds awakened by the hunting horn...

The coffin entered, borne on the shoulders of four bandsmen. It all seemed wrong somehow, but it had been in the Will of Nicholas Crake that these friends of his should carry his coffin and be pallbearers. Fourteen of them in the town band uniform in procession and then the widow on the arm of her brother. She looked like a bride in black and some form of macabre wedding march ought to have greeted her arrival in church. Her heavy veil was lowered, and her head was bowed. Her brother didn't seem to know what to do with his hat. The two children followed like strangers who had just drifted in on the off-chance and found themselves in the funeral procession by mistake. Nita had on her black costume; Alec wore what looked like holiday clothes. They seemed forlorn; afterthoughts, supers, invited to the ceremony at short notice. The bandsmen, met at the door by Mr Roebuck with a surplice hanging from his huge paunch like a tent, deposited the coffin. Someone had forgotten to erect the catafalque and two of the undertaker's men ran out with two trestles and a board, manoeuvred them with fumbling hands and arranged the coffin on them. Then the scene-shifters of this strange drama withdrew and left the stage to Mr Roebuck. He intoned in a twanging nasal voice, the congregation rose, and the band played one of Nicholas Crake's favourite brass band hymns.

There had been some debate at the meeting of the band which chose the musical accompaniment of their president's funeral. "Let's give 'im *A Day's March Nearer Home,* he always liked it," said one faction, but they were outvoted by the supporters of *Glory for Me*.

When all our labours and trials are o'er,
And we are safe on that beautiful shore...

At the first blast of brass, everybody jumped as though the roof were caving in. It was like a tornado, the equal of which had never been heard in St Sepulchre's before. It shook the ancient timbers and brought down dust from the beams overhead. Uncle Bernard corked up his ears with the promised cotton-wool, like somebody getting ready for a journey by plane. Sir Ronald Goosenargh smiled to himself. He thought of his old friend's last joke with delight. And he almost laughed outright at the sight of this large, very respectable, orthodox congregation singing the romping revivalist hymn. The band, having played the air, waited and then led the singing louder than before. Not only that the drummers, warned beforehand by the conductor to "'old themselves in", were carried away by emotion and gave it all they'd got. It sounded like a piece in the class of *1812,* describing an artillery battle. One by one the assembly joined in, self-consciously, outraged, watching one another from the corners of their eyes.

Oh, that will be...
Glory for me...

Tom Trumper from his stall bellowed with incredible fervour, his large eye all the time fixed disapprovingly on the widow who remained seated and still, unaffected by this hurricane of song, an enigma behind a black veil. The racket had penetrated Uncle Bernard's cotton-wool and his face was convulsed with rage and tics...

The hymn died away and Mr Roebuck's voice sounded thin and pale after it as he took up the service. Tom Trumper was whispering to his next-door neighbour, his eye still on Dulcie Crake. The vicar droned on like a talking machine. His voice rose and died away, then rose again... The dead who die in the Lord...

Men's works live after them... Our dear brother... Justice, mercy, love... Asleep in Jesus... For ever with the Lord...

Nobody seemed interested. All their faces wore a stony, monumental look except that of the bass drummer. He was weighing Mr Roebuck in the balance and finding him wanting. Drummer's wife was a spiritualist, spoke at meetings, held séances, brought home brothers and sisters in the cause for sittings with planchettes and tables. His missus had a much better gift of the gab than Roebuck. Drummer felt neglected and out of it as he sat at home, silent, listening to his wife and her friends in their orgies. Jealous, too, now and then, when the brethren held her hands and even gave her what they called "kisses of peace" as they departed. Now he felt quite proud of his missus. In Chune with the Infynyte... Passed over... Called 'ome...the Unseen Watchers of our daily round...the Inh'effable... Snatches of his wife's outpourings passed through his mind and he thought them streets ahead of Mr Roebuck's phrases, h'educated though the vicar might be... Drummer realised that he must have nodded off for they were singing the Nunc Dimittis and they were standing to watch the coffin and the black figures go down the aisle into the open air. The sun was shining without warmth, a pale, watery light, and the east wind blew down the main street. The Mayor was hoping they wouldn't be long in the icy crematorium otherwise he was sure he'd be the next. He had to prod the Town Clerk awake...

The bearers placed the coffin in the hearse, and the widow and her brother entered the first cab. Uncle Bernard had removed the plugs from his ears, was still having difficulty with his hat as he handed his sister into the vehicle, and then followed her, his thin hair blowing in the wind, his nose livid with cold, his eyes glassy and wild. He sat beside her, folding himself in the narrow space like a great jack-knife. Nita and Alec were next in the family sports car...

The crowds gathered on the long flight of stone steps which

led from the church to the street. Those who were going to the crematorium waiting for their cars; others standing watching the strange last journey of the man who seemed without an enemy in the town. Beatrice Kent and her husband were first in the line waiting for transport. She had been reluctant to break the old tradition of her family whereby the women stayed at home whilst their men carried their kin to the grave. But her sister-in-law's fantastic conduct called for someone to correct the balance, and she had joined the rest. Colonel Bulshaw, in ancient mourning garb, bumbled beside Dr Bastable, huge and puffing from the cold.

"Heard what's bein' whispered, Bastable?"

The doctor looked annoyed. He had given the death certificate with certainty. Pneumonia and heart failure; but the cause of his old friend's sudden relapse had baffled him.

"Yes... A lot of poppycock..."

"Think so? I don't. Won't think any blasted funny thing that woman does is poppycock. I've met a lot of bad women in my life, Bastable, but Crake's wife has 'em all beat for badness. You know what's bein' whispered...?"

"Yes, I said so, didn't I? Somebody had better be careful. Slander, you know..."

"All the same, I'd like to bet..."

"Come on... It's our turn. There's your car. Let's be gettin' along. I've a surgeryful waiting for me..."

They climbed in the Colonel's enormous barouche, driven by an ancient whiskered retainer more skilled with horses than engines. With a jerk, they joined the procession. The band hadn't been asked to play Crake to the crematorium so made their way there by short cuts, arriving ahead of the cortège. They had heard that it was usual for loud-speaker music of a solemn kind to be played during the committal and were determined to rescue their late president from such an indignity. They were waiting on the steps for the coffin, the chimney of the furnace scattering all that was left of the previous ceremony in a long banner of smoke. They carried the body inside again; Mr Roebuck intoned the committal and pressed a button. The coffin slowly rolled behind the purple curtains with the municipal monogram inscribed upon them in gold. The band played him off.

...And here I pitch my roving tent,
A day's march nearer Home...

There was something almost jolly about it. The tempo got out of hand. They seemed to be *hustling* him away... By the time they all got back to town, there was nothing left but a handful of grey ashes and wisps of dark smoke drifting over the garden of rest to join the low clouds over the town. But that didn't stop the whispering. A snatch of sentence, a few words at a time. It all grew and formed a pattern. Rich and poor, respectable and despised, they all listened and asked for more. By the time the mourners had dispersed, it was everywhere. Dulcie Crake had speeded her husband's death by laying him naked to the keen wind blowing in at the open window. Tom Trumper saw the judge at the window when they went there carolling... Naked to the waist...trying to close the wind out... Tom Trumper thought at first he had come to throw them some money... Then *she* dragged him back in the room. Not only Tom, either, saw it... Some of the others...

A constable told the Chief about it all when he returned to the station. The Chief was cross and ordered him to be quiet. But he didn't like it. It meant trouble and he was all for a quiet life. The Superintendent of Police, however, who was there, smiled sardonically. He gave the Chief a disrespectful, feline look. He was like a large, ruthless hawk, the terror of wrongdoers, his underlings, and all the small boys of the town. Mothers of undisciplined children only needed to say, "I'll fetch Superintendent Simpole to you," and all was quiet. He was tall, dark, wiry, with a long cadaverous jaw, slightly askew, dark waxed moustache and a thin, cruel mouth. "The man's a ghoul…no warm blood in him," said Colonel Bulshaw, Chairman of the Bench of Magistrates. "But, damn, he does the job properly. I hand it to him there." And he was right.

Simpole's dark, beady eyes glowed with the idea of a new crime, however faintly mentioned.

"I must take a walk round and see what I can hear," he said, and curtly leaving the room, slammed the door.

"Rude devil," said the Chief to himself. "By gad! If it's true, I'll see that he doesn't hound her down, at least. I detest stoats…"

They mentioned it to the Mayor when he returned to his parlour. Mr Huxtable nearly cried with temper.

"Leave me alone," he said. "As if I wasn't ill enough without all this silly talk. I'm going home to bed and I don't want to hear about it…"

That wily lawyer, the Town Clerk, listened sleepily to somebody who whispered the poison in his ear on the way back from the funeral. He looked round furtively lest anybody should overhear. "Tell me more," he said.

It had grown so bad that, as the car bearing the widow and her brother passed through the town on its way back to Beyle, accusing, savage, unsympathetic eyes followed it in its course. Some were even tempted to throw stones at it. Tom Trumper was back in his grocer's shop, adding fuel to the flames. The place was crowded.

"Has somebody told the police…?"

"It ought to be investigated…"

"I jest see Simpole. He looked 'ot on the trail already…"

"Once he gets 'is claws in 'er, it's all UP for 'er…"

They bought soap and tinned goods they didn't want, just for the pleasure of turning over the outrage with Tom Trumper in his shop. The interior was still filled with the trappings of Christmas past. Boxes of crackers, candied peel, preserved and dried fruits, nuts, basins of Christmas pudding, tangerines and dates. Trumper was improving the shining hour and disposing of his surplus. No need to mark down the prices. One after another he packed the good things in customers' bags and baskets and they accepted them in exchange for gossip and theories. Tom rubbed his hands under the counter. At this rate, he'd soon clear the lot and repay his seasonable overdraft at the bank!

The cafés were full too, and, although it was only around noon, the bandsmen had gathered in the pub over which they practised twice a week to discuss the case and try to make up their minds about it.

"Glory for me!" said the drummer, who had been suppressed altogether at the crematorium and felt it keenly. "Glory for me! It'll be glory for 'er, if wot they say's true..."

Nita and Alec had gone for a run in the country. Alec was in search of a quiet inn where he could drink his fill and maybe find a buxom barmaid to fondle. The thought of going home to a household of crêpe and maternal misery made him feel sick. Nita, on the other hand, felt the need of the quiet and the comfort of sweeping bare fields, leafless hedges and deserted lanes. The majesty of winter which matched the bleakness she felt inside her. She could not bear to go back to Beyle. Alec, ever ready to turn an event to his advantage, agreed to the trip. A queer way of behaving on the day of the funeral; but the Crakes were a queer lot. He got his beer and sat with his arm round the landlord's daughter whilst his sister walked beside the stream and watched the flight of the wild duck as they fled from the fowler's gun...

Nita did not know how far she walked. She lost count of time and place. All she knew was that it was quiet, and she was alone. Finally, she became so preoccupied with thoughts quite remote from the present that her grief for her father lost shape and definition and she was only aware of a dull spiritual ache like a deep-seated diffused bodily pain. The lane ended in a stile giving access to a large field in which two horses were grazing. They lifted their heads and solemnly regarded her as she stood undecided... In the distance a car horn sounded impatiently. Alec had tired of beer and dalliance and wanted to move on. He could not rest anywhere for long. Nita almost ran back the way she had come. There was no sign of the car. At the village inn the girl Alec had been fondling met Nita at the door. She looked defiantly sheepish and red-faced.

"He said he was going. He waited a bit and then said to tell you he wasn't waiting all afternoon. I looked up a bus to Tilsey. It goes in twenty minutes. He said if you came back to take it... He said he was going for a few drinks at the airport..."

He said... He said... He said...

Nita despised Alec and despised the girl, so obviously bemused by her brother's charms and eager to pass on, word for word, all he had told her. As though he might return and reward her for her good offices by a lot more cuddling and shallow flattery!

"Very well," she said, "where does the bus start?"

"It comes in from Bishop's Cree and stops here. Won't you come in and wait?"

Nita entered and sat in a corner of the bar. The place was tricked-out in cheap modern brass and bottles of coloured drinks. The girl was still all agog...

"Is he your brother?"

"Yes..."

"You come far? Do you live near here?"

She was arch and trying to find out if there were hopes of more amorous visits from Alec.

"Not far... Tilsey..."

"Oh. I come into Tilsey sometimes..."

Was the girl expecting to be asked over to tea next time she came? Nita strolled to the door and was thankful to see the bus approaching down the village street. She bade the girl goodbye and stopped and boarded it. She sat, numb with a sense of loss and dreading her return to Beyle without her father there. She descended at the Market Place in Tilsey, suddenly realising that she must have automatically paid her fare. She was clutching a ticket but didn't remember taking it from the conductor… As she stood recovering herself, a farmer passing in a shooting-brake hailed her and offered her a lift. He took her right to the gates of Beyle.

The sun was low as she entered the house. Mists were rising and hung over the grounds a foot high, like dirty cotton-wool. Nita entered by the side door which was loose. A kettle was singing on the hob of Elspeth's kitchen; she made innumerable pots of tea for herself all day long and kept water forever on the boil. But the old woman was nowhere to be seen. Nita stood in the hall and listened to the familiar sounds of the house; the grandfather clock ticking at the foot of the stairs. It gathered itself together with a whirring of wheels and choking noises and struck five. Whereat the bracket clock in the dining room repeated the hour, having previously chimed in broken tones because one of the bells was loose. Nick had been tinkering with it the week before. Tears burned at the back of Nita's eyes to think that but a week ago when she had hurried down to see him, he had been surrounded by wheels and cogs from the clock and had confessed in his quizzical way that he was unable to sort them out.

Nita wondered where everyone had got to. Surely, Dulcie and Uncle Bernard had returned. She mounted the stairs in search of them…

Down the hill to Beyle a man was walking. He wore tweeds and heavy brogues and was smoking a pipe with great enjoyment. Middle-aged and greying over the temples, he carried himself like a young man, strong, well-knit and tall. Ahead of him ran a bobtail sheepdog chasing a ball which she brought back to her master time and time again. Neither seemed tired of the monotonous game. He threw the ball, she chased and caught it, brought it back, deposited it carefully at her master's feet; and then the process was repeated. As the dog ran after the ball, her master walked briskly.

Since Littlejohn had adopted Meg, the sole relict of a

murdered man, he and his wife had said goodbye to holidays in which the dog could not join. So devoted had this waif become that she went off her food if Littlejohn was absent from home for long.

"She's a bind, but she's worth it!" he said, and here she was again spending Christmas with the Littlejohns in Oddington, two miles from Beyle, where ex-Chief Inspector Shelldrake, once of Scotland Yard, was keeping an excellent pub in his retirement...

Man and dog separated again as the ball flew and bounced past the iron gates of Beyle, and, as the dog leapt to catch it, the front door opened, and a wild-eyed girl rushed down the steps and ran screaming along the drive. The dog dropped her ball, stared at the running figure and, with a quick leap, placed herself protectively between her master and the gesticulating figure.

"In there... In there... My mother... He has killed her..."

And with that, she fell unconscious at the Inspector's feet. The dog stood by, bouncing the ball, waiting for Littlejohn to throw it again...

4

DEATH AT BEYLE

At first, Littlejohn thought he was becoming involved in another family quarrel, a domestic fracas in which words like *murder* and *killing* are bandied about lightly, and hysterical people rush out of doors to raise the neighbourhood. He picked up the unconscious girl, hastily carried her indoors and laid her on the nearest couch, his astonished dog following closely on his heels still bouncing her rubber ball in the jealous hope of providing a counter-attraction. The house was quiet and the blinds, still drawn for the funeral, gave it an eerie, uncanny air. The Inspector pulled back the curtains of the room he had entered and examined the features of the girl. She was breathing steadily, and he felt he could safely leave her whilst he tried to get help. He went into the large hall.

"Hullo!" he called. "Anybody in?"

His voice echoed through the building but brought no response. One after another, he entered the dark rooms downstairs but found them all empty. The fires were out, and they smelled of soot and mould. He was just making for the telephone, which stood on a table in the hall, and searching his memory for Shelldrake's number when suddenly everything began to happen at once. An old woman in faded black opened the door, entered and stared at him.

"What do *you* want?" she said.

A sports car drew up at the still open door, and a young man, slightly drunk, emerged unsteadily, mounted the front steps, stood on the threshold and regarded Littlejohn and the old woman owlishly.

"Gatherin' for the funereal bake meats?" he asked, and without more ado turned to the old woman and ordered her to make his tea.

"Where've you been?"

"To my sister's… Nobody suggested that I came to the funeral. I wouldn't have come in any case. Proper Crake women don't attend…"

Littlejohn mightn't have been there!

"I found a young lady unconscious in the drive," he said. "And I brought her in and put her in the room to the right there. She said someone had been killed…"

The old woman and the young man looked at each other and then at Littlejohn.

"She must have meant my father… I'll go and see…"

Alec reeled off in the direction of his sister. The Inspector was just beginning to tell Elspeth more details when a third and more spectacular entrance was made.

A gaunt, wild figure appeared on the landing at the stair-head. He looked like Don Quixote taking the part of King Lear. In his arms he bore the prostrate body of a woman. Step by step, he descended, muttering to himself in a broken voice, for all his bony frailty carrying the well-made body easily and steadily.

Elspeth rushed to meet him.

"Mr Bernard… Mr Bernard. Whatever have you been doin'? What's 'appened?"

The man she called Bernard ignored her. Where he thought he

was taking the body, nobody could guess. He came on inexorably. Littlejohn quickly crossed the hall and intervened.

"What are you doing with that...?"

Uncle Bernard regarded him with glassy eyes. The Inspector steered him to an oak settle in the hall, took the body from him, and laid it down. No need to ask what had happened. The woman was dead. He turned to Uncle Bernard and shook him. It seemed to set the old man in motion. He ran and knelt down by the body again, rubbing the hands, stroking the brow...

"Dulcie... Dulcie..."

"She's dead..." said Littlejohn.

Elspeth uttered a wild scream and covered her face with her hands. Her shabby hat slid to the back of her head revealing a large bruise on her brow.

"I know she's dead. I'm a doctor..."

Uncle Bernard drew himself up as he said this and then bent down, opened the front of the loosened dress of the dead woman and revealed a large pad of lint strapped to the skin with plaster. Savagely he tore away the dressing and laid bare a wound which might have been made by a stiletto, right through the heart.

"I did what I could... It was no use..."

Uncle Bernard sadly shook his head. Littlejohn wondered what he was talking about for the woman must, with a clean blow such as that, have died instantly.

"What...?"

His words were cut short by the entrance of Alec. He had a brandy bottle in his hand and had obviously been drinking again. His sister followed. They both tried to speak together. For one who had just recovered consciousness and one who was half drunk, they were a very quickly collected pair.

"What the hell...?"

"Why have you brought her down...?"

Nita staggered back a little and then joined the group round the body.

"He killed her... He did it... He was standing over her with a knife..."

She pointed at her uncle who recoiled and flailed the air with his long arms as though avoiding the plague.

"You are mistaken, my dear... She was the dearest thing in the world to me... All I have to live for... She was lying there when I found her... I did what I could..."

"You killed her..."

"What the hell...?"

Elspeth started to wail, a long, shrill cry and, moaning, said she knew it would happen. The spirits had warned her...

"Be quiet, all of you...! Go to the other room and stay there. I'll ring the police..."

"The police!"

Uncle Bernard looked surprised. As though somehow it would be possible to settle everything quietly without interference from outside.

"Yes... Right away..."

Littlejohn crossed to the telephone and picked up the receiver. Then he paused, for the door opened and there *were* the police. A tall, dark, diabolical-looking man with a waxed moustache and a crooked jaw loomed between the daylight and the dark hall. He was dressed in the uniform of a superintendent of police and carried a heavy stick and gloves. He remained without speaking for a minute and then joined the group with long catlike strides.

"What is going on here?"

He spat out the words and looked straight at Littlejohn as if suspecting him of causing all the trouble. The dog, standing silently by, bared her teeth at him. Littlejohn raised a hand to quiet her.

"I'm Inspector Littlejohn..."

"Indeed!"

It was obvious the newcomer resented the intrusion.

"Well...?"

"I'm staying at Oddington on holiday. I was passing, and this young lady ran out and brought me here. She mentioned someone had been killed. I came in and found this..."

Nita pointed at Bernard.

"He did it. I saw him..."

"She lies, Superintendent... I found her..."

The police officer raised a long hand.

"That will do. All in good time. Where are you from, if I might be so bold..."

The voice was ironical; Littlejohn might have been masquerading as a policeman! He handed over his card. The Superintendent glanced at it; then he looked again more carefully this time. He seemed a bit taken aback for a second or two then he recovered.

"My name's Simpole. I'm Superintendent of the Tilsey police. I'll ring for help."

He said it in a tone of dismissal; he evidently felt quite capable of handling the situation without outside assistance. He crossed to the telephone with the same padding steps, dialled a number and, without any explanation, ordered a sergeant and two men to come to Beyle at once and bring the surgeon.

"Now..." he said, returning. "Now. Tell me what all this is about..."

Nita could not contain herself.

"I came home about five o'clock and found him..." She levelled an accusing finger at her uncle again. "I found him bending over my mother with a knife in his hand."

"Yes... What then?"

"I ran out for help and then I fainted."

The Superintendent turned to Littlejohn.

"Is that true? You didn't say she fainted."

The Inspector could feel the deep antipathy of the other officer.

"I haven't said anything yet. I'm quite at your disposal though."

"It can wait…"

He strode over to where Alec was sitting on the stairs, his head in his hands, trying in a befuddled way to understand what had happened.

"Where were you?"

"Who? Me?"

"Yes… You… Where were you?"

"At the airport, having a drink."

"Who with?"

"All alone. Didn't want company. Can get drunk without any help."

"Faugh!"

Simpole turned rapidly on his heel and stood before Uncle Bernard. "What have you to say?"

He seemed quite without respect for the family or the age of the strange old man.

"I was in my room… I came out for something…"

"What did you come out for?"

"I wanted bread from the kitchen to feed my rats…"

"Your…? Never mind. Go on."

"I found my sister lying in the doorway of her room. She had a terrible wound… I dressed it and tried to revive her, but I failed…"

"No wonder you failed with a wound like that! Where is the knife?"

"In my room. It is a stiletto she used as a paper-knife. One of my father's…"

"Very foolish of you to remove, or even handle it."

"What did you expect me to do, Superintendent? She is my sister. I couldn't…"

"I don't want to argue with you. You had no right to touch the knife if you found her dead…"

Suddenly the old man drew himself up to his full height.

"I will do as I like in my own house… Or rather, my own

home. I am twice your age, Superintendent, and I am a fully qualified doctor. I demand that you treat me with the dignity and respect due to me..."

"I beg your pardon, *doctor*..."

He said it sarcastically and Littlejohn felt his blood begin to boil. Much more of this and he'd have to put this ill-mannered fellow in his place.

"And you? Here, don't go."

Elspeth was making for her own quarters. She was scared of the formidable officer now fixing her with his ruthless brown eyes.

"I was just going to..."

"Never mind what you were going to do. I want to ask you some questions. Where have you been all afternoon? I didn't see you at the funeral and you're clad in outdoor things..."

The old woman's lips tightened.

"I've been to my sister's in Oddington."

"All the time?"

"From eleven till just now, when I got in. I found *him* here."

She indicated Littlejohn as though he were responsible for all the turmoil.

"So the house was empty during the funeral?"

"Yes. I locked up."

"What time did you get back, *doctor*?"

"Who? Me...? I got back with my sister about two..."

"What did you do then?"

"We ate the cold meal Elspeth had left and drank a bottle of champagne..."

"Funny stuff for a funeral..."

"We neither of us wished to make tea. We opened the first bottle I could find in the cellar. We felt the need..."

"Yes. What then?"

"You will find the remains in the dining room..."

"I'm not interested in the remains. What did you do, *doctor*?"

"I went to my room as soon as the meal was over. I played the piano a bit and then carried on with my experiments. I then thought I'd better feed my rats. I am experimenting in..."

"What was Mrs Crake doing meanwhile...?"

"She went to her room to lie down. She had drunk rather a lot of the wine."

"And that was the last you saw of her?"

"Yes. Until I found her..."

"Quite dead..."

"Not at all. She was dying, but not dead."

"Oh. Did she say anything?"

"One word only. She asked for the police..."

"She did, did she? Quite a natural thing in the circumstances. What was the one word?"

"'Police,' of course."

"Nothing more...?"

"No... I think she died then..."

"You think?"

"Yes. I was very upset..."

Littlejohn felt sorry for the old fellow. He seemed utterly bewildered.

"Don't you think...?"

His words were cut short by the arrival of the sergeant and his retinue. Littlejohn felt he could do no more good there. The Superintendent obviously resented his presence and Simpole's methods filled him with distaste.

"I'll be getting along, if you don't want me further..."

Simpole nodded. He expressed no thanks nor asked any advice.

"You'll be hearing from me later, Inspector. We'll want you at the inquest, of course."

"Very well. I'm staying in Oddington at the Bull's Head, Shelldrake's place. You'll find me there."

"Good bye, then."

Simpole turned to his men and started ordering them about without another word for Littlejohn, and the Inspector, calling his dog, left them.

At Shelldrake's place in Oddington, another surprise awaited Littlejohn. A police car stood at the door of the Bull's Head and in the bar he found Simpole sitting with a glass of beer, hobnobbing with the ex-Chief Inspector. Simpole rose and stretched out his hand to Littlejohn.

"I came right away to make my peace with you. Sorry I was so gruff at Beyle. I had to be though..."

Shelldrake, fat, peaceful and worldly-wise after thirty years of Scotland Yard, gave Littlejohn a broad wink behind the Superintendent's back.

"You two've met before, I hear... What'll it be, Littlejohn?"

"Beer for me, Shelldrake, please..."

Littlejohn was puzzled. Simpole was a different man now. Must be the type who becomes obnoxious the minute there's any official business to be done, thought Littlejohn, and he shook the offered hand. Simpole was almost jovial; as jovial as his satanic appearance and crooked jaw would allow.

"You see, Inspector, everybody at Beyle is quite mad. If you don't bully them about, you get nowhere. Cloud-Cuckoo castle I call Beyle; and now there's been a murder there. What we're going to do, I don't know. It was bad enough when we prosecuted that old maniac, Bernard, for cruelty to animals. They behaved like a race apart. We let it drop for the Recorder's sake. We all liked him. But this is something we can't gloss over, or the Crakes wriggle out of. So, you see, I treated 'em rough. Sorry if I included you in the rough-house. I didn't want to spoil the atmosphere I'd created..."

"That's all right... Think no more about it. I'm on holiday so can't claim any special privileges..."

Shelldrake winked again and smiled to himself.

"No, you're not," he said. "Things have been moving fast.

Whilst you were covering three miles from Beyle to here, Scotland Yard's been consulted. You're in it now — officially."

Simpole smiled a frozen smile.

"The Chief Constable, to whom I reported as soon as you left, insisted on calling in Scotland Yard. You see, sir, the Crake family are an unusual lot. The late Nicholas Crake was Recorder of Tilsey and there's been a bit of trouble about his death already. I don't know why the Chief's in such a hurry, but he telephoned Scotland Yard right away. They said you weren't far away and could undertake the work and they're sending down a Sergeant Cromwell to help..."

It was obvious Simpole was making the best of a bad job. He didn't like it at all, especially after the way he'd first met Littlejohn, but he was trying to make amends as graciously as he knew how.

Littlejohn was due back on the morrow. This probably meant another week or so with the Shelldrakes. It suited him, and it would certainly suit his wife.

"I don't think there's anything else to tell you, Inspector. You were there from the start and know as much about it as I do..."

"The doctor confirmed the cause of death?"

"Yes. He says it would be impossible for her to say a word to her brother, as Doane asserts she did. Death was instantaneous. The old boy's just beside himself that's all. Doesn't know what he's doing..."

"You said there'd been trouble there already..."

"Yes. There's a rumour round that the dead woman killed her husband. He died from pneumonia, but the doctor was baffled as to why he did die. It's said his wife hurried him off by opening the window and letting the east wind blow on him. They say she stripped the bed and him."

Littlejohn felt a bit nettled. This wasn't police procedure at all; just plain gossip.

"*They...?* Who are *they...?*"

Simpole finished his beer.

"It's all over the town. It seems that Tom Trumper, the grocer, saw Crake at the window trying to shut it and saw his wife drag him away. Trumper takes a crowd of carol singers round every Christmas, and they called at Crake's sister's place not knowing he was there and ill. They started carolling full blast, and then Crake appeared, stripped to the waist, Trumper says..."

"Is Trumper reliable?"

"None better. A solid, religious British citizen."

"And you've investigated all this?"

"No. I only heard about noon, and, before I could question Mrs Crake, she'd been killed. It's going to be a hard nut to crack. There are quite a lot of people won't mourn for her. In fact, I could count the likely suspects on the fingers of both hands."

"For example...?"

"Crake's sister for a start. She doted on him and hated his wife. Not without reason. Dulcie Crake treated her husband badly. Affairs all over the place. Left him to fend for himself and worried him to death with her antics. Beatrice, that's his sister, must have had a pretty long account to settle there. To say nothing of the fact that Beatrice's husband was sweet on Dulcie for quite a while."

Shelldrake stretched himself and helped himself and his guests to more bottled beers.

"Nothing much ever reaches Oddington," he said comfortably. "For which I'm truly thankful. Had enough of scandal and crime when I was earning my daily bread..."

"The town's full of Dulcie Crake and her ways. This will be a nine days' wonder and no mistake."

"Any other suspects?"

Littlejohn wished they hadn't handed over this case to him. It was time he had a change from small-town crimes and tittle-tattle. He envied Shelldrake his comfort and peace of mind.

"There are the children, too. She's their own mother, but you wouldn't think so. Nita, that's the girl you found in the drive, left home because of her mother's spite. Dulcie was all for the boy, Alec. Nita was Nick's girl and now that he's dead, and with such a rumour flying about as to the cause of his death, she might have done anything. She's hysterical and quite capable of violence. It was she who reported her uncle for the animal offence. If it was true that Dulcie caused Nick's death, I wouldn't put it past Nita. She's a nurse, with plenty of nerve."

"And Alec…?"

"His mother doted on him, but he's a waster. All he wanted his mother for was what he could get out of her. His father's dead and I suppose has left all to Dulcie. Perhaps Alec saw a chance of getting hold of the money quickly. I really don't envy you your job with that crazy lot. They can't give a straight answer to the simplest question. They're all mixed up and all of them born liars. How Nicholas Crake stood it all these years is a mystery to me…"

Shelldrake emptied his glass again.

"What is a man to do who's caught like Crake must have been with a mad, uncontrolled woman. Does he leave home? Chuck up his job? Run off with another woman, perhaps one he doesn't want, simply for spite? Hundreds of men in the same position put up with it out of decency, or conservatism, or else pity for their wives. Their lives are set; they don't want to change simply because one human being chooses to make them unhappy. Or they don't, on principle, want to cause a scandal. Or again, it's quite possible to be sorry for a sinner, or one who can't resist her impulses, or even who's merely selfish. Some men, and Crake was the type, regard such things as mental illness, a sort of inherited curse, and feel sorry for the victim just as if they were ill from a malignant disease…"

Simpole sneered and laughed.

"Quite a philosopher, Mr Shelldrake, since you left the force. But were you one when you were on the active list? I'll bet you weren't. We're surgeons, in a way, in the police. We cut the cancers out of the public body. It doesn't do to have pity when you're dealing with criminals, does it, Inspector?"

Littlejohn's dog was looking at him with melting, adoring eyes. He felt a warm gush of gratitude and almost unworthiness flow through him.

"I see you have your own philosophy on these things, too. Personally, I agree with a much greater detective than I can ever hope to be, albeit he was fictitious. Pointing out a vile criminal to his friend, he said, in Baxter's words, 'There, but for the grace of God, goes Sherlock Holmes'..."

Simpole laughed outright.

"Sherlock Holmes! That's a good one! You mean to say you model yourself on..."

"Time, gentlemen, please," said Shelldrake heavily." The ladies are due back from their trip to town and if there's nothing done when they get back, there'll be hell to pay. So, come on, Littlejohn..."

Littlejohn wondered what in the world Shelldrake had to do before the ladies returned but admired his old chief's curt dismissal of Simpole. The Superintendent rose and straightened his uniform.

"Thanks for the beer, Mr Shelldrake, and for the pleasant talk. I must be getting along. See you at the inquest tomorrow if not before, Inspector. Inquest's at two-thirty... Goodnight..."

"I don't like that small-town cop," said Shelldrake, when Simpole's car had gone. "He's burned up with ambition and frustration. I don't envy you your job. Let's have another beer till the women get back..."

5

INQUEST

Mr Gladstone was Coroner of Tilsey, and, when people heard his name, they expected something good. When, however, they learned the rest of it, they laughed. It was Harold. Harold Gladstone; the two didn't seem to mix somehow. His father had wanted William Ewart, of course; but his mother's father was Harold, and Harold it had to be. Not that Mr Gladstone minded. All he cared about was music of the sinister variety, like the villains' arias in *Tosca, Faust, Rigoletto* and *Othello*. He had them all on records, croaked them to himself in a horrible monotone when alone and hummed them softly when his court was in session. On the day of Dulcie Crake's inquest, he couldn't get Mephistopheles' Serenade out of his head. He chirped it to himself and softly clucked the accompaniment.

"Pom, pom, pompom...pink, pank, ponk..."

Mr Gladstone sat in a kind of pulpit above the well of the court. He was true Victorian in his cut of clothes which, by the way, were rather shabby. The Coroner had quarrelled with his tailor about increasing prices, stamped out of the shop and tried to persuade a multiples store to cater for him. When the manager had seen the narrow trousers and high lapels which Mr Gladstone sported, he'd bowed him out. So now the Coroner was awaiting an up-rush of courage to go back to his old purveyor, who was ready for him with a long-rehearsed rebuke...

The courtroom was crowded. The whole affair shook the town to its roots. Press men everywhere, people rushing hither and thither twittering and talking, queues for the inquest, and even charabancs bringing people in from the nearby country places. It was bad enough Dulcie Crake giving her husband his death of cold, as the rumour said; now, somebody had murdered *her*. It was as good as going to the pictures! There were bets laid as to who it might be. Bernard, Nita, Alec, Beatrice and Arthur Kent, and even old Elspeth were on the list. Some people nodded wise heads and mentioned other names associated with Dulcie Crake, men and women her promiscuity had involved. The inquest was timed for two-thirty in the Town Hall. At one they had to close the doors of the courtroom which wouldn't hold another soul. The crowd expected a good show and they got one!

Mr Gladstone hummed to himself and eyed the audience quite unperturbed. He looked like a respectable murderer himself. Crippen in the chamber of horrors at Madame Tussaud's! Round, clean, bald, intelligent head; grey moustache; gold-rimmed spectacles; and air of complete innocence. He beamed down from his perch, took out his fountain-pen, unscrewed the cap, and laid it precisely down beside his sheets of foolscap. He gave the little pile a gentle pat in time with his humming. Ponk, pom, pom...

"Call Alexander Crake..."

There was a small jury and Mr Gladstone nodded genially to them. They, all seven, rose and bowed like a lot of dolls on wires. They were delighted to be chosen for the event and to share the dignity and best seats.

Alec Crake rose from beside Mr Trotman, the family solicitor. Trotman was a fat, pompous ass with a profile like that of a decadent Roman emperor and a roving eye for the ladies. He was utterly dependent on his clerk, a little weasel of a fellow who was ever at his elbow. Alec was wearing his red tie and sports attire which included a dark red jacket and suede shoes. At the sight of him a mild roar of disapproval wafted round the court like a rising gale. He was merely required to give evidence of identity. This he did with perfect grace and lack of feeling, and then stood down. Mr Trotman tried to look professional but not in the least friendly towards his client. He himself was dressed like a floor-walker in a large shop.

Next, the doctor. This happened to be Dr Bastable, who was police surgeon as well. He rose and lumbered to the box, an enormously tall and heavy man, very kind-hearted and tender-handed for one so huge.

"The cause of death was a knife wound through the heart. The knife, a weapon of the stiletto type..."

Mr Gladstone made a little gesture like that of a conductor bringing in the flute in an orchestra, and his clerk at the desk below produced the dagger in question and passed it to the doctor.

"Yes... That could easily have been the weapon, sir.

"Pray proceed..."

"The weapon entered the chest below the left breast and slightly to the right, between the ribs, and penetrated the right ventricle. Death would be instantaneous..."

There was a murmur of admiration for this expert statement and the members of the doctor's panel present preened themselves at such an honour.

"Could the deceased have spoken after it...?"

"I cannot see how that was possible. Of course, sir, one cannot be dogmatic. But in my experience and scientifically speaking, any noise from the chest would be purely reflex..."

"I see."

Everybody held their breath. You could have heard a pin drop.

In the middle of the hush a drunken hiccup was heard and the man responsible tried to look as if he hadn't done it. Mr Gladstone paused and looked perplexed.

Murmurs of sympathy rose, and Mr Gladstone nodded to the assembly. It was all very friendly and informal. They were like that in Tilsey. All pals together!

Bastable had done his duty and was thanked. It was as much as the crowd could do not to give him a round of applause when he stepped down.

"Miss Juanita Crake..."

Nita, all in black, took the stand. They could only see her lips move as she recited the oath from the card sympathetically handed to her by the coroner's officer.

Mr Gladstone played a few bars of *Faust* on his desk with his fingers.

"Speak up, my dear. Don't be afraid..."

The audience muttered a mass approval of this. They all agreed that nobody was going to hurt poor Miss Crake. "Now... Tell us in your own words, please, what happened on the afternoon your mother was...ahem...died..."

Nita had been sitting on the other side of Mr Trotman from her brother. It was obvious that the lawyer was acting *in loco parentis* as well as her legal guardian. He patted the girl's hand before she left him and told her not to be afraid, *he* was there. She now gave him a wan look and smiled. Another sympathetic murmur rose in the air. Good old Trotman; the friend indeed!

Nita was as pale as death. It was obvious that she would only pull through with difficulty. Since the shock of her mother's murder, she had been staying with friends and had hardly slept.

"I returned from Bishop's Idley, where I'd been with my brother. We'd parted at Idley and I came to Tilsey by bus. Mr Spencer, our neighbour, gave me a lift home in his van. It was five when I got there... The clock was striking..."

She paused, as though listening again for the chimes. Another expectant hush filled the room. Nita looked around as if seeking help, or to gather her thoughts. Mr Trotman rose, padded softly to her side like a huge up-ended carp, and whispered to her, "Go on, my dear. Don't be afraid…"

"That's right, Miss Crake. Take your time. It's all right…"

Mr Gladstone beamed at her and whistled gently through his teeth the perpetual satanic air from *Faust*.

"'Neath your window...pom, pom, pom, pink..."

"There was nobody there. I looked in all the downstairs rooms and then went upstairs. Right on the landing…"

Her voice grew shrill and accelerated. People felt their spines crawl and talked about it afterwards.

"Right on the landing, I saw my uncle. At his feet was my mother and he was holding a dagger dripping with blood in his hand…"

Ohhhhhh! The audience looked at one another and then at the Coroner, as if expecting him to do something about it at once.

"Steady…"

Mr Trotman administered comfort and security.

"What then, my dear?"

"It was right in the doorway of my mother's room. He had killed her…"

Uncle Bernard, although not under arrest, was accidentally sitting between two policemen. He was wild and dishevelled when he arrived, but now he looked wilder than ever. He staggered to his feet as though baring his breast for a mortal blow. Nita turned to him and pointed a trembling black-gloved finger at him.

"HE KILLED MY MOTHER…"

"I didn't… I told you, I found her…"

Someone shouted from the back, *"Sit down..."* Uncle Bernard was spoiling the show! Chipping in before his cue!

"Silence!!" said Mr Gladstone and whipped off his spectacles just to show he meant it." Let us confine ourselves to facts, Miss Crake; not your opinions, which will be struck from the records." The two policemen ministered to Uncle Bernard in no uncertain fashion. One looked to be reading him a lecture on good manners. The old man cringed and was mute.

Mr Trotman was helping Nita to her seat. Someone at the back could be heard asking for air. A woman had fainted.

"Make way... Get her in the open air... Air! Water!"

Nita finished her evidence sitting by Mr Trotman. She ran out for help at once and fainted in the drive. That was all.

Uncle Bernard's turn came.

"Your name is Bernard Doane; your age is sixty-seven; you are a qualified medical practitioner, retired; and you live at Beyle House...?"

"Yes, sir."

Uncle Bernard had assumed a strange dignity. He stood at attention to take the oath and kissed the book with reverence. His thin hair was on end and he passed a long hand through it and restored it to a semblance of neatness. His bearing towards Mr Gladstone was one of great respect.

"Might I make just one correction...? I qualified in Spain and never practised in this country, sir..."

Pooh! You could hear the assembly say it. They wanted none of his acting. They wanted him sentenced for murder and, in their ignorance of his powers, hoped Mr Gladstone would get on with it.

But Mr Gladstone was equally kind and courteous. He recognised a kindred spirit and deep called to deep. He asked the questions himself. Bernard Doane told of leaving his room to feed his rats (noises of disgust from the crowd) and finding his sister lying stabbed in the doorway of her room.

"I removed the dagger. It was her paper-knife and very sharp. I tried to do what I could... She died in my arms..."

Someone said *"Booo!"* and this made Mr Gladstone angry. He slapped his desk with the palm of his hand. "Any more of that and I'll clear the room..." Several people turned on the booer and rebuked him.

"Did she say anything?"

In spite of Dr Bastable's statement, the Coroner persisted.

"Yes, sir. She said simply 'Police...' Her meaning was obvious... She had been murdered and was trying to tell me to inform the police..."

"You are a doctor, sir?"

"Yes..."

"You have heard Dr Bastable's comments on this point?"

"I have, sir, and I respect them. But, quite apart from what we as doctors know is possible, I was there when she spoke. I KNOW. Doctors can only surmise..."

"That is so... What happened next?"

"I tried to dress the wound and applied stimulants. I know now that it was hopeless, but in my then distressed state, I tried to perform miracles. She was dead..."

His voice broke. The more compassionate members of the gathering felt deeply sorry for him. Among them was Littlejohn, seated with the Chief Constable and Superintendent Simpole in the well of the court.

"I lifted my sister and carried her down... There I met an Inspector... Mr Littlejohn, I think, who was very kind... The police arrived and took over... I think that is all, sir."

He looked very old and broken as he took his seat between the two bobbies again. It seemed the two constables were the only friends he'd got. They made room for him on the bench and the heavy one of the two smiled politely at him.

"Superintendent Simpole..."

Simpole rose, crossed the court with swift steps like a cat, and took the oath. Littlejohn watched Simpole closely. He couldn't quite make head or tail of him. In a private interview before the inquest, the Chief Constable had told Littlejohn quite plainly why he'd been so quick in calling in Scotland Yard.

"Simpole, our Superintendent here, is a dark horse where Mrs Crake is concerned. It's said he was one of her great admirers if not more than that. We've no proof; only rumour. During a case where her brother was involved in cruelty to animals with his vivisection experiments, Simpole spent quite a lot of time at Beyle. He and Mrs Crake were very friendly; I know that. And the prosecution was eventually dropped. It caused a lot of local talk and scandal. You quite understand my position, therefore. I can't accuse Simpole; but I can't let him carry on this murder investigation on his own. Why! The feller may have done it himself...!"

Awkward!

On his way to the stand, Simpole staggered slightly, quickly recovered himself, took the card for the oath, and recited the words. Littlejohn, watching his eyes, noticed that whilst pretending to read, the Superintendent was doing nothing of the kind. His eyes wore a glazed look, as though he were far enough away from the court, and his jaw was set in grim determination to keep control of himself.

"I arrived at Beyle just after five. I wished to see Mrs Crake. There had been rumours in town about the circumstances of her late husband's death, and I wanted to question her informally with a view, if possible, to dispelling them..."

Another murmur like a rising wind through trees passed round the room. Mr Gladstone's mouth opened loosely and then closed again. Simpole turned on the audience a look of steely disdain, hating them and knowing all the fickle, ignorant, gullible tricks of crowds.

"I found..."

And he went on, in a dull monotone, to describe the scene at Beyle when he arrived there. He then stood down and, turning his head in the direction of his seat beside Littlejohn, marched back to it with the precision of a sentry. He sat down without a word and Littlejohn observed great beads of sweat on his forehead.

"Inspector Thomas Littlejohn..."

You could hear the crowd settle voluptuously in their seats like a cinema audience when the feature is announced.

Now for the star turn! The *Tilsey Daily Bugle* had told them all about it that morning.

BEYLE MURDER.

CHIEF CONSTABLE PROMPTLY CALLS IN SCOTLAND YARD.

FAMOUS INSPECTOR ALREADY ON THE TRAIL.

Their eyes shot out like organ-stops as the Inspector rose and took his place in the witness box. The jury eyed him over and whispered together. Everybody expected an immediate solution and arrest. Uncle Bernard — that foreigner! — had met his match at last.

Littlejohn told the Coroner how he had arrived on the scene and what he had found. That was all. A murmur of regret and dissatisfaction rose in the body of the hall. They hadn't had their money's-worth. What did they pay taxes for?

All the time Mr Gladstone knew he was going to adjourn. The preliminaries were merely to establish cause of death, identity, and to enable him to issue a certificate of burial. He turned to the jury.

"I shall now adjourn this inquiry pending further police investigations..."

From the point of view of the sensation-mongers, it was a sorry flop! They waited, expecting the hand of the law to be laid on Uncle Bernard's arm. Instead, they saw Littlejohn, after a hasty word with Simpole, speak kindly to Bernard Doane, and those standing near heard him offer the old man a lift in his car. The pair of them left the room and entered the police vehicle at the wheel of which sat a lugubrious officer in a bowler hat and mourning clothes, ready to drive them off.

"This is Dr Bernard Doane, Cromwell. I've promised him a lift home to Beyle. Drive on, and I'll show you the way..."

The crowd melted and formed smaller knots; some went to the local pubs for fuller discussion; others made for Trumper's Stores (Established 1858) to learn more of what the oracular proprietor thought of it. Mr Trumper was at his best. Still wearing his hat and in his shirt-sleeves, he expounded police strategy.

"They're lyin' low, till 'ooever done it's off his guard. Then...then..."

He drew narrowing concentric circles round a sugar lump on the counter as though that object was animated and quite off its guard as well.

"Then...THEY'LL POUNCE!!"

He brought his heavy palm down on the sugar lump and converted it to granulated. Everybody jumped and looked suspicious of his neighbour...

At Beyle, Uncle Bernard took them to his own room.

"It's the only place where there's a proper fire. Nobody seems to bother about keeping the house warm anymore..."

He looked distracted. Elspeth had been living at her sister's since the second tragedy. According to her second-sight, other catastrophes were in the offing and she wouldn't sleep another night under the roof of Beyle. She came, made the beds, laid out the food for the day in the dining room, and then stole away. Nita had gone off with Mr and Mrs Trotman, who had taken her under their wing, and Alec had presumably left on another of his drinking tours.

"I'm sorry the place is rather a shambles... But I can offer you a glass of excellent Tio Pepe... No...?"

He showed them round the rooms. In one corner, the great

bed; under the large window, his piano, with music scattered about as though somebody had been hastily rifling the music cabinet. On the walls were reproductions of Goya paintings, a coloured print of Augustus John's portrait of Suggia, and a genuine full-length oil of a very beautiful young woman in black with a mantilla. The figure, tall and graceful, poised as if to begin a Spanish dance, looked ready to leap from the canvas at the first bar of the music.

"My sister when young… She grew larger and coarser… Who would not, with the life she led…? But she was always beautiful, even in death. She filled men with madness. All except Nicholas Crake. She filled him with fire at first; then he turned to ice. She was as God made her…"

He shrugged his shoulders. "God have mercy on her. Here is my laboratory…"

Little cages with rats and guinea-pigs and mice, all imprisoned and restless for their freedom, or else hungry. The aroma which usually surrounds such creatures was missing presumably killed by the fluid which shone bright green in little bottles attached to the cages out of reach of their occupants. There was a bench filled with all sizes and shapes of glass vessels. Some of the receptacles were large globes, almost like round electric bulbs, of scintillating, iridescent glass. They might have been used for imprisoning fire spirits or shadows. The books scattered everywhere were on esoteric subjects… Alchemy, necromancy, antiquities, customs, ancient and modern medicine. Old leather and calf-bound treatises as large as a man could carry, side by side with new red and green works on morbid psychology and modern clinical practice…

"I have my work. It takes up most of my time. That and music…"

They went back into the bed-sitting-room and sat down. The old man seemed to think that he had to entertain them. Cromwell looked at Littlejohn out of the corner of his eye, but the Inspector's face was bland and good-humoured.

"Now, sir. Will you please tell me something about the life under this roof before the deaths of the master and mistress of the house?"

"Of course. Ask what you will..."

"First of all, did you say they were estranged?"

"Yes; they went their own ways. It was a misalliance from the start. He was a good man, completely immersed in his work, which was the law. He married my sister in a rush of passion. Her beauty was like wine; intoxicating. Men could not leave her alone. Nicholas was her lover for a time; then he became her husband. You understand...the typical English husband. His attention was divided between her and his work and he would not allow her to invade his working territory. She was Spanish by nature. She did not understand it. She expected marriage to be a permanent love-affair. To Crake, marriage meant a little love, a lot of responsibilities, a fine home and a fine woman to grace it, work, hard work, to keep the ménage running... To my sister, it meant love first, the rest after. They didn't agree... He became more and more engrossed in his work and she sought pleasure elsewhere. She had not far to seek it."

He recited it all without blame or malice. He might have been describing the habits of a couple of the occupants of his little cages.

"Where did she seek it...?"

He shrugged his shoulders and flicked his long fingers about.

"How can I say? Men came and went. They drove her home; then they called and took her away; but always brought her back. She insisted. She was Catholic and thus bound for ever to her husband."

The idea sounded a queer one, but Littlejohn didn't pause to discuss it.

"Who were these men...?"

Uncle Bernard looked outraged.

"Who am I to accuse anyone? She was murdered. Struck down in rage or jealousy. It is your business to discover who did it."

He rose and poured out a glass of sherry for himself in an exquisite old wine glass, a long, thin, beautiful rainbow funnel.

"You won't…? Please excuse me if I drink. I have had very little food for several days…"

He sipped the wine, then drank it slowly and refilled his glass.

"All the same, sir, you'll help us find the culprit with a lot less trouble if you name the men who associated with your sister."

"You could count them on the fingers of one hand, sir. She was not promiscuous…You must not think she was…was…loose…"

"I didn't suggest it. But the names…"

"You will smile and be incredulous. Besides, I was not my sister's keeper. I didn't follow her around. I only saw…well…the ardent glances…surreptitious often…of those who came here. That superintendent who tried to bully me, for example. She completely charmed him. He dropped his ridiculous case against me with a caution, on account of my sister. He actually said I ill-used animals. I am not a cruel man, gentlemen. I always give an anaesthetic before I operate…"

"But what when they recover from it?"

"I see they do not suffer. But my work is important. One day I shall lay bare secrets which will astonish the scientific world and completely overthrow materialism… I could…"

His eyes glowed as he lost himself in his obsession…

"The names of the other men, sir?"

"The policeman called several times. His visits always happened to coincide with Nick's absences. The Superintendent was in a particularly favourable position in that respect. He knew everything about everybody."

"They were lovers?"

"No."

"You seem very sure of it."

"I am. I knew my sister. I knew when she was playing at love and when she was seriously engaged in it. Simpole was for ever outside the pale. He was mad about her, and her invulnerability made him more mad. He is not married; his career is his all. But before Dulcie, career, reputation, all...went by the board. But not his caution. Few people outside this house knew of his visits or of his passion. He hid it all behind that diabolical mask of his."

"The others?"

"How was I to know the lovers? They did not parade themselves before others. The admirers, the jealous, the ones crazed with desire...yes...I saw them round her like moths round the flame. Even with their wives...they forgot they were not alone."

"Who did?"

"Arthur Kent, her own brother-in-law... Trotman, the family lawyer... Francis Alkenet, at the big house down the Oddington road and a millionaire... I remember the dinner parties we held here. They ruined Nick for his wife spent so much on them. The lights and the food and the music. Perfect settings for love and for Dulcie. All the men...harmless ones, like Bulshaw and Huxtable and Dr Bastable, would roll their eyes at her and flatter her and perhaps envy Nick a little. But Kent and Trotman and Alkenet hardly troubled to hide their feelings. They vied with each other for her favours; made their wives look small and ugly and blush for very shame for them. And Nick would be the perfect host, calm, unaffected, wrapped safely in the mantle of his philosophy. Had she run away with any of them, I don't think he would have cared. Although she was my own beloved sister, I tell you, such an event would have been the end of a long agony for him, the release after spiritual and physical imprisonment..."

"Were the three you mentioned your sister's lovers?"

"My dear sir! Trotman! I have seen him. Fat, cruel eyes and mouth, tall flabby figure, completely selfish and a sensualist. No! Never! But Kent... Alkenet. Kent with his culture, his veneer of indifference hiding an iron will, ambitious and single minded in pursuit…maybe. Alkenet…certainly. A horse-rider, a dare-devil, sophisticated and old in worldly knowledge, perfect in technique in handling men, women and livestock…no doubt about it…"

He was cut short. The front door slammed. Running footsteps mounted the stairs, and the door of the room flew wide open with such force that the projecting key struck the oak panelling and splintered it.

Nita, her hair flying wildly, her eyes flaming, her breast heaving with fury, ran to her uncle and struck him across the face.

"They didn't arrest you… They let you free when they ought to have hanged you! You and my mother danced with my father dead in the house and now you drink to her speedy forgetting…"

She seized the glass from his hand and flung it in the fireplace where it shattered into a hundred pieces.

"If they don't hang you, I'll kill you. Do you hear? I'll kill you. You told her to kill my father… Then you killed her…"

And she raised her fist and smote him heavily in the mouth until the blood spurted, and, in sheer self-protection, he returned the blow, hard, with the back of his hand across her tightened throat. Then she collapsed in a heap on the floor, sobbing. He bent and stroked her hair.

"My poor Nita. I know your grief because I feel the same myself. Only mine will not relieve itself in tears. Only when I have killed whoever brought this upon us will I rest…"

She looked up at him with a changed look. He offered her his hand and helped her to her feet, and then she kissed him tenderly on his bleeding lips.

6

LEPERS' HOLLOW

Littlejohn and Cromwell waited patiently until this emotional family scene had ended. Cromwell said later, he wondered if the Crakes were always like that. His stolid, English character was aghast at the idea of brawling and drawing blood one minute and the next, kissing and making friends. "It takes me a long time to get really hopping mad, but, when I do, it takes everybody quite a while to get over it," he said, and he meant it.

"Do you both think you can now answer a few questions?" asked Littlejohn, when the storm had subsided. Nita and her uncle seemed completely reconciled without so much as a word of explanation or apology. The fact that the old man had expressed a desire to kill her mother's murderer seemed enough for his niece. She forthwith dabbed his swelling mouth with her handkerchief, staunched the blood, hurried to his laboratory and came back with a dressing and plastered the now shapeless top lip with lint.

When Littlejohn spoke, they both looked surprised to find him and Cromwell still there.

"By all means, Inspector. But I seem already to have answered so many questions. Are there more?"

Uncle Bernard said it with difficulty for his wounds made articulation thick and his Don Quixote moustache was now bristling from his upper lip like a shaving-brush.

"Very many more, sir… For example, did you hear nothing going on whilst your sister was being murdered? Was there no scream, no conversation, no sound of voices at all?"

"Nothing, Inspector. I admit, I was engrossed in my work, the door is a thick one, as you can see, and the house is large and rambling. I heard nothing."

"And you, Miss Crake… You got home at dead on five. Did you see nothing suspicious, either?"

Nita was sitting now on a stool by the fire which she had made up with fresh logs from the chest. She looked fresh and alert after her emotional scene with her uncle as though some mental safety valve had been in operation and done her a lot of good.

"No… Definitely no. There wasn't a human sound in the house. That's why I came up and discovered what I did. It was so unearthly quiet that I ran upstairs when I found nothing below."

"You met nobody on your way here?"

"No."

"Tell me, please, had your mother any enemies who might have wished her dead?"

Nita looked Littlejohn straight in the face. Her lips tightened, and a stubborn light came in her eyes.

"That's not fair, Inspector. It means telling you a lot of private things about our family that ought not to be divulged. I'm sorry, but I don't wish to answer…"

Littlejohn accepted and lit a long cheroot which Uncle Bernard offered him from a small tub. He'd done it before he realised quite what he was doing and Cromwell, also politely asked if he smoked, did the same, rather amazed at the boss being so sociable at such a moment.

"I'm trying to make all this as easy as I can, Miss Crake. I must tell you this, however. The Coroner's inquest on your mother has merely been adjourned. If we find those who could help us in our inquiries are going to be uncooperative, we have powers to reopen the inquest and have our questions put to those concerned under oath, and, if they choose to remain unhelpful, they will be liable to punishment for contempt of court. I'm asking you these questions informally. It is less embarrassing for you to help me now than in open court..."

"It isn't fair... It's not just..."

"Do you wish to help us find out who killed your mother?"

"I don't know..."

She seemed to be labouring under severe mental strain and unable to make up her mind one way or another.

"*You don't know*? That's a strange answer. Are you trying to shield someone?"

"Not particularly. But...well...my mother..."

She screwed up her will and blurted it out, quickly and excitedly, as though she might change her mind if she didn't say it right away.

"I didn't like my mother. I may as well be quite candid. You'll only get it elsewhere if I don't tell you. I loved my father and I thought she treated him very badly. I don't care what *you* think, Uncle Bernard... I nearly hated her..."

Uncle Bernard removed his cigar. He had been calmly listening, eyeing his niece as though appraising her character and power.

"Go on, my dear, I shall understand. I know you loved your father..."

"Yes, I did. And she treated him like a dog. And he was such an angel about it. It was a disgrace... She deserved..."

The rest was lost in a storm of weeping. The girl had borne much before the tragedies at Beyle and now was at her wits' end.

"There were others who thought as you did?"

Littlejohn asked it gently as the tears subsided.

"That's what I object to. There were mother's friends, and

father's. I'm on father's side, and I won't betray the others who are..."

"You are not betraying them. In fact, you will be helping them. We shall find out in other ways and all will be under suspicion. If you tell us now..."

"What good will it do...?"

"Leave us to judge that."

"Yes, my dear... You'd better tell the Inspector," said her uncle.

"The first was Auntie Bee... Father's sister, Beatrice. She *hated* mother. The feeling was mutual, I think. They had some terrible scenes and ended by not seeing each other for years till daddy insisted on being taken to auntie's house in his last illness. My aunt never wished daddy to marry mother. In fact, it's said she never wanted him to marry at all. They were so happy at home. But daddy fell in love and it was broken up. It's said Auntie Bee married Uncle Arthur in a sort of reaction..."

"You confirm that, sir?"

"I do, Inspector," said Uncle Bernard. "I know more than Nita of all the quarrels, almost violence, that occurred between Mrs Kent, that's the Bee Nita mentions, and my sister, whenever scandal got round...and that was often, I can assure you with great regret."

"And this went on right until your father's death? There was no reconciliation?"

"None. In fact, I heard... It was Alec who told me, and he thought it rather a joke... I heard that Uncle Arthur was sweet on my mother latterly..."

"Have you anything to say about that, Dr Doane?"

"I mentioned his name to you before Nita came in, you remember. It was quite true. My sister, in one of those strange bursts of childish confidence which she reserved for me, informed me that Beatrice had found out too. Arthur had told her and had said that he daren't risk a scandal. His position would not allow it.

Dulcie took that badly. She wasn't used to being dismissed. She did the dismissing herself, as a rule."

"You think she might have threatened Kent...made a fuss... have seemed likely to cause him to regret the association?"

"That may have been. She said nothing about her feelings in the matter, but, if I'm any judge of my sister's make-up, Kent's cooling-off would add fuel to the fire, if only by increasing her desire to satisfy her own vanity."

At times Uncle Bernard had a strange, detached, scientific way of dissecting even his own nearest and dearest!

"I'll make a note of that and follow it up..." Cromwell had already done so in his little black book. "Anyone else?"

"Elspeth hated her, too. She treated her like a dog. Poor Elspeth..."

"The old servant I met?"

"Yes. She's been with the family since daddy was a boy. But she would never have stabbed anyone. She's too afraid of violence. Sometimes, when rumours have reached her, and she's been sorry for daddy, she's talked about drowning and poisoning rather wildly, but never of stabbing... She only stayed here for daddy's sake, and now she's getting ready to go..."

Littlejohn felt it would be unwise and perhaps indiscreet to discuss her mother's lovers with Nita, especially after Uncle Bernard had already given them a lead.

"Now, this dancing business," he said. "You said something about your mother dancing with your father dead in the house. Was it some kind of wake...like the Irish affairs...or what?"

Nita had evidently forgotten all about the dancing when she became reconciled to her uncle. She was beginning to cast angry looks at the old man again.

"She's dead now and I can tell you," said Uncle Bernard. He was quite calm about it, even relieved, as though wishing to get rid of some dread secret like expelling a morbid foreign body.

"It was all very simple in itself, yet it was so dreadful during her life. It was a secret between her and me...though Nick discovered it. She was a sufferer from tarantism..."

Nita's eyes opened wide.

"Whatever's that? I'm a nurse, but that's a new one to me..."

Uncle Bernard smiled.

"I don't expect you've ever come across it. It isn't found much in these parts. It is caused by a bite from a tarantula, a spider, found in Spain. Your mother suffered from it. When she was a girl, she was gathering corn at a farm where our family were spending a summer holiday..."

"But surely, Uncle, that didn't affect her forever after."

"Yes... Even if cured at the time, the pain and attendant symptoms return every year at the same period..." Nita laughed incredulously.

"But that's ridiculous! This isn't the Middle Ages. Modern science could soon put her right."

"You don't understand, my dear..."

"What is there to understand? To go on suffering from such a thing was madness..."

"Hardly. The symptoms are like those of apoplexy. My sister was very beautiful, but do you think any man would have married her, knowing she suffered from a taint like epilepsy or apoplexy...?"

"But if she were cured...?"

"The usual treatment was applied in Spain and it wasn't until she returned to England that other measures were mentioned. I continued the treatment here. She refused to have another doctor attend her. It was like defacing her beauty, she said, to parade her infirmity. At first, the regular recurrences were easily coped with, but later, excitement sometimes caused them to return. Your father's death brought on an attack..."

"What was the treatment?"

"Music..."

"I don't believe it. It's just another of your own mad ideas..."

Uncle Bernard sighed and crossed the room for one of his large volumes. He turned over the pages. "Here is an authoritative English work on Materia Medica…listen…"

He commenced to read in a dull sing-song:

"Francis Mustel, a peasant bitten by a tarantula...fell as if struck by apoplexy. Knowing the remedy, his friends fetched musicians. When the patient heard their playing, he began to revive, to sigh, to move first his feet, then his hands, then his whole body. At last, he took to dancing violently. Two hours after the music began, he sweated freely and regained perfect health. Every year at the same season, the pain and symptoms returned, and they could always be averted by music. If the imminent paroxysm was not averted, he was found struck down as at first and was restored in the same way..."

"May I see the book, sir," asked Littlejohn.

The old man passed over the volume. It was a standard work.

"Are such patients dangerous during attacks?"

"No, Inspector. They are helpless. But, as intense emotion might bring on a fit and, on such occasions, music and dancing restore the patient, anyone finding my sister apparently enjoying music and dancing at, let us say, a time of grief or mourning, would think her very strange. They might even…"

"If they were near and dear to the dead, they might even hate your sister and vent their rage on her for her callousness?"

"That is so."

Nita wrung her hands and looked haggard.

"That's how I felt about it."

Littlejohn flung the stump of his cigar in the fire.

"To return to our other business… Do either of you think Mrs Crake was capable of doing what rumour says she did: exposing her husband to cold night air whilst he was helpless with pneumonia and aggravating the disease till he died of it?"

The pair of them answered almost together.

"No!"

"My sister was callous about her love affairs. Many women are. The sight of the rejected lover attempting to frustrate by his pleas or actions the development of a new love makes the woman despise and ill-treat him all the more. Dulcie was like that. But to kill in cold blood…never…"

"Very well, sir. This…this…dancing mania, or whatever we care to call it… Who knew about the complaint?"

"Nick knew, of course. One can't live in marriage with a sufferer from it and not find out. She had an attack shortly after they got back from their honeymoon, here. I happened to be handy and she soon recovered under the usual regimen. It was never spoken of. She refused to let Nick call in the family doctor, insisting that I take the treatment. That is why I came to live here and not, as I know Nita and Alec think, to sponge upon my relatives…"

"I'm sorry, Uncle…"

"But did anyone see the dancing cure in operation, doctor? Somebody who might not have known the reason for it?"

"Elspeth has frequently seen us… And Beatrice… Beatrice came just after Dulcie lost her third and last child. She came upon us here suddenly, just as Dulcie was recovering. I had been playing… The Tarantella is the usual dance tune, significantly enough. There was a fearful scene which, for Dulcie's sake, I could not avoid by explaining…"

Cromwell, sitting there with his bowler balanced on his knees, looked dazed. He was longing to get away and breathe the fresh air and see normal people again. This lot were quite mad! Music, dancing, tarantula spiders! What next?

"Your sister made a will, sir?"

"Yes. She left all she had to Alec…"

Nita sprang to her feet, her eyes blazing, and her cheeks flushed.

"I knew it! She always hated me. Well, he can keep it all. I don't want her beastly money, such as it is. She hadn't much, according to her talk. She was always pestering daddy for more."

"She had a good reason, my dear," said Uncle Bernard." She knew you could always look after yourself. You're your father's daughter, my child..."

"I'm not a child any more. And I *can* look after myself..."

"Alec, she knew, never would be any good. He has his mother's self-indulgence, irresponsibility and sensual nature. She knew he would die in the gutter or become a criminal rather than work for his living. So, the ten thousand pounds left to your mother in your father's insurance goes to Alec, in trust. He can't get the lot. It's to be invested in an annuity to make sure he doesn't dissipate it and leave himself penniless almost at once."

"Ten thousand pounds! Poor daddy... She never deserved him. I'm glad she's dead. She was bad...rotten..."

"I won't have that. She was a poor weak creature, for all her beauty."

"I never want to hear her name spoken again!"

These family upheavals were instructive and informative in the case and the two police officers sat quietly by, listening without interruption. They might not have been there in the heat of some of the arguments.

"So, I'm to go penniless, then. I can't understand Daddy..."

"He didn't forget you, either. This house is yours now your mother is dead."

"What! This mausoleum! I don't want it. You can have it, Uncle. Once I go, I'll never come back here. I hate the place. Beyle! Do you know what its real name was? What the old people round here used to call it? The House in the Lepers' Hollow. That's what it was called. How right they were. Now that daddy has gone the whole place seems unclean...diseased...rotten... I won't stay another night here."

"With the exception of his life insurance, which he always said was his duty to his widow, your father left you all he had. He knew your mother would favour Alec, so he made provision. There is probably money for you as well. Mr Trotman should know. He will be reading the wills tomorrow."

"I've just come from there. He said nothing."

"Not until the family is assembled. It wouldn't be right."

"There won't be any money. That's certain. Mother screwed every penny from daddy. He'd nothing left…" She rose quickly.

"I'm going now. I'm packing my bag and leaving for London at once. I won't even stay for the funeral. In spite of mother, real Crakes never attend family funerals. They never have done, and I'm a Crake…"

And she left the room without another word.

Littlejohn rose, and Cromwell followed suit.

"Mr Trotman was a family friend, then?"

From what he'd heard of Nicholas Crake, Littlejohn was surprised that the judge had favoured the flabby lawyer who had been in the Coroner's court earlier that day.

"The firm always handled the family legal business. It was really Mr Trotman's father who was Nick's friend. Old Samuel. I guess when the old man died, Nick just let the son carry on. There are other partners, of course."

"But the present Mr Trotman deals with the estate of Nicholas Crake?"

"Yes. There's another reason too. Arthur Kent, who married Nick's sister, Beatrice, is a partner in Trotman's firm. Nick never liked Arthur. Less of late too since his affair with Dulcie. But perhaps for Beatrice's sake, he put up with it."

"We'd better call and talk to Trotman tomorrow. Mr Crake might have left quite a sum to his daughter."

The house was uncannily still as they rose to go. Dusk was falling and, as usual, mists were rising in the hollow. Lepers' Hollow. Littlejohn wondered how it got its name. Certainly it was, as Nita had said, an unwholesome spot.

"What are you going to do, sir? The house is deserted. If Miss Nita leaves, there'll be nobody to look after you."

"I can look after myself. This is my home, if Nita will let me stay. My work is here. I couldn't manage elsewhere. I must get on with my work..."

"Medical research, sir?"

The old man looked cunning but did not answer.

"I'll see you to the door, gentlemen. The place rambles a little..."

Uncle Bernard rose to escort them. There was no sign or sound of Nita. They descended the stairs.

The great hall was gloomy, and they could only with difficulty see their way safely down. Uncle Bernard snapped on a switch.

The mass lying just near the door had looked like a dark mat in the half-light, but now it took proper shape. It was a body, sprawling with arms and legs spread-eagled. They hurried down, the two detectives well ahead of the old man. It was another corpse, done to death this time by a savage blow from behind. Littlejohn turned over the body. Uncle Bernard was at their side. He uttered a wild cry and covered his face with his hands.

"When is it going to end...?"

"Who is it?"

"Arthur Kent!"

Littlejohn felt the cheeks. They were quite warm. The man must only just have died. He flung open the front door and looked down the drive. Not a soul in sight. He ran round the house, struggling through the riot of briars and weeds, but found nobody about.

Then he and Cromwell began a systematic search of the rooms on the ground floor. They were shabby and cold. One of them, a large dining room with its long mahogany dining table and tall tapestry chairs, must have been lovely in its good days. Now... moths and cobwebs. The whole ground floor was deserted.

"They'd have had to pass the door of the room we were in to

get anywhere else," said Cromwell after they had entered the first two rooms on the upper corridor and found nothing. "And Mr Bernard's door was open all the time. It even looks on the servants' staircase to the attics. By the way, where's Miss Nita...?"

She might have heard his question for she appeared at a door farther down the passage.

"Do you want me?"

"Have you seen anybody about since you left us, Miss Crake?" asked Littlejohn.

"What's the matter?"

"Your uncle, Mr Kent... We've just found him dead in the hall. He has been murdered..."

She dropped the bundle she was holding.

"Another...?"

And then she burst into uncontrolled laughter, high pitched and hysterical. Littlejohn hurried to her and shook her hard.

"Come, come. This won't do. Pull yourself together. Did you see anybody...?"

"No. No..."

She said it quickly, evasively, and Littlejohn knew she was lying.

"You saw someone, and I want to know who it was. Now...tell me, Miss Crake."

"She'd nothing to do with it... I won't tell you. Go away and leave me."

"Not till you tell me whom you saw."

Uncle Bernard was back. He had climbed the stairs soundlessly and was standing listening, expecting the worst.

"Tell them, Nita. It won't do any good. Was it Alec?"

"No. I might have mistaken the car. It went away before I...before I..."

"Whose car was it?"

"Uncle Arthur's..."

"Did you see him come here?"

"Yes... I saw his car at the gate as I was resting in the morning room. Then it went away..."

"You knew he wasn't driving it. Who was in it with him? Was it your Aunt Beatrice?"

Her eyes opened wide.

"She didn't do it... She couldn't... She wouldn't."

"But you saw her in the car and you saw her drive off later..."

"She was going through the gate... It was getting dark... I must have been mistaken..."

"So, it *was* your Aunt Beatrice...?"

For answer the girl screamed and lapsed into hysterics again.

"Look after her, sir," Littlejohn said to Uncle Bernard and then he and Cromwell went round the house and locked doors and windows.

"And now, you will both come with me and stay elsewhere than here for the night," he said to Doane and his niece when they got back. Nita was weeping but calm and the old man moved like someone in a dream.

"You'd better come with us and we'll find you some place for the night... In the circumstances, it had better not be the Kents' home."

"Better try the Trotmans," said Uncle Bernard and lapsed into stunned silence.

They telephoned for the local police and soon a sergeant, two constables and the doctor arrived. Bastable looked ready to do a lot of talking, but Littlejohn gently waved him aside and indicated Nita and Uncle Bernard, waiting mutely, to leave with him. The old man was wearing his astrakhan coat and holding the top hat he'd worn at the funeral. Littlejohn took it from him and changed it for a soft felt.

"Where's the Superintendent?" he asked the sergeant.

"He's been out since the inquest. I left a message..."

"I'll be back as soon as I've made a call or two and seen Dr Doane and Miss Nita safely somewhere."

The sergeant looked up at Uncle Bernard and smiled. Dr Doane. That was a new one! Balmy Bernard was the name they knew him by locally.

"Okay," he said, forgetting his place for a minute.

Uncle Bernard was fussing and trying to get a word in.

"Give me my own hat; this isn't mine. It's too big for me."

Littlejohn could have laughed outright at the sight of him, the opulent-looking homburg down to his ears. He gave Uncle Bernard back his topper and the old man flung the felt back on the hat-stand.

"We're ready..."

7
COMMOTION AT ST MARK'S

Cromwell summed it all up in his customary fashion.

"Two murders and not a pot washed!"

They pulled up at the studded oak door of St Mark's, and Littlejohn rang the bell. They were certainly there whilst the news of Arthur Kent's murder was fresh. It was going to be Littlejohn's duty to tell his widow of his death.

A cheerful, red-faced girl opened the door.

"Come in. I'll tell Mrs Kent you're calling..."

Beatrice Kent came to meet them at once. Littlejohn felt sorry for her. She had been utterly devoted to her brother, he'd been told, and now she looked to have taken the judge's death very badly. All her colour had gone, and her complexion was like parchment. Her fine dark eyes were feverishly bright in their shadowed sockets, as though she wasn't sleeping well.

"May we have a word with you in private, madam?"

"Is it about my brother...?"

That was apparently all she thought of.

She led the way into a small cosy morning room where a bright fire was burning and offered them a chair apiece. Then she sat on the edge of a small sewing chair as if she didn't intend staying long.

"Yes...?"

"I'm sorry to have to tell you, Mrs Kent, that your husband has met with an accident..."

The impact of the news was not very marked. Beatrice Kent rose and stood relaxed, ready to sit again when the tale had been told.

"Is he...is it serious...?"

"I'm afraid he's dead, madam."

She seemed more puzzled than distressed.

"But I left him not more than half an hour ago. I dropped him at the gates of Beyle House. He was going to see the children about their plans. I was driving home and gave him a lift from town to Beyle..."

"Did you go in the house, Mrs Kent?"

"No..."

"May I ask why? You were their aunt, weren't you?"

"Yes; I was their nearest relative. But Beyle has been extremely distasteful to me for many years. I never got on with my late sister-in-law and stopped calling. I saw no reason for resuming it. Nita and I are friends, but Alec and I have nothing in common."

"I... By the way, madam, if you don't feel up to answering questions at present, please say so. We can call again."

"Please go on, Inspector. I'm waiting to learn how my husband met his death. Was it a road accident?"

"No. He was murdered! Struck down on the threshold of Beyle House..."

That did it! Mrs Kent sat down, overcome. It had seemed previously that her face could not turn paler. Now, the remnants of blood drained away leaving her the colour of putty.

"No... No!... No!!"

She was losing control. She'd been through so much in the past days that the limit had been reached. Out in the hall they could hear Margery, the maid, talking on the telephone in muffled tones. The milkman had rung up to ask her to go to the pictures. Cromwell hastily called her and asked her for some brandy. Margery, torn between her milkman and her mistress, decided in favour of the latter, told the phone she'd ring back later, rushed to the dining room and returned with a bottle.

"What's the matter?"

"Mrs Kent isn't very well..."

"What have you been doing to her...?"

Margery, still brandishing the three-star bottle, took her mistress in her arms and pressed her head to her ample bosom.

"There, there, Mrs Kent. Whatever is it?"

"Mr Kent...your master...is dead. He's been murdered..."

It was now Margery's turn to emit shrieks. The policemen were kept busy dosing the women from the bottle. They both seemed to recover together, their colour flooded back at the touch of the old brandy, and they comforted one another in turn.

Margery was indignant.

"Well...? What are you waiting for, you two? Haven't you done enough? Better leave her to me."

"No, Margery. They've both been very kind and want to ask me some questions. Go and make us all some tea. We need it."

The maid eyed the two detectives reproachfully, as though they might have killed her master between them, and then left slowly. On the way she dialled the dairy, told the milkman in an enigmatic voice that she couldn't see him that night, and then hung up and went to make the tea. The milkman, suspecting a rival, spent the night contemplating throwing himself in the river, but, thinking better of it, proposed and was accepted by Margery the following day. When all was settled, they went to keep a milk-bar at Leamington Spa... But that doesn't concern us here...

"You say you left your husband at the gates of Beyle, Mrs Kent?"

"Yes. Then I drove on at once."

"Whilst you were at Beyle, did you see anyone else about the place? In the grounds or on the road…?"

"No. There wasn't a soul about."

"You say you picked up your husband at his office. Did you call for him?"

"No. He had the car with him. After the inquest, I stayed for lunch in town. He said I could call for the car when I was ready to go home. I did some shopping and went for it. It's usually parked in a side-street near the office. Arthur, my husband, was sitting in it waiting for me. He said he was going to Beyle House and would like me to drop him there on my way home. He would catch the bus at the gate later. I drove him there, left him, and came on here."

"Why did he suddenly decide to go to Beyle?"

"I didn't say he suddenly decided to do anything, Inspector. It must have just cropped up…something which made it necessary…"

"This is all very difficult. Whoever killed him must have seen you drop him, followed him in, and struck him down. Miss Nita saw you both from the window…saw you leave…"

"Did she?"

It was said unpleasantly. Mrs Kent resented being watched, it was clear.

Littlejohn could have sworn that, in some way, Beatrice Kent was relieved by her husband's death. It was hard to believe that she had just been bereaved swiftly and violently. Once the initial shock of the murder had passed, she had recovered full possession of herself.

"Had your husband any enemies, madam?"

She was suddenly on her guard, watchful, suspicious.

"What do you mean?"

"Just what I said…"

"That someone hated Arthur enough to kill him?"

"Yes."

"I don't know. He never told me of any enemies. He never told me much."

This was inviting inquiry, but Littlejohn let it go. All in good time.

Margery arrived with the tea and poured out three cups. Cromwell put on his best smile.

"Mind if I take a cup with you in the kitchen, miss? There are one or two things I'd like to ask you…"

Littlejohn, with difficulty, kept a straight face. Margery had flushed the colour of a geranium. Instinctively it flashed in her simple mind that he had designs on her! She tossed her head.

"I can look after myself. I should have been going out with my young man, but…"

She thought she'd better let him know from the start that her heart was given to somebody else. But she was flattered, and stayed, waiting for the next move.

"What do you wish to ask her?"

There was a rasp in Mrs Kent's voice.

"Perhaps she can tell us something useful about one or another of the recent deaths, madam. We'll have to question her sooner or later."

"You will, will you? I like your impertinence. As if I knew anything about it."

"Go along the pair of you and get your cups of tea…" Littlejohn always supported his sergeant and Cromwell cast him a grateful nod.

The coloured portrait of Queen Victoria, cut from a 1901 Christmas almanac by Margery's late mother and carried about like a sacred relic wherever her daughter went, stared at Cromwell in stony disapproval. The sergeant gave the Old Queen an apologetic look.

"Take sugar?"

"Yes, please."

Cromwell smiled, carefully laid his bowler on the kitchen sideboard and drew up a rocking chair to the fire.

"That's right. Make yourself at home. Would you like the wireless on, as well?"

Margery was thawing. Impudent banter was her way of showing a return of her good humour.

"No… I want to talk to you, Margery. You said this has stopped you going to see your young man?"

"Yes; but he can wait. The master doesn't die every day."

She suddenly seemed to realise for the first time what had happened.

"Isn't it funny talkin' like this. The master mightn't be dead at all the way we're carryin' on. When my pa died, the 'ouse was like bedlam. Everybody cryin' all over the place, ma with 'ysterics, me struck all of a heap and couldn't do a hand's turn to help myself, and that's the way it was till after he was laid away. Then ma got married agen…"

"You're right. Doesn't seem like a house of mourning, does it?"

"But he was never at home. Thought of nothing but work…or so you'd have thought. Neglected poor Mrs Kent shameful. I don't know how she stood it. I know what my ma would have done… and *did*. Pa once got sweet on one of the flighty young things in the shop he worked in. 'Ought to be ashamed of yourself and you with daughters older than her,' said ma, when told. And she emptied a pan of cabbage water over his head. 'And that's what you'll get every time you come 'ome with face-powder on yer, or lipstick on yer hanky,' she says. It cured pa good and proper. But of course, Mrs Kent's too much of a lady. She just bore it…"

"He was a one for the ladies, then?"

"I shouldn't be talkin' like this and him not yet in his grave. But, as you said, I'll only be asked it all later, didn't you? So, I might as well speak first as last."

"That's right."

Margery was enjoying it. She poured out another cup of tea for Cromwell and gave him a piece of her own-made slab cake.

"He wasn't here, there and everywhere. It was just Mrs Crake he was sweet on. Eyes for nobody else when she was about. Disgraceful, I call it!"

"What kind of man was he?"

"Cold as ice to most people, includin' the missus an' me. Ordered me about just like he talked to the dog."

She indicated the spaniel sleeping in the corner. He hadn't shown a sign of interest in the company and was busy dreaming in his basket, whimpering and thrashing about convulsively as if in the throes of a hard afternoon's rabbiting.

"I wouldn't have stayed but for the missus. One of the best, she is. I'll be sorry to leave her."

"Thinking of leaving soon?"

She looked coy, stretched out her sturdy legs to the fire and started to rock voluptuously in her rocking chair.

"There's four of them want me..."

She said it with a show of indifference; it didn't matter how many of them wanted her or how hard, she was the one who was going to say "when".

"He'll be a lucky chap, whoever he is. You'll not only make him proud of you, you'll give him a good cake, too."

"Go on with you."

Cromwell looked at Queen Victoria apologetically again and she gave him back a frosty, regal stare.

"Mr Crake died here, I believe."

"Yes. Pewmonia, they said. He was that poorly when they brought him here. Must have had it on him for days before he fell sick. You oughtn't to speak ill of the dead, but Mrs Crake was a devil. Look at her with the master. Shocking. She couldn't leave the men alone. And on with the new and off with the old, as they say... Or should it be the other way about?"

"It's all the same. Do you think one of his rivals for Mrs Crake might have harmed Mr Kent?"

"Why should they? Mrs Crake was dead by that time..."

"Yes, that's true. But suppose somebody knew something about Mr Kent and Mrs Crake and tried to..."

"Blackmail! You talk like a tuppenny book! Blackmail in Tilsey! Why; they only do that in London and big cities..."

Margery had evidently been educated in the true penny novelette tradition where the innocents of the provinces need to go to the evil cities to be victimised.

"Besides, Mrs Kent knew all about it. She hated Mrs Crake. Not only because of her and Mr Kent but more because of the way Mrs Crake treated Mrs Kent's brother. Doted on Mr Nicholas, did the mistress. I don't blame her. If I'd a brother like him, I'd dote on him. Poor Mr Crake."

Margery shed a tear or two. It was evident the dead judge had not been without his supporters.

"Is there any truth in the rumour about Mrs Crake opening the windows when her husband was ill and, so to speak, starving him to death?"

Margery agitated herself to and fro enthusiastically in her rocking chair.

"I don't know. If you ask me, it was all UP with him when he got here. So ill, he was. I'd believe anything of that Mrs Crake, but why should she want to kill her husband? She was having a good time. He let her have all her own way. She did just as she liked. Why kill the goose that laid the golden eggs?"

"Let's see; wasn't it the Christmas carol singers who said they saw him at the window?"

"Yes... That Tom Trumper. Him and his carol singers! He says it's for charity. But if you saw the condition they're in after one of their rounds of the town, you'd know *whose* health they were looking after. A lot of proper old topers. They was, as like as not, as tight as drums when they got here. I slept through it all myself, but I've seen 'em in years past. They *imagined* things... Have a piece of my Christmas cake...?"

She'd taken to Cromwell, that was obvious. Nobody but her special friends, like the milkman, ever got helpings of Margery's special cake. She emerged with a rich, dark slab, lost in concrete-like icing and rocky marzipan.

"There! Try that..."

The Old Queen looked icily on whilst Cromwell mastered his helping.

He congratulated Margery unctuously on her cooking and then got back to business.

"So, you think the affair of exposing Mr Crake to the east wind was all a tale, Margery?"

"Or else he was delirious and when they struck up their carols, he got up and thought he was throwing them some coppers or somethin'. Naturally, Mrs Crake would try to get him back to his bed. If that's what Old Trumper saw, there's no harm in it. It would do Mr Crake a lot of harm, but you can't hold Mrs Crake responsible for it now, can you?"

"No. That's quite a theory. You defend her as if you liked her."

"I never. But right's right, isn't it? Besides, I don't hold with killing people. Wrong as she might have done in life, nobody's any right to hasten her end."

"Were the Crakes and the Kents very friendly?"

"No. Mrs Crake and the mistress were daggers drawn. Mrs Kent couldn't stand her on account of what she did to Mr Nicholas. Then, when Mrs Crake and the master got sweet on one another...well... They didn't visit one another much. Until Mr Nicholas was ill, Mrs Crake hadn't been here for a year or more."

Strangely enough, whilst Cromwell was pursuing his inquiries below stairs, Littlejohn was following similar lines above. Mrs Kent thought exactly the same as Margery about Tom Trumper and carolling party.

"A lot of old topers. Trumper might have imagined it. Or my

brother might have heard them singing and got up to the window. His wife would naturally try to pull him back. They had been singing quite a time when I awoke and sent them away."

"The rumour started with Trumper?"

"It seems so..."

"I must have a word with him about exactly what happened..."

"I have thought a lot about it. My sister-in-law treated my brother shamefully. But I cannot believe that even *she* would do such a thing to him. Had I believed it, I would gladly have killed her myself."

"Where were you at five in the afternoon after the funeral of your brother? You mustn't mind my asking. It is a matter of routine."

"I haven't an alibi, if that's what you're after, Inspector. I was very upset about the whole affair. In our family, the women don't attend funerals. But my sister-in-law insisted on going to Nick's and making quite a show of herself in widow's weeds. My brother would have hated it. I had to go, in the circumstances. When it was over, I came home and stayed indoors until dinner, at seven. Margery was out, so nobody could testify..."

"Not even your husband, were he still alive?"

"No. He went back to the office."

"And now about your brother's will, Mrs Kent. I believe he left the bulk of what he had to his wife..."

"Who told you that?"

She raised her head sharply and snapped out the question.

"Dr Doane..."

"Doctor...? Oh, I beg your pardon. It seems strange to hear Uncle Bernard called that. How did he know?"

"I didn't ask the source of his information. He said there was a considerable sum for insurance and little else but Beyle, which was to go to Nita."

"My brother was a strange man. Singularly impersonal when it came to doing his duty. He covered his life for ten thousand pounds which was to go to his widow on his death. He told me that, when he died, Dulcie wouldn't be able to do a thing if she weren't left provided for. In his own words, she'd die in the gutter. So he took out a large insurance. It was a terrible drain on his resources. He had to undertake other things besides court duties. He was rather eminent in company law and did a lot of private work. He also wrote a book or two which brought in royalties. They are standard authorities, I gather, on company matters. Then, of course, Beyle went to Nita. He knew very well that Alec would help his mother to dispose of the insurances and regarded him as well dealt with especially as Alec was supposed to be studying to become an architect. He'll never make much of it."

"And now Alec inherits the ten thousand?"

"Did Uncle Bernard tell you that, as well?"

"Yes."

"I didn't know, but I'm not surprised. He was the apple of his mother's eye, and, of course, Nita has her own profession, and, unless I'm very mistaken, her looks will serve her well in the marriage market."

Littlejohn looked hard at Mrs Kent. The way she spoke, there was no love lost between her and Nita, either.

"How did your brother expect Nita to be able to keep up Beyle without money to do it? It's rather a ruin now; it will be worse in a few years."

"He left her Beyle *and* the residue after Dulcie got the insurance. I recollect his telling me about his will and how he would try to amass some ready cash to leave her..."

"Is there likely to be much?"

"I don't know. There ought to be quite a sum. He once said that he forced himself to make ends meet on his salary. That's why Beyle is so tumbledown. When we were children there, it was beautiful..."

"So he tried to save his fees and income from his books...?"

"Yes. They ought to be considerable."

"Do you know who the executors were?"

"My late husband and his partner, Mr Trotman. So far, I haven't heard a thing about their duties. I guess Mr Trotman, being a lawyer, will now handle everything."

"And now about Alec, Mrs Kent. So far, he hasn't returned home since the inquest on his mother..."

"He is probably drinking somewhere. He's thoroughly dissolute. He was badly brought up when a child. Nita was neglected, but Dulcie seemed to try to make Alec a part of herself, sharing in her escapades, even when he was quite small."

"I'm surprised your brother allowed it."

"Had you known Dulcie, you wouldn't have been. After the birth of Nita, she seemed to go morally all to pieces. Nothing Nick did was of any use. She was a disgrace to him. He had ample grounds for divorcing her but would never agree. I pleaded with him to get rid of her. All he said was, 'I married her and I'm responsible for her. If I let her go, she will soon go to the dogs. My presence is the only curb she has.' And that was true, although it wasn't much use."

"I don't understand it at all, Mrs Kent. Here is a man well thought of, with possibly a great future, marries a woman quite unsuited to him, allows her a free hand in her disreputable conduct and lets her drag his good name..."

"Stop! I won't hear of such a thing! Nick's name has always been good. It was better for the saintly way in which he treated that wicked woman!"

"But, as a rule, when such a marriage goes on the rocks, there is good reason for it. A psychological reason, I mean. One of the parties, or both, simply drives the other to desperation. But from what I hear of Mr Crake, he was the last person to drive a wife on such a course."

"That is true. He didn't do it. They were happy together for many years. Then, she just went mad. It *was* madness. They were a queer family. Look at Uncle Bernard... And I once met their father. He was a dipsomaniac! They had to put him in a home now and then. Finally, he died from it."

"Were you aware that Mrs Crake suffered from a kind of dancing malady caused by the bite of a tarantula spider in her youth?"

Beatrice Kent's eyes opened wide.

"Whoever has been telling you that tale?"

"Uncle Bernard."

"He seems to have told you quite a lot. No. I never heard such fantastic nonsense before. Nick... Was he supposed to know?"

"Uncle Bernard said so. He said that was why he, Dr Doane, was allowed to live there; because he knew how to deal with Mrs Crake during the attacks."

"I never heard such nonsense! Bernard Doane came to Beyle for a so-called holiday. He was penniless, except for a very large collection of gold coins said to have been collected by his father. He provided pocket-money for himself by selling his silly medals, or whatever they were, and sponged on Nick for the rest. His holiday became protracted to a regular residence. Nick tolerated it, as he did many other things, because Dulcie wished it. It is sad that, in spite of all she did, he loved her to the end."

"He must have been a very fine man."

Beatrice Kent rose like one possessed.

"To me, he was the finest man who ever lived. And let anyone beware who says otherwise, yourself included, Inspector."

"Where did Doane live before he came to Beyle?"

"In rooms in London. It's said he was in practice in Madrid at one time. But he threw it up for music and then made a miserable failure at his first concert. He must have been in England twenty years or more."

"When did he come to Beyle?"

"Shortly after Nick's marriage."

"That tallies with his own story."

"So, he's been telling you his sorry story. He's very plausible and has managed to eke out a very comfortable existence for many years through his pathetic tales. He's as mad as the rest of his family..."

Her sentence was interrupted by a violent ringing of the doorbell. They heard Margery hurry to answer it, but, before she could ask any questions or announce anybody, loud footsteps thudded in the hall, and then, in the doorway of the room in which Littlejohn was sitting, appeared Alec. He was drunk and held himself upright with difficulty. He did not see the Inspector and went straight to his aunt.

"Alec! What are you doing here in that disgraceful condition? You ought to be ashamed..."

"Go on, go on, complete the sentence, Auntie Bee. I oughter to be ashamed and my mother not yet in her grave... Very unkind of you, I must say, when I've walked all the way from Beyle to express my condolence. We oughter get together, you an' I, Bee. Fellow-mourners; simultaneously bereaved, so to speak. I left the police busy on the body, Auntie... Gave 'em a very satisfactory alibi... Twenty-four people can testify I've been all the afternoon at the airport bar. No' so bad, eh?"

"Alec! Control yourself... This is no time for levity..."

"Levity? Who? Me? No, Aunt. You know as well as I do what I'm thinkin'. Somebody's avenged my mother... You know as well as I do who we think murdered her. Uncle Arthur did it because she insisted on lovin' him and wantin' to tell all the world she did, when all the time Uncle Arthur had got tired of her and wanted to be his old respectable self again... We know, don' we?"

"You're drunk..."

"I maybe... I maybe... But how does it go: *In vino veritas*. What are you doin' here? Din' see you..."

Alec turned and spotted Littlejohn sitting in the gloom outside the orbit of the standard lamp.

"What are doin' here? Bloody copper. Damn snoop... This is a family affair. We'll settle it our own way. Gerrout..."

He made as if to do violence to Littlejohn, tripped over the carpet, and measured his length on the floor. There he remained, swearing and snorting, until Cromwell, who had followed him and was standing keeping Margery quiet in the doorway, helped Littlejohn to raise him and throw him on the couch like a sack of potatoes. There Alec at once fell asleep and there they left him, snoring, to the tender mercies of his aunt.

8
DISCOMFITURE OF TOM TRUMPER

Cromwell halted in front of an old-fashioned shop with a bow window which held an excellent position in the High Street. In banner headlines, ornamented with holly and mistletoe, was emblazoned:

TRUMPERS FOR VALUE AND SERVICE.

Beneath it, in smaller type:

ONLY NORFOLK POULTRY SOLD.

In the window itself stood a plaster Santa Claus bearing a banner like a fire-screen:

A MERRY CHRISTMAS TO ONE AND ALL.

The figure had, until Christmas Eve, nodded jovially with the help of clockwork but, in its frenzy of greetings, had dislocated its machinery and now held its head pathetically awry with stiff-neck. A sign between the first and second storeys announced what everybody knew by heart:

B TRUMPER & SON, GROCERS,
AND WINE MERCHANTS.
EST 1858.

B Trumper had been with God (we hope) over twenty years, and now the son ruled alone.

The shop was dark inside and smelled, on this particular morning, of cinnamon, a bag of which had been accidentally burst. The floors were of old wood and the counters, where most used, were hollowed out by generations of customers. The shelves which ran round the place from end to end and from counter height to ceiling were full of good and bad things, particularly in the section which held strange kinds of canned fish. Facing you as you entered, the wine department stimulated your thirst with its bottles of coloured alcohol in many forms, and a large card:

BONAVENTURA (ENGLISH) PORT.

Mr Trumper's recent unofficial appearance in the Crake affair had improved his Christmas trade to the extent of clearing out most of his seasonable fare and now a solitary stack of plum puddings in basins and a box or two of withered looking almonds and peanuts were all that remained. An easel supported a blackboard on which was written in coloured chalks amid a flurry of snow, holly and mistletoe:

TRUMPERS WISH YOU
A HAPPY NEW YEAR.

SEE IT IN WITH OUR MONSTER
TWO-GUINEA BARGAIN PARCEL.

1 Bott Australian Sherry.
1 Bott Bonaventura Port.
1 Bott Cocky Dick Cocktail.

"Yes?" said someone hopefully to Cromwell, who was reckoning up in his own mind whether or not the parcel was a bargain or a fraud.

"Yes?"

The questioner was a large, portly man in a huge white apron like a tablecloth tied round his middle. He wore lozenge-shaped spectacles and had wrapped some wool round the bridge to prevent their lacerating his button-nose. His grey, drooping moustache added a touch of permanent melancholy to his face. He was busy piling up items from the shelves on the counter as he read them from an order book.

"Mr Trumper?"

"Did you want to see 'im? I'm not 'im. But I'm manager 'ere, and if there's anythin' I can do…"

"I'd rather see Mr Trumper, if I may."

"You travellin' for somethin' because we shan't be orderin' till we've stock-took on the 31st?"

"No. I'm from the police. Will you tell him I'm here?"

The man in the apron placed his two palms flat on the counter and leaned confidentially towards Cromwell.

"And not before it's time, eether. Shameful the gossip that's goin' on. I'm surprised that Tom Trumper should countenance it. I was with them carol singers and I didn't see nothin' of all that's bein' scandalously talked of. Poor Mr Crake…"

"I'd like a word with you after, then. What did you say your name was?"

"Call me Oscar…"

Oscar's surname was Bloater and he didn't like it. In fact, he'd contemplated changing it to Bloader or Boater, but his old father, still living at eighty-four, had kicked up such a fuss that Oscar had given up the idea. It had been his downfall economically, however. At one time, he'd been sweet on Tom's daughter and Tom had talked of making him a partner. But the father, having envisaged *Trumper and Bloater* on the sign over the door, had finally blown cold on the matter; and the daughter, contemplating changing a name like Trumper to an even worse one, had run away with a wine traveller called MacNamara and divorced him for one called Heginbotham. Mr Bloater was bitter. He was too old to change his job, but he never lost a chance of secretly doing down Tom Trumper. He made horrified gestures to anybody who inquired about the tinned fish and whispered here and there that an eighteen-shilling bottle of Tally-Ho Port would cheer you up for letting-in the New Year far quicker than *two* bargain parcels.

"I'll call Mr Trumper, and if you'll have a word with me when you've done with 'im, I'll tell you a thing or two..."

Mr Trumper was in the back room mixing bottles of Cocky Dick for his festive customers. One of gin to four from an unlabelled bottle which looked to contain homemade Vermouth, and a dash of bitters. "Taste it," said Mr Trumper genially, after introductions had been effected. "Bloater, the assistant in the shop, says you want a word with me?"

No wonder he wanted to be called Oscar! thought Cromwell.

Mr Trumper might have been Bloater's brother except that he looked twenty years older and wore steel-framed pince-nez instead of spectacles. These balanced precariously on the end of his nose as he measured out the ingredients of his potions. Cromwell took a drink from the proffered measuring glass. The liquor crossed his tongue and palate very benignly and he was just about to congratulate Mr Trumper on it when it struck his stomach like a soft-nosed bullet. He hiccupped violently and held on to the table for support.

"He, he, he," cackled Tom Trumper. "Got a bit o' kick, wot?"

Cromwell felt like one who has been given an explosive cigar.

He could have kicked Trumper's large rear, which shook like a jelly in his mirth.

"I want to ask you a question or two, sir," he said formally, and took out his little black book to make it look official. Mr Trumper grew solemn, removed his pince-nez, shut them in a spring box with a loud bang and indicated that he was ready.

"Did you really see Mr Crake naked at the window with his wife helping him to catch his death of cold on the night before he died…or had you all been drinking Cocky Dicks and didn't know what you *did* see?"

The bad wine had gone to his head now and he didn't care a damn how Trumper took the question.

"'Ere, 'ere, 'ere. What you getting at? I said nothin' about seein' Mrs Crake doing any such thing to her 'usband. All I said was 'e was at the window and his wife pulling of him back into the room…"

"Did you actually see it?"

Mr Trumper cleared his throat and paused to consider. Cromwell hiccupped softly and cleared his own throat too.

"Now, look here, sir," he said gravely. "This matter is very vital. In fact, a man's life might depend on it…"

Mr Trumper took a drink of his homemade Vermouth from the measuring glass.

"'Oose life?" he asked, and he put on his pince-nez again.

"Never you mind, sir. Police secrets. But I can tell you that the thing will soon be aired in court, and, if you assure me that you did see Mr Crake in the circumstances mentioned, you'll be called upon to repeat it in public under oath."

Mr Trumper paused.

"Let me give you another drink, sir. A proper one, this time. Good sherry, eh? That was just my little joke. I mixed it different just to have you on… I'm a proper one for my little joke."

Cromwell assumed his most disapproving air.

"Was the affair at St Mark's a little joke as well, Mr Trumper?

Because, if it was, it was in very bad taste, like the one you just played on me. Come now, sir, I've no time to waste."

"Oh, very well, if you've no sense of 'umour... Strictly speakin', I didn't see it myself. Not with my own eyes. But one of my choir saw it and told me. I...ahem... I..."

Mr Trumper began to look queer. He licked his dry lips and mopped the sweat from his shiny forehead.

"You mean, you passed it off as if you'd seen it, sir. You took the limelight, so to speak."

Tom Trumper grew humble.

"I didn't see any harm in it. A tradesman like me 'as to 'ave somethin' to chat about to his customers. It's part of the goodwill is a choice titbit of noos. It 'ad happened, so I didn't see any wrong in passin' it off as if I'd seen it myself."

"No? Who did see it?"

"Willy Kneeshaw, one o' my basses. He told me..."

"When did he tell you?"

"The follerin' morning when the noos got round town as the Recorder was breathin' his last. 'No wonder,' says Willie, callin' in the shop for his deliveries — he runs the van for me — 'No wonder he's on his last legs'...and he tells me the tale."

"And that's all there is to it?"

"Yes. Sure you won't 'ave a little proper sherry...?"

"Nope. Enough's as good as a feast, sir, thank you all the same. Where can I find Willie?"

"He's out with the van now. He lives at Bright's Buildings across the way, in the 'ouse on the top. He's caretaker of the offices there and runs my van in his off time..."

"Right. I'll be off then, sir, if you've no more to tell me. Have you?"

"Only that Mrs Crake owed me quite a bill. Never 'ad any money. The Recorder used to settle them for her, although I did hear he allowed her enough for all she wanted and more besides. But she couldn't make ends meet. Poor Mr Crake..."

"Very well, sir, thanks. Good morning."

"Good mornin'. No 'ard feelings. Just my little joke."

"I ought to charge you for obstructing the police in the discharge of their duties..."

And with that, Cromwell passed into the shop. Mr Bloater was serving a lady but hastily disposed of her. Then he removed his large apron as though it might impede him in his chat with the police. He looked hard at Cromwell's flushed face.

"You been getting cross, sir?"

"No. Drinking Mr Trumper's poison. Cocky Dick, indeed!"

"You don't mean to say he's tried that trick on you. Give you a drink from the Fernet Branca bottle instead of the Vermouth! That's one of his so-called jokes. He's got a nerve tryin' it on the police! But then, 'e never had a sense of wot was proper. I see him peepin' at us through the glass door, so I'd better tell you. I was with the carol singers. I'm a bit of a tenor myself. All I want to say is, neither Trumper nor anybody else saw Mr Crake at that window. I was *there*. I'd have known. How 'e has the nerve to say he saw it... It was the next to the last place we'd to call at. We sang *'Ere we come a-Wassailing* and *Midnight Clear* and then out comes Mrs Kent an' stops us. Her brother was ill on 'er 'ands, she said. So we went off. Usually have a good spread at the Kents. But this time we 'adn't. Although I say it myself, the 'ospitality we'd already received by the time we got to St Mark's was enough to stop us seein' very much. All we could do was *sing* and that off pitch, as you might say. And Tom Trumper was as bad as the rest. Half tight and more. I see no Mr Crake at the winder and I was right under it, singing away for dear life. That's as true as I'm here..."

From behind the glass panels of the back room Mr Trumper was watching them. He had changed his steel-rimmed pince-nez for shell-framed spectacles, the better to see what was going on.

"Who is Willie Kneeshaw?"

"Our van man. Drives the horse and cart. Can't be trusted with the motor van, so we just use him and the old vehicle at rush times. He's caretaker of a block of offices. All he's good for really. A bit simple. Difficult to make him understand sometimes and as difficult to get him to talk."

"He seems to have talked to Mr Trumper, though. It seems he was the one who saw the scene at the bedroom window."

"Wot! Well, I never! Now what's afoot, I wonder? Why should Trumper be so interested in idle gossip of that sort that isn't true and make out he saw it when he didn't, and then say it was Willie as is a bit short in his wits just to get out of it."

"He said it was gossip and good for trade."

At this, the glass door opened, Mr Trumper appeared and made for the front door. He had removed his apron and was wearing a tall, black bowler hat.

"Good day," he said very formally to Cromwell. "I'm jest going to the bank. I want to see *you* when I get back, BLOATER," he added ominously and offensively to Mr Bloater and closed the door with a bang.

"Well!" said Bloater. "Wot's he up to? He's not goin' to the bank at all, if you ask me. He put all his takin's in the night safe last night and the manager won't be there yet. It's market day and Grimes, that's the manager, always goes to the markets branch before he turns in here. He's off somewhere else. I wonder where? Did you hear 'im at me? As if he was goin' to give me the sack? As if he *could*? This shop's mortgaged to the hilt. I've a thousand pounds loan money in this show too, *and* he can't repay. He was hard-up when my mother died, and he persuaded me to invest what she left me. Promised a partnership and went back on 'is word..."

"*Is* he hard-up then?"

"Since these chain stores opened up here, a lot of his trade's gone. The shop's mortgaged and he's been over-drawn at the bank. The manager's been after him, I know."

"Well, I must be off, Mr Bloater. Thanks for what you told me. Be seeing you again, I hope."

"Yes, sir. I'll let you know if I get the sack."

On his way to the police station Cromwell passed the post office and called in to buy a stamp for his daily letter to his wife. In one of the telephone booths, he recognised the tall bowler hat of Mr Trumper. Tom didn't notice Cromwell. He was too engrossed in his call. Whoever he was talking to must have been giving him a rough time for Trumper kept mopping his brow and between his neck and his collar with his handkerchief. He looked very unhappy.

Littlejohn was with Mr Trotman discussing the will and other things, and Cromwell called at the police station to wait for him. Superintendent Simpole was in his office surrounded by papers and looking more sardonic than ever.

"Been calling on Trumper, I see..."

"How did you know?"

"I don't miss much that goes on in this town. Were you confirming the tale about Crake's behaviour and his wife's attempt to murder him when Trumper and his crew were singing carols, like a diabolical accompaniment, under the window? Because, if you were, I could have told you all you want to know..."

Simpole's voice was acid.

"Yes. And by the way, sir, we're not here deliberately poaching on your ground. We were *invited*, you know. So don't take it so badly. We only want to cooperate."

"Sorry. I'm a bit sore about this. I could have managed very well myself. But to return to Trumper. He didn't see what he said he saw, did he?"

"No. He said somebody called Kneeshaw told him."

"Kneeshaw! The local simpleton. Murders, ghosts, parachutists during the war, Loch Ness monsters in the park lake...it's always Willy Kneeshaw who sees them! If you want to set a rumour flying round the town to suit your own purposes, you say Willie saw or did something, and it's off. However, I got that much from

Trumper myself. I intend seeing Willie as soon as our wholesale murderer will give me a minute or two to spare. Now it's Arthur Kent..."

"I'm going to see Kneeshaw myself as soon as he gets back from delivering the groceries. Meanwhile, could you help me trace a telephone call, sir?"

Cromwell told Simpole about Trumper's haste to telephone from an outside instrument after his interview with him.

"Hmm... Could it be that somebody has put Trumper up to spreading the rumour with a view to implicating Mrs Crake?"

"You mean somebody who intended killing her all the time so he spread the tale around to turn people's eyes to one of the family, out for revenge on her for Mr Crake's death?"

"You read my thoughts like a book, Sergeant. That's it."

As he talked with Simpole, Cromwell noticed that he was furtively trying to conceal an object lying on his desk by shuffling it in a pile of letters. It was a large magnifying glass. He wondered what the Superintendent had been up to and why he wanted to hide it. Had he been snooping round like Sherlock Holmes with the glass or what...?

The telephone bell rang and Simpole answered it.

"Lucky that owing to the war this place isn't yet on the automatic telephone. The call from the first box in the post office at eleven-ten was to Trotman, the lawyer. You've so scared Trumper that he's been taking legal opinion and asking friend Trotman for guidance!"

Simpole cackled mirthlessly. Cromwell sensed in the laugh how much on edge the Superintendent really was.

"Well... And are you and the Inspector any nearer a solution of the murders?"

"No, sir. It might be anybody. Mrs Kent has no alibi for Mrs Crake's murder; nor for her husband's really..."

"Yes, she has. I followed the pair of them out to Beyle. I intended seeing old Bernard, but, finding them just ahead of me, I travelled slowly to make sure they weren't bound there too. They were. I saw Mrs Kent drop her husband at the gate and drive off. I followed her part of the way, as I'd another call to make. Thought I'd let Kent get his business done at the house and then return after. When I got back, I found my men in and Kent dead on the mat! I've already told Littlejohn."

"As for Alec," added Cromwell after a pause to digest the strange news, "he seems to have alibis in one bar or another all over the place."

"Not exactly. Only at his favourite one, the airport. And there, I doubt if I'd take their statements for gospel. They'd damn their immortal souls for a glass of whisky and all hang together. What about Nita?"

"No watertight alibi in either case. Uncle Bernard has none in the case of his sister, but Inspector Littlejohn and I were with him when Kent was killed."

"You'll have a job sorting that lot out and I wish you luck. I'm working independently on a line or two myself. I've a lot of local knowledge to draw on, you know."

"Have you any theories, sir?"

"Plenty. I'll tell you quite candidly, I'm out to show the Chief Constable I can solve this case myself…"

Simpole cast a queer sarcastic look at Cromwell.

"I thought if we cooperated…"

"We'll do that when I've found the culprit. I have my pride, you know. I've done the dirty work of this district for fifteen years, and now, when a real sensation and a chance to show my metal comes along, the Chief calls in an outside force. It's not good enough. I'm not blaming you, Sergeant. You've to do as you're told, just the same as I have. But I'm not having you or anybody else picking my brains and getting the credit…"

"I'm sorry you're taking it that way. Inspector Littlejohn will be…"

"I've told him the same thing."

Cromwell remembered the Chief Constable's reason for calling in the Yard over Simpole's head. He'd been in love with Dulcie Crake himself! There was nothing more to be said.

"Well, sir, I'll not take up your time. I'll just sit here and read my notes till the Inspector calls, so you can get on with your work."

"I'd rather you waited in the room next door, if you don't mind. I can't concentrate with anybody else at my elbow."

Cromwell stiffened huffily.

"Very well, sir. I'll go there... Good morning..."

"Be seeing you later..."

The sergeant made his way to the waiting room next door. Then he discovered he'd left his bowler hat behind. Hastily he returned, tapped on the door marked "Superintendent Simpole" and entered. Simpole was again examining a document through his large magnifying glass. He hastily thrust both in his drawer and turned on Cromwell with momentary anger in his eyes.

"Well...? What now?"

"My hat, sir... I forgot it."

Cromwell hastily collected his property and left the room, aware that Simpole was looking strangely ashamed about something.

"What about a cup o' tea" said the large sergeant, who just happened to be passing. "It's long past my elevenses and I'm as dry as a bone."

"I don't mind if I do, thanks."

"You look a bit put-out," said the sergeant over the steaming cups of what turned out to be coffee. "'As the Super been havin' a go at *you*, too?"

"Not exactly. But between you and me, Sergeant, his manners might be improved."

"You're right there. He's given me a 'ell of a time this mornin' so far. The last month or so, he's been absolutely unbearable. I'm thinkin' of askin' for a transfer or else chuckin' up and keepin' a pub, if things go on like this. I can't stand much more."

"What's the matter with him?"

The sergeant passed a huge hand across his brow.

"Ask me another. He's like one who's been crossed in love. He's a bachelor, you know. Lived with his mother till she died two years ago and now he's very comfortable in nice cosy digs, kept by a maiden lady — a *real* lady. But it's not the life for a man, you know. Look at me. Five children, all grown up now, but as 'appy as the day is long if only Simpole will let me be..."

He looked ready to break down and howl.

"Once we all got on fine together. Now he won't have anybody in his room while he's workin'. Seems to want to be all alone as much as he can. Time was when him and me would sit there comparin' notes for hours. Now...well... I'm not wanted. If my work was going off, I wouldn't mind, but it isn't... I say that without boasting, Sergeant..."

He took a large gulp of hot coffee in his emotion and became convulsed.

"God! That's 'ot. And they always bring me coffee when I want tea. What's the *matter* with everybody? 'Ave they all gone mad? Or is it me?"

He turned his blue childish eyes in dumb appeal to Cromwell.

"Do you ever see him using a magnifying glass on papers?"

"So *you've* seen it too! You're a sharp 'un, you know. Proper Scotland Yard sleuth'ound..."

He gave Cromwell an admiring look.

"Yes. That's another thing. That magnifying glass. I think he thinks he's Sherlock Holmes, you know. Candidly..."

The sergeant solemnly pulled himself together to impart a profound truth.

"Candidly, I think the Super's goin' off his chump. Work and worry's gettin' him down. He ought to find himself a good wife to take his mind off things..."

And with this sage prescription for his chief's complaint, the sergeant-in-charge rose, wiped his ginger moustache on the back of his hand, and gathered the two cups on his big fist.

"I must be off, else I'll be fallin' foul of him again. So long, sir. Be seein' you again, I 'ope..."

That night, Superintendent Simpole hanged himself in his own office thereby confirming the sergeant's views and giving the town something more exciting to talk about.

9

MR TROTMAN CONDESCENDS

Trotman & Co occupied the best suite of offices in Bright's Buildings. Outside the front door, which opened on a large square with grass and old trees in the centre of it, stood a sumptuous car; Littlejohn had a bet with himself that it belonged to Mr Trotman. It added the final touch to the sensualist lawyer with his Savile Row clothes, his exquisite linen, his white well-tended hands and his fastidious manners. His name was on the appropriate doorplate of the office.

TROTMAN & CO.

Solicitors & Commissioners for Oaths.

L Trotman, MA.

A J Kent, LLB.

J Skrike.

Mr Skrike, whoever *he* might be, brought to your mind a half-naked poor relation with his absence of degrees and his plebeian name. He did most of the work.

Littlejohn paused before a large oak door marked Mr Trotman. Next door there was one, Mr Kent. Both said peremptorily, Private, so the Inspector entered the General Office, the door of which bade you Come In. Mr Skrike, in a glass-partitioned cubby hole, was busy conveyancing, a girl was brewing tea, and a small office-boy with red hair was sticking labels on old envelopes with a view to their use again for humble clients. Mr Trotman was keen on economy for everybody but himself.

"Yes, Chief Inspector Littlejohn," said the boy. "I'll ask him right away, sir." He rummaged in a drawer which presumably held his own property and brought out an album.

"Could you please give me your autograph, sir?" he asked.

Littlejohn's photograph had been in the *Tilsey Magnet* that very morning and this was the price of fame. He signed the book.

"And would you please put 'Scotland Yard' as well, Chief Inspector?"

"Just plain 'Inspector', sonny," said Littlejohn and did as he was bidden. The boy thereat ran all the way to Mr Trotman's room where, in view of his recent contact with one of his personal heroes, he treated his boss with less respect than usual.

"Send him in," boomed Mr Trotman. "And say 'sir' when you address me, boy."

"Okay," replied the boy and, on the way back, wondered to himself if he could wring another autograph from Littlejohn and sell it to other admirers.

Mr Trotman rose as the Inspector entered, but, instead of offering his hand, he gave a little bow and bade Littlejohn be seated. The room was large and airy; the furniture sumptuous and comfortable, especially Mr Trotman's working-chair, padded in soft leather, slung on springs and swivels. His desk was of choice mahogany, a period piece. The walls were half covered in calf-bound volumes; the rest held very nice etchings. Over the fire-place hung a large oil-painting of an obvious and very venerable Trotman in whiskers and high collar.

Mr Lancelot Trotman looked like a very well-bred fish. Small head with pale blue cod's eyes; a perfect sweep of chest and belly which seemed to curve right to his feet; and as he walked his legs moved from the knees only in a paddling motion, like swimming in air. The short fin-like arms, the white flapping hands and sensual lips which had a half-drinking expression permanently upon them, the straight nose. It was as if a magician had taken a large carp from a pond, blessed it, and sent it to Savile Row with orders to get dressed and become a man.

"Ha, Inspector. I wish you could have put off this visit until another day. I am naturally distressed by the violent death of my partner and very occupied. Is it urgent?"

The voice was deep and unctuous. There was little evidence about the place of its owner's being busy, but he was obviously on his guard about something from the start.

Littlejohn felt a bit nettled.

"I won't keep you long, sir. And all my business here is urgent. With two people murdered in as many days, it's bound to be urgent. We don't want a third victim on our hands."

"Of course not… What do you want of me?"

"You are the Crake family lawyer, I gather, sir. Mr Bernard Doane tells me Mr Crake left the bulk of his money, except the house, to his wife and that she in turn left her share to her son. Miss Nita gets Beyle House. Is that so?"

Mr Trotman had risen with an expression of horror on his face. His eyes opened very wide revealing bloodshot whites behind the blue. He loomed over Littlejohn for he was quite as tall as the Inspector and considerably heavier, most of it flabby flesh.

"How dare he? How dare he? I say. That information was confidential and only told to him in confidence by my late client, Mrs Crake. It's outrageous of him to talk about it all over the town."

"He hasn't talked all over the town. He's told me at my pressing request."

"I'm surprised at you, Inspector. You should have come to me."

"Suppose we leave that side of the argument, sir. Was my information correct?"

"Substantially, yes. Substantially..."

When he mouthed a good word, he repeated it like a diner coming back for a second helping.

"Miss Nita was being saddled with a liability in being left Beyle, wasn't she? Even her father's money didn't go to her on Mrs Crake's death; it went to Alec."

"That is right. Miss Crake is not the residuary legatee...residuary legateeeee." He mouthed it again with relish. His bright white dentures flashed as he spoke, and he passed his hand nervously over his well-groomed head.

"But I don't see how this affects your case, Inspector."

"We have to establish motive, sir. By the death of his mother young Mr Crake inherits about ten thousand pounds. Miss Nita inherits a tumbledown house. There's quite a difference."

"You are not suggesting that Alec killed his own mother. That is preposterous."

"No, sir. He seems to have had alibis of sorts given by his drinking companions at the airport bar."

"A wastrel, sir...wasting his substance in riotous living... riotous living, I say."

"How came he to become so degraded. He's barely in his twenties. And with such a father too."

"He was his mother's constant companion. I'm afraid the company he met was not very edifying...not edifying, I say. His mother was a very fine-looking woman. Culchahed, too. I say, culchahed... But she sought the company of artists, bohemians, loose-living people... Fond of the picturesque and unusual...the picturesque and unusual. It might have suited her, but it didn't suit the boy. He was taking alcohol out of bravado at a very early age, much to his mother's amusement."

"But did his father tolerate it?"

Mr Trotman lolled back in his opulent chair and waved his white hands about on the ends of his short arms.

"My dear Inspector. Have you realised what it means for a public man to resist the wishes of a wilful and strong-minded wife, I say, wilful and strong-minded...? She prefers a certain course of reckless conduct. He may forbid it, but can he stop it? If so, pray tell me in what way. Can he shut her up in a room and turn the key? Can he incarcerate her? I say, incarcerate...Or can he beat her to enforce obedience? Can he, a judge, take her to court? Can he sue for judicial separation and cause a scandal and odium on his good name? I say, ooohdium. He was a great churchman, Orthodox Church, although his wife was a Roman Catholic. He felt very keenly the duties of a husband. The same applied to the boy. He couldn't be always watching him. He had his work to do. He sent him away to school, but his mother brought him back and found a tutor locally...one who would let the lad free when it suited Mrs Crake to have his company... Oh, no, my dear sir. Oh, no. It wasn't as easy as that. The result was Alec became an idle and dissolute wastrel at a very early age. An idle, dissolute wastrel..."

Suddenly another look of horror came into Mr Trotman's eyes. Littlejohn followed their direction and saw outside a fellow with the bullet head and stiff hair of a simpleton leaning on the sumptuous car at the door, lighting a clay pipe. This done, he lolled a little more on the bright bonnet as though deriving great satisfaction from the act, and then moved to the shining radiator, the top of which he breathed upon and began to polish with his coat sleeve.

The red-cheeked diminutive junior clerk arrived in response to Mr Trotman's wild signalling on the bell.

"Tell Kneeshaw to get away from my car. That's the second day in succession... I say, in succession. I don't want it breathing upon and I don't want the bonnet polishing. Tell him so at once and tell him, if he values his job, to keep away from it."

"Very good."

"And call me 'sir' when you address me. You may go."

Mr Trotman turned his purple face to Littlejohn.

"The impudence of the present generation… I feel appalled… I am upset. The death of my partner…your questioning which is far from pleasant for me, and now this… I feel very upset, I say."

Littlejohn didn't know what he was expected to say to that but saw the perky junior sending the man called Kneeshaw about his business. They seemed on very good terms and the lad was showing the simpleton his autograph album by way of impressing him.

Mr Trotman beat impatiently on the window with his signet ring and flapped a white hand. Thereupon the party broke up after Kneeshaw had imposed a final polish on the radiator of the car.

"Where were we?"

Mr Trotman oozed back in his padded chair.

"You knew the Crake family very well, sir?"

"Of course I did. I went to school with Crake. We're both natives of this town and were very good friends. That's why I am so upset."

Mr Trotman was contemptuous and sorry for himself at the same time. His petulance made him nervy and jerky. He kept twiddling his fingers and pulling his copious and sensual nether lip.

"What about Mr Bernard Doane? He's lived with them quite a long time…"

"As far as I recollect, he came for a holiday with them soon after their marriage and stayed on. Imposed himself upon them… imposed, I say. I would not have stood it, but Crake was a strange mixture. A strong man on the bench but, in private life, anybody's fool. Too charitable. I'd have sent the fellow packing…"

Mr Trotman, with a sweep of his arm, consigned Doane to an imaginary limbo.

"Was Mrs Crake in good health always...?"

"Good heavens! This reminds me of a proposal for life insurance instead of criminal investigation! Yes, of course, she was. Why do you ask?"

"I have, in the brief time I've been here, sir, gathered quite a lot of background about the Crake household. In Mrs Crake I seem to see a very attractive woman married to a kindly, well thought of, influential local man. The kind most women would be flattered to marry. Yet, here we have a woman who, after her marriage, seems to deteriorate morally at a remarkable rate and in a very strange manner. She seems to relish dragging her husband's good name in the mire. She is, if I may speak ill of the dead, promiscuous, carrying on love affairs here and there, even corrupting her son by making him her companion on her questionable career..."

Mr Trotman levered himself forward in his spring chair and flung himself heavily on his desk, leaning across at Littlejohn like somebody about to practise on terra firma the leg strokes in swimming.

"Wait! Who has told you all this? It is scandalous! There has been a lot of gossip, I admit, and I admit too, that Mrs Crake was not above reproach. But promiscuous, promiscuous...my dear sir, never! Promiscuous...never..."

He flopped back, and the chair groaned on its springs.

"Alkenet... Does the name convey anything, sir?"

"Of course it does. Alkenet is an old friend and client of mine. What of him? Crake's neighbour at Beyle... Their two houses are in what was once called Lepers' Hollow... Historical spot, you know...historical..."

"He was Mrs Crake's lover?"

Mr Trotman actually blushed. He might suddenly have stumbled across Mrs Crake and Alkenet indulging in their illicit amours.

"It is said so. But why bother about Alkenet...? Oh, I see... You are thinking he might be involved in the case... What do the French call it...? *Crime passionel... Crime passionel...* yes...*passionel...*Ah... Well, Inspector, in this case you have a perfect alibi. Never a better. Alkenet has for the past month been in a private ward of the local hospital with a broken neck! Yes, a broken neck. He took a bad toss whilst out hunting, broke his neck, and has been a prisoner in plaster ever since. He's doing very well but quite unable to move to say nothing of committing a crime."

"That lets him out, sir."

"I rather think it does. And now, Inspector, will that be all? I am very occupied."

"You are Mrs Crake's executor...and her husband's, sir?"

"Yes. Why? The death of my partner, Kent, leaves me sole executor in each case now."

"As far as you are aware, sir, did Mr Crake leave any available monies to his daughter for carrying on the house? In other words, having left specific legacies to his wife which he knew would eventually reach his son, did he set anything aside in cash for Nita to keep up Beyle?"

Mr Trotman looked hard at Littlejohn and pondered deeply.

"That is really too much, Inspector...or would be had there been any such funds. The wills have not yet been proved and it would ill become me to make them public at this juncture... Public at this juncture."

"Thank you. Which means Miss Crake may have nothing. The house, if I'm any judge, is a liability. Funny that... A man like Judge Crake to do that. It's not in character, especially as he was so fond of her."

"Nothing funny about it, Inspector. Crake died suddenly and certainly was not advanced in years. He had hoped, he said, to set aside something for Nita when she and Alec were launched on their careers and no further liability in that respect... I cannot discuss the matter yet... I..."

Mr Trotman looked annoyed at the very idea of Littlejohn's lack of tact. Then his face changed, and he rang the bell. The boy put in his head.

"Boy! Kneeshaw is at the car again, breathing on and polishing the bonnet. Tell him, for the last time, to go away!"

Littlejohn smiled to himself at the pantomime.

"Okay."

"Don't dare to say okay to me…and call me…" But the red head had vanished.

Outside, the comedy was resumed. The boy approached Kneeshaw who by now was polishing the chromium radiator cap with his own dirty handkerchief. This time, however, the junior clerk got a different reception. Mr Kneeshaw was annoyed. He seemed to be telling the boy so and threatening him with violence. Mr Trotman, snorting hard, rattled on the window again with his signet ring and flapped at Kneeshaw to go away. The simpleton did so with great reluctance, like a dog ordered by his master to drop his bone. At length he obeyed, but, as he shambled off, he turned and faced Mr Trotman, raised his outspread fingers to his nose and cocked a snook at him.

"Oh…" exhaled Mr Trotman, as though somebody had knifed him in the lungs. "Oh…"

He sagged in his chair at this affront to his dignity.

"Is there really anything more, Inspector?"

He was pleading to be left alone.

"No more, sir, thank you."

Littlejohn left him, and Mr Trotman took a long drink from a whisky decanter in his filing-cabinet, sat in his swivel chair, put his head in his hands and made little moaning noises, very sorry for himself.

The telephone bell rang; listlessly he unhooked the instrument and what he heard galvanised him back to life…

Littlejohn joined Cromwell at the police station.

"What are you doing here sitting like a patient in a doctor's surgery...?"

"The Super's turned me out of his office. Can't work, he says, with anybody else in the room. The sergeant-in-charge says Simpole's going potty."

"I'm very sorry for Simpole. He's got a lot on his mind. Let's go for a coffee somewhere and talk."

They found a café and compared notes over coffee cups.

"If you're wanting a word with Willie Kneeshaw, as he's called — sounds like a made-up name to me — I think you'll find him back from his grocery round. He caused quite a diversion while I was at Trotman's by a desire to polish Trotman's swell car by breathing on it and rubbing it down with a filthy handkerchief, greatly to the annoyance of the owner. In fact, I left them in a state of hostilities with Willie thumbing his nose to Trotman..."

Cromwell found Kneeshaw emerging from the coal-hole of Bright's Buildings where, presumably, he had been stoking the boiler and trying to creep up the flue. His hands and face were coal black.

"Hu," said Willie in response to Cromwell's polite good morning. He tried to wipe the dirt from his hands on the rag he'd used for Trotman's car; his grimy face seemed to satisfy him, and he left it alone. There was dust in his bristling hair and on his shaggy moustache. He was tall and well-nourished with large ears and a cranium as shallow as a saucer.

"I want a talk to you, Willie," said Cromwell and handed Kneeshaw a shilling to encourage him.

Willie bit the shilling to make sure is wasn't cardboard, pocketed it, sat down on a box in his cubby hole under the stairs and tried to light a short clay pipe. Cromwell offered him a cigarette which he tore up and inserted, paper and all, in his pipe. He lit it and puffed out clouds of smoke, a sight which gave him so much satisfaction that he laughed aloud and called the sergeant's attention to the fact that his pipe was smoking. This he did by pointing to it and ejaculating "Zmoaking", with great glee. He began to regard Cromwell favourably as the author of this natural phenomenon and indicated a chair without a back on which Cromwell sat himself.

"You a bit of a singer, Willie?"

"Good zinger… I like a good zing."

"Carol singing?"

"Ah. Comfort and joy…"

"Comfort and joy… Oh, yes…"

Cromwell's infinite patience and quick wit brought to light, at length, that Willie was a member of Tom Trumper's waits and his sole and solo function during their carolling was to put in the repeat bass-line, "Comfort and joy" of *God Rest You Merry Gentlemen*, at the top of his voice. He gave Cromwell an example of this with such power that people in the offices above put their heads round the doors to see if there was a fire.

When quiet had been restored, Cromwell again began his patient inquiries in the meantime maintaining good relations with Willie by breaking up his stock of cigarettes and stuffing them in his pipe. He did this with certain hard feelings for they were of an expensive brand especially bought for him at Christmas by his mother-in-law. However, he consoled himself by calculations of the difference due to him on his expenses sheet.

"Did you go to Judge Crake's…no…I mean Mr Kent's carolling this year…?"

"Ah…we did. Got sent away. Made me mad. We allus got a good feed from Mrs Kent. Mr Crake was there, ill, so she sent us off… Got no feed."

He said it with intense annoyance, as though Crake had no right to be breathing his last with Willie in good voice and the Christmas bake meats waiting for him after his Comfort and Joy.

"Did you see Judge Crake? I mean was he at the window when you were singing, Willie?"

A cunning look crossed the simpleton's face. Then it turned to glee as though, even if he were simple and publicly acknowledged as such, he still had a bit of power of his own, something people wanted which he could only divulge if he liked.

"Hu," he said and grinned all the more.

Cromwell passed him another of his threepenny Christmas cigarettes.

"Ask Tom Trumper," said Willie after he had got his pipe burning again. "Ask Tom Trumper."

"I have done. He says you saw him. Did you?" Willie paused and rubbed his dirty chin.

"Ask Tom Trumper."

Cromwell rose with a show of petulance. In his hand he held half-a-crown for Willie to see. Then he shrugged his shoulders, tossed the coin jauntily in the air, and thrust it back in his trousers pocket. Willie grew very disturbed. He indicated the broken chair and his pipe, which was empty again.

"No, Willie, I'm off. I thought you were a clever chap. This isn't getting us anywhere, you know. I'll go and ask Mr Trotman."

Willie rose to his feet shouting maledictions against Trotman, thumbing his nose again at the lawyer's imaginary presence, and uttering epithets against him too indecent to print.

"To 'ell with Trotman. He doesn't know nothin'. He wasn't singin'. He didn' hear Tom Trumper say as he see Judge Crake fightin' with Mrs Crake at winder. An' he didn't hear Tom Trumper a' tellin' of me to say as I seen 'em, as well. Trotman don't know nothen..."

And then Willie chuckled as if something had tickled his unusual sense of humour.

"He don' know nothen'... Neether does Trumper and neether does Willie..."

"So it was all just a tale...?"

"Trumper gave me a job and a Christmas pudden..."

"So's you'd say you saw the judge...?"

"Ah. But don't you go tellen. Don't matter much, though. Me

job's finished now as Christmas's over and the pudden's eat and can't be got back..."

Willie bit the half-crown and placed it with great satisfaction in a purse from his pocket. He seemed more engrossed in the box containing the last of the expensive cigarettes which the sergeant gave him than in the contents. There was an embossed gilt replica on the lid of the medals won by the makers with their products, and Willie indicated that he proposed to cut out the panel and ornament the wall of his home with it. He led Cromwell from his lair in friendly fashion, gripping his arm like a long-lost buddy, saw him to the door, spat on a highly polished car standing there, and then returned to contemplate the medals again.

10

PANIC IN TILSEY

At two in the morning Littlejohn was wakened by Shelldrake knocking on his door.

"Chief Constable on the telephone, Littlejohn."

Colonel Morphy didn't waste much time in explanations.

"Simpole's committed suicide. Can you come at once?"

Littlejohn had barely time to wash and dress before a police car arrived at the hotel and took him back to Tilsey.

"You *would* be a policeman," said his wife as she sweetly answered his goodbye and nestled back under the bedclothes.

Simpole had been working late into the night. The sergeant-in-charge had expected that; it was nothing uncommon. The Superintendent usually packed up about midnight. He'd recently been so keen on nobody disturbing him that the bobby had hesitated even to take in a cup of tea when the light continued to burn at well after one. There had been an ominous silence in the private office, and, in the end, Sergeant Budd had tapped and peered round the door, thinking the boss had fallen asleep. Instead, he found him hanging from a hook on the wall. The picture of the Tilsey Watch Committee, 1897, which had occupied the hook for more than fifty years, had been carefully placed in a corner. Simpole had used a long ventilator cord from his window, and, if it had stretched another six inches under his weight, he wouldn't have died for his feet would have met the floor. The police surgeon said Simpole had been dead an hour when they found him.

The whole business shook everybody at the police station. Simpole had been rather repulsive in appearance with his pale diabolical face and the waxed moustache which did not improve it and made him look more like Mephistopheles than ever. He had too, been unbearably officious and stern at times, intolerant of mistakes, asking no help and volunteering very little. A queer, lonely man whose way had been increasingly lonely and barren since the recent death of his mother of whom he thought a great deal. His mad infatuation for Dulcie Crake, known only to the few, had jeopardised his career and made him a problem to his superiors. Now, he'd taken a way out. With all his faults, he never earned hatred from his men however hard he treated them. He was capable of sudden acts of great kindness and humanity. He reserved for himself alone the right to deal with wrong-doing or slackness in the force. Whatever he did or said to the men, he always stood between them and defended them against anybody else, no matter who it might be. And every Christmas he handed to the treasurer of the policemen's treat for the poor of Tilsey: a packet containing fifty one-pound notes and threatened what he would do if their source was made known.

"He must have driven himself out of his mind with one thing and another. He's had too much on his plate," said Colonel Morphy when he and Littlejohn got together alone at last. They were in the Superintendent's room. The body had been removed, but nothing else had been disturbed.

There was no suicide note, no message to indicate the cause of it all. The "In" tray on the desk was empty and the" Out" tray full, as though the dead man had finished his day's work, risen without any fuss, and simply hanged himself.

"Yes, and, on top of all his troubles, Simpole was going blind."

Littlejohn's voice was full of compassion.

"What? He never said anything to me about it."

"Did you expect him to? I only discovered it by mistake. It was the way he behaved at the inquest on Mrs Crake that made me suspect it. He seemed lost in the room like somebody in a fog and gallantly struggled not to reveal it. I looked at his eyes, and, if you got them in the right light, it seemed obvious the man had cataracts coming..."

"Still... That would have been curable... An operation and he'd have been all right."

"I agree. He'd got pretty near total blindness too. My colleague told me he caught him this very afternoon using a magnifying glass which he quickly concealed when anybody entered. That's why he said he couldn't work with anybody else in the room. Think of it...a policeman... It must have been hell."

"But it's all so daft when an operation would have put him right."

"An operation would have involved wearing spectacles afterwards, which is hardly to be contemplated for a man of his type and in his position... A Superintendent with bad eyesight, you know. But apart from that. Have you thought what his greatest trouble must have been? It was that he'd have been off duty during the unravelling of this Crake case. Simpole was terribly upset when you sent for me. He showed me how much he resented my presence here, yet tried, in his way, to be decent personally, but not officially. Why? I think because he was afraid I'd come across something which would incriminate him and blast his career in his absence. What could it have been?"

"I'm damned if I know. You're not suggestin' that he might have had a hand in the murders?"

"No. I don't think that. But suppose I came across something in my inquiries which incriminated him...say some letters among Mrs Crake's correspondence? They might have been in her desk, or even in her box at the bank. And all the time these inquiries were going on, Simpole was a lame duck, half blind, pretending to see or else in hospital with his eyes bandaged. Nobody can tell the agony Simpole must have suffered if what I think is true."

"Poor devil... She seems to have driven him quite off his head..."

The clock on the tower struck five. It was dark and damp outside and Littlejohn, looking from the window to the square below, could see the reflected lights of the police office glowing on the wet pavements. It was all terribly quiet. Not a sound or a footstep, as though all the constables were moving on tiptoe or else sitting in silence out of sorrow for the man they found so difficult yet respected so much whilst he was alive.

Morphy sat down heavily. He was a tall, lean retired Army man, one of the last of his kind in police administration. Simpole had never been very close to him; too cold and inhibited, but a very efficient officer for all that. A constable entered quietly, laid down a tray with tea on it and withdrew after a silent salute.

"Thanks, officer..."

Littlejohn filled his pipe and lit it.

"Now what?"

"Had we better look through his desk, sir? That will be the first thing."

"Better get it over, then."

They examined the papers spread on the top of the desk first. Nothing but official documents. The drawers too, neat and orderly, contained only official stuff. If the dead Superintendent had any private papers, they must have been in his rooms; he had recently sold his house. The tragic reading-glass was tucked among some papers in the top drawer along with a diary, official issue, marked "Superintendent Simpole" on the outside.

Littlejohn sat down and thumbed the book. It was almost full and already the new year's issue, a replica of the one they were examining, was in the drawer with a few entries already scribbled in it. The word "Salary" towards the end of each month told its own tale and notes like "Police Sports", "Children's Treat", "Police Conference", and "Old folks", at Christmas, showed that Simpole had at least been getting ready for the New Year and not contemplating taking his life before it came in.

"Do you know when these were issued, sir?"

"Yes; I got mine last week. The constable had a stack of them. I got mine first."

"So between last week and now, Simpole has decided to end it. He evidently expected to be functioning well into the New Year, judging from the way he's anticipated events by transferring them from the old diary to the new."

There was nothing much to guide them in the rest of the new book. The old one was a more difficult problem. Every day held some entry or other, often a complete page of them, entered in Simpole's precise, sprawling hand.

"I'd better take and go through this, sir, if you don't mind. It may give us a lead..."

"By all means..."

As they finished the tea, Littlejohn turned over the last few pages of the diary.

"There we are, sir..."

He showed Morphy several entries.

N Crake died.
Doctor... Coroner... Trumper... Beyle.

"Those must be the appointments he made arising out of Nicholas Crake's death. He told me he was investigating a rumour that Mrs Crake caused her husband's death... That'll be it."

"Very likely, sir. Look there..."

Just a pathetic scribble in pencil.

DC Murdered. Beyle.

Scotland Yard called in.

"That must have been a very bitter day for Simpole, Littlejohn."

Then:

A Kent, murdered. Beyle.

And finally, a few brief notes on Simpole's last working day, again pencil scrawls, as though he hadn't time or inclination to continue his usual neat entries in ink.

Shotter: South Counties... 10.30.
Sharp, Phillips... 11.30.
Mansion House 05433.

That was all.

Morphy looked over the top of his spectacles at the entries.

"Shotter... That's the manager of the South Counties Bank here in Tilsey; and Sharp, Phillips are local Stock and Share Brokers. Mansion House... That's a phone number..."

He rubbed his chin.

"Could it mean he was in financial trouble or something? Banks, stockbrokers, phone numbers in the City. Was he sellin' securities or trying to borrow money or...or what?"

"This book contains only his official entries, as far as I can judge. Those interviews must concern a case he had in hand. Did the Crakes bank at the South Counties...?"

"Yes, I think so. The City Treasurer's accounts are there, and most officials keep them at the South Counties for convenience too. Yes; so did Mrs Crake. She gave my wife a cheque for some bridge debt or other not very long ago. My wife asked me to cash it for her... It was on the South Counties."

"I must follow this up in the morning, sir. I don't think there's much more we can do until then..."

The way back by road took the police car past Beyle House. The route was as black as ink for no sign of dawn was showing. Lepers' Hollow held a belt of mist like dark cotton-wool and the headlights of the car came back in their faces. Littlejohn got out and led the way through the valley with his torch. Below, he could hear the stream rattling over the stones, and, in the woods round Beyle, owls were calling. At the bridge in the hollow itself, the fog was thickest, and then, as the road rose, it gradually cleared, and the way became quite visible again. There, in the valley, Beyle House, its feet lost in the mist, its towers black against the surrounding night, thrust its gloomy mass to the sky, and, as if to accentuate the darkness of the rest, a light shone from beneath one of the towers. It was in Uncle Bernard's room. Littlejohn wondered what the crazy old doctor was doing at that hour but was too tired to satisfy his curiosity. Shelldrake was waiting with hot coffee at his pub.

Next morning panic broke out in Tilsey. The strange death of the Recorder; two murders; and now the Superintendent of Police had committed suicide! Trumper's shop did a roaring trade again. It had become a Mecca for those seeking news and theories about the recent crimes. Greatly to the disgust of Mr Bloater, nourishing in his bosom his secret hatred of his employer, Tom Trumper expressed fantastic opinions about the murderer and even conjectured that the Superintendent had been assassinated.

"Thugs," he breathed hoarsely, for he had been doing some drinking to quiet his nerves since his ordeal of the day before with Cromwell. "Thugs can make garottin' look like suicide by 'angin'..."

A customer fainted and was given a small portion of English Brandy. Mr Trumper's Bargain Parcels of New Year Good Cheer sold like hot cakes and he was obliged to leave Mr Bloater in charge of the shop whilst he withdrew to the room in the rear to mix more Cocky Dick potions.

Littlejohn had a long talk over the hot coffee with his old chief, Shelldrake, after returning in the small hours.

"We've discovered one or two important facts about these crimes," he said.

"Go on… Tell me."

"In the first place, the tale about Mrs Crake's killing off her husband by exposure is probably quite untrue. Someone deliberately set it around. We'll find out who did it. Meanwhile, I think it was done by somebody who had decided already to kill Mrs Crake and was trying beforehand to make the crime look like a bit of family revenge. When we get down to brass tacks, nobody actually *saw* the thing done. Trumper, who the rumour said actually witnessed it, now denies it and tries to blame a half-wit who helps him a bit and who goes with the carollers whether they want him or not. The half-wit blames Trumper… So, there we are."

"But who can it be? Was it Simpole?"

"I hardly think so. We never thought to check his movements, of course, when the crimes occurred, but, until I'm satisfied that nobody else did it, I shall give Simpole the benefit of the doubt. He resented my intrusion, of course. As I told the Chief Constable, I think he was afraid I would find something which would implicate him, not perhaps in the killings, but, shall we say, in his relations with Mrs Crake. He seems to have been infatuated with her."

"Could there have been blackmail in it?"

"That's what I'm wondering. Judging from some notes he left in his diary, he might have been a jump ahead of Cromwell and me. He might even have been on the track of the murderer. Then he commits suicide. The murderer might have turned on him and threatened to ruin him if he pressed the case."

"Meaning…he knew something dangerous for Simpole…?"

"Yes. Tomorrow I'm going to try to follow Simpole's tracks round the town and see where they'll lead me."

The clock in the hall struck seven…

"I'll try to get an hour's sleep and then a bath. Then I must be off. We've a busy day in front of us."

There were special editions of the local paper out as Littlejohn crossed the Town Hall square to the South Counties Bank. People were buying them eagerly and reading them in the streets. Knots of idlers were gossiping at corners and the seats round the flower beds in front of the Town Hall were filled with grim-looking men, arguing, remembering things, surmising about Simpole and his fate. As Littlejohn passed along, all eyes seemed to turn to him. He wondered what had happened until he bought a paper himself, and, beneath a large sombre photograph of Simpole in full uniform, he saw a smaller picture of himself." The Man on the Case. Famous Yard Man on the Spot."

The bank manager received him as if he were a lifeline thrown to a drowning man.

"It's a good thing you're here, Inspector, now that the local police have been thrown into confusion."

The bank was very imposing, an old private one absorbed by the larger body. There were stained-glass windows and large oil-paintings of grim bankers, dead and gone, on the walls. The seven tellers spread along the vast counter made a brave array and were frantically trying to count cash as their customers talked about the local sensation. They all looked up as Littlejohn entered. You could have heard a pin drop. It was as if he had called to single-out the killer and bear him off to the scaffold without more ado.

As soon as Littlejohn's card was handed in to Mr Shotter by a smiling clerk, who passed it over with a gesture which implied "Now we're all right", the banker emerged from his private office, wrung the Inspector warmly by the hand, took him in his lair, closed the door, and said how glad he was to see him. He was a tall, straight man who looked like a butler when attired in formal clothes. In the tweeds and little bowler which he wore on Saturdays and half-holidays in keeping with the spirit of leisure, Mr Shotter looked like a respectable bookie, whilst in his full evening clothes at a Masonic function, he could easily have passed for a Victorian diplomat, there to sign a secret treaty.

"Superintendent Simpole was here yesterday. He seemed quite all right. This news is altogether staggering."

He was turning grey with little sideboards in front of his large ears, and he had a hawk-like nose and kindly grey eyes. He wore an air of personal bereavement because he felt that as the one who paid Simpole's salary and sat on the bench of magistrates served by the dead officer, he had somehow been part of the civic family.

"Was Simpole hard-up?"

"I beg your pardon."

Mr Shotter wasn't used to being asked such questions in his capacity as banker. It wasn't playing the game to ask a man's banker the state of his account.

"Was Simpole short of money?"

"No. He was nicely off. But that is, of course, in confidence."

"Of course. Now, please tell me something else, sir, also in confidence. Did Simpole's account show any evidence of payments-out which might have been blackmail?"

Mr Shotter leaned against the wall for support. For the most part, he was used to quite a humdrum provincial existence here in Tilsey. Now matters were getting a bit beyond the bounds of his experience.

"Blackmail! My dear Inspector. Whatever makes you suggest such a thing? I thought it only occurred in crime stories and on the films. Simpole? Blackmail? But he was the police. You don't blackmail a policeman."

"Don't you, sir? All the same, are there any suspicious items in his account? He kept it here, didn't he?"

"Oh, yes. I can soon tell you, but such a thing couldn't occur to Simpole…"

He rang a bell and a clerk entered, hurried off for the ledger, and quickly returned. The banker made no fuss at all about showing Littlejohn the account. He was so anxious to prove his case that he overcame his natural caution. He was right. The entries were quite straightforward: income from salary; expenditure for his rooms, his tailor, his bookseller, his club. No large withdrawals over two years at least.

"And now, sir, would you tell me what brought the Superintendent here yesterday morning at 10.30?"

Mr Shotter cast an admiring glance at Littlejohn. This was really Scotland Yard at work! Tactful, bland, polite, omniscient. He sang the praises of the police and Littlejohn that evening at his Masonic lodge.

"Yes. He called to make an inquiry about the late Mr Crake's affairs. It was most irregular, of course. But I knew Simpole well, knew his undoubted integrity and trusted him with the information. I will tell you in confidence. He had been obtaining details of Mr Crake's estate. It seems that now that Mrs Crake is dead, as well, a large sum passes to Alec Crake, and Nita, the daughter, is left with Beyle and the residue of the estate. Simpole was trying to find if there was any residue. In other words, had Mr Nicholas Crake amassed other funds for his daughter? I made an exception upon Simpole's promise to see me protected by the Courts if the information should need to be made public."

"Will you make a similar deal with me, sir, and tell me what you told Simpole?"

"Yes. Crake, by the royalties on his books and by special counsel's fees over and above his standing salary as Recorder, had amassed a considerable sum in a number two account. I think that must have been an absolute secret, Inspector, for there were special instructions that only the judge must be given the statements of account or details of transactions on it. I will tell you that he amassed over a period of years, ten thousand pounds in the account."

"Ten thousand!"

"Yes. No wonder he wished it kept a secret! Had Mrs Crake known, she would never have left him alone until she got it. I can tell you, sir, her extravagance was appalling!"

"And the money is intact, sir?"

"Not in the account; no. I told Simpole and he seemed very gratified for some reason."

"Was the money withdrawn by the judge?"

"In a way; yes. To avoid death duties, he appointed trustees for his daughter's benefit and the funds were withdrawn and invested in their names."

"Who were they?"

"His own executors, Mr Arthur Kent and Mr Trotman, the lawyers."

Littlejohn whistled to himself. Simpole certainly *had* been a jump ahead!

"And were the investments lodged with you for safe keeping?"

"No. You know how close some lawyers can be. They are so very independent! After the funds had been invested, we lost touch with them. Trotman & Co have accounts with other banks in town, you see. We keep part of their business... As for the rest..."

Mr Shotter shrugged his shoulders.

"Can you tell me how the money was invested, sir?"

"Yes. The cheque withdrawing the funds was made payable to Sharp, Phillips & Co, the local stockbrokers."

"Ah!"

"I beg your pardon, Inspector..."

"Superintendent Simpole left you to call on them, yesterday?"

"Yes. He said he was going..."

There was a sudden interruption caused by a huge woman wearing a fur coat. A middle-aged, spoiled child face was thrust round the door. The head was wearing a fur cap to match. Then the mouth opened.

"Ah… There you are, dear…"

And the fur coat walked into the room.

"I'm engaged, my dear…"

"I won't keep you a minute, Claude…"

Mrs Shotter was in the habit of breaking in on her husband's seclusion whenever she was in town.

"I've forgotten my cheque-book and I've just seen the sweetest…"

"You'll excuse me, sir, if I get along? Thank you very much."

"My wife, Inspector; this is Inspector Littlejohn, of Scotland Yard, my dear…"

The banker might have been introducing the bank messenger or the carpark attendant for what it mattered to Mrs Shotter! She had a one-track mind of great determination and had just seen the very hat she wanted. Littlejohn escaped.

Sharp, Phillips & Co occupied two rooms above Trotman in Bright's Buildings. Mr Sharp was in active control; Mr Phillips was his father-in-law, at present a guest in a home for inebriates.

"What can I do for you?"

The office girl had led the Inspector into a cosy room with little sign of stockbroking going on in it. The only brokers Littlejohn had previously dealt with were defaulting or decamping ones. Mr Sharp looked as if he might join one or another of such categories sooner or later. A little dapper man with a large nose, a clipped moustache, thin receding hair which matched his thin receding chin, and the cocky manner of one who had been poor and suddenly found himself very well-off through marrying the boss's daughter. He walked flat-footed and moved with little skipping steps.

"What can I do for you?"

Littlejohn produced his warrant card.

"Was Superintendent Simpole in to see you yesterday, Mr…?"

"Sharp's the name. Yes, he was."

He sniffed hard and cleared his throat like a dog barking. "Will you kindly tell me what he called about, sir?"

"Well... It was clients' business and very secret. I don't mind telling you what I told him, but you'll have to keep it under your hat."

"I'll see you're protected if I have to make it public."

"Right. Well, it concerns an important firm of solicitors in this town, so, if you blow the gaff, I'll be for it..."

"I said I would see you protected, sir. What was it about?"

"Well... Some time ago, Trotman & Co invested some trust funds for Mr Nicholas Crake on behalf of his daughter, Miss Juanita. The Superintendent wanted to know if the investment was sold later. That was all."

"And *was* it sold?"

"Yes, it was. Nearly a year ago."

"What was done with the funds, sir?"

"The cheque was handed over to Trotman & Co. I don't know why they did it, or where the money went. It may be they were changing investments. There was certainly capital improvement in the stock and it paid to sell for the profit."

"What was the stock, sir?"

"War Loan, all of it."

Mr Sharp lit a cigarette, leaned back in his chair, and put his hands behind his head.

"Did Superintendent Simpole want to know anything else, sir?"

"Yes. He asked how it was transferred. I said by Bank of England transfer signed by the two trustees..."

"Messrs Trotman and Kent?"

"That's right. I told him, and then he asked if it would be possible for anybody to see the transfer. I said I didn't know. That rested with the Bank of England Stock Office."

"Do you know Mansion House 05433, sir?"

"Of course. Our London broker..."

"Did you give that number to the Superintendent?"

"Yes. I told him they might help him. I wasn't familiar with London practice to that extent, but they'd tell him how to get the transfer, if possible..."

"Who handled the deal at Trotman & Co?"

"Mr Kent, I think."

"Many thanks..."

Mr Sharp pranced before Littlejohn and opened the door for him. In the outer office, a ticker started to pour out slips of tape...

Back at the police station in the Town Hall, Littlejohn telephoned to Scotland Yard, described the investment and the transfer and asked them to get it, if possible, from the Bank of England.

"I'll send you specimen signatures of the two parties. See if the ones on the transfer are genuine, please."

It wasn't difficult getting signatures of the two lawyers from the court archives. They were always signing something.

"And, by the way, you might do something else for me. This is a bit more difficult and you may not be lucky. But, contact Spain... Yes, Spain. I want as much information as I can get about a Dr Bernard Doane. He left Spain, I gather, about twenty-five years ago. The starting place should be Madrid University where he says he graduated in medicine. Also, was there ever a Doane on the Spanish consular staff...? Yes, I know it's a tall order and may come to nothing. On the other hand, we may be lucky...! Thanks..."

As he telephoned, Littlejohn had been watching a constable who had entered and apparently wanted to speak to him. The bobby stood first on one foot then on the other; then with both feet on the ground he performed a little heel-and-toe dance which made the room tremble.

"What is it, constable?"

"A Mr Alec Crake has called asking for you, sir."

"Is he sober?"

The constable's mouth opened; then he grinned. The Inspector would have his little joke!

"Oh, yes, sir. He told me to tell you he knew how somebody murdered Mr Kent without being seen."

"He did, did he? Well, that's something fresh. Sober and cooperating. Good. Show him in, please."

Alec Crake must have been right outside the door. He entered at once, sober, washed, shaved, dressed in a decent suit, and looking steady and a bit chastened.

"A great shock, Inspector… Arthur Kent…and now Simpole…"

He opened his mouth as if to speak again, but, instead, he pitched forward on the floor in a dead faint.

11

THE TERRIFIED PRODIGAL

For a minute, Alec Crake lay on the floor like one dead. No vestige of colour in his face; his cheeks sunken and corpse-like; his nose pinched; his closed eyelids, charred-looking, dark rings under them; and his upper lip drawn back in a half-grin over his even teeth. Littlejohn slipped his pocket flask from his hip and poured a few drops of brandy between the clenched teeth. Almost at once, a pink tint returned to Alec's skin; then he opened his eyes and tried to get to his feet.

"Steady… Let me help…"

"I can manage… I feel a damn fool. Did I faint?"

"Yes; how long is it since you had a decent meal?"

"Two days…"

"Meanwhile, you've lived on gin or whisky?"

"That's about it…"

"Then, as you say, you're a damn fool. Whatever's got you in this state?"

"I just felt everything was on top of me. I feel a lot better now. I came to see if I could be of any use."

"Good! But why this change of heart?"

Alec looked a bit awkward.

"Things have brightened up a bit for me. I got this telegram an hour ago. It was like a tonic to me..."

He pulled from his pocket a ball of crushed paper, smoothed it out, and handed it to Littlejohn. It was a cable from Paris.

SO SORRY TO HEAR OF MOTHER'S DEATH. WAITING FOR YOU TO BRING ME HOME. DON'T BE LONG. LOVE. GINETTE.

"Well?"

"I was engaged to Ginette. She threw me over just before father died. Took up with a chap who called himself my pal. I took it badly, I guess. She was everything to me. I was just bringing her home to meet mother when she walked out on me. Now it seems all right again..."

It was obvious that something violently emotional had happened to Alec. He was sober, his eyes were bright, and he was full of a new and feverish vigour.

"That's why you made a thoroughgoing beast of yourself instead of supporting the family in its trouble?"

Young Crake gave Littlejohn an odd, slightly apologetic look.

"Yes..."

"So, it wasn't grief at the death of your parents?"

"Don't be callous, Inspector. My mother's death was a ghastly blow on top of Ginette..."

"Why not your father, too?"

"That was different."

"You didn't care much for him?"

"Let's not discuss that now. I hear that Simpole's dead. Is it right he killed himself?"

"Quite right. By the way, what was it you said about your knowing how Kent was killed?"

"You searched the house, Nita said. All the rooms the murderer might have hidden in, and he couldn't have got upstairs without passing Uncle's door, and you were in the room with Uncle. Even the stairs to the servants' quarters are visible from uncle's room. That right?"

"Have you been going into this with Miss Nita?"

"Yes. After I got Ginette's telegram, I went home and talked to her. Then I came straight after you. I want to help clear all this up. Now that Simpole's out of the way, I'm scared. If I'm not careful, I'll be the next."

"Why?"

"There's a plot to wipe us all out. I'm quite sure... We're all doomed. I didn't care before, but now that Ginette..."

"Don't be silly. And don't get hysterical. Tell me about where the murderer hid himself whilst we were hunting for him."

"In the room under the stairs. You'll have noticed that the staircase is all panelled-in. Well, there's a hidden door which gives into the cavity under them. We used to play in it when we were kids. It's not been used for years. There are old golf-clubs, croquet tackle and the like...relics of happier days, you might call them... stored there. Well, I opened the place this morning. Someone's been in lately. There's a patch of dust gone where he sat on an old hall chair that was there..."

"Are you sure?"

"Yes... I told the bobby who, since mother died, has been a sort of shadow hanging round the place. They keep relieving him, but he keeps turning up again like a bad penny. I told him, and he said he'd telephone the fingerprint men. I hear the technical staff with their cameras and gadgets haven't been much use, so far. In other words, science hasn't been able to help you."

"That's quite right, but that doesn't say it won't later on. So, they're in the cubby hole already. That's good. You've saved me a bit of trouble. This means that if the murderer did hide there after he killed Kent, he was someone familiar with the house."

"Yes... I suppose quite a lot of people knew of the place. It was always being opened in the old days, to get out the tackle for games on the lawn, but I guess that for over a dozen years, nobody except Elspeth, chasing dirt, has ever been in."

"Where is Elspeth these days?"

"Still at her sister's in Oddington. She's scared of the house now."

"Which reminds me, you said you hadn't had any food. We'd better see about a sandwich or something for you. Could you eat something?"

"Yes, if I could have some tea with it. I'm dying for tea."

Littlejohn rang the bell and a policeman put in a rather scared face at the door. Only Simpole had been used to ringing that bell and it had given him quite a turn! He smiled with relief.

"Could you get this young man a bite of something from the canteen, please, constable…and some tea?"

"Yes, sir. Right away."

It wasn't long arriving, and Alec tackled it ravenously.

"Will you answer a few questions now?"

"Yes…"

He eagerly poured out more tea and drank deeply.

"What did you want to know?"

"Some very personal things. Tell me something of your early life… The way you were your mother's companion as a child… How she took you away from boarding school and gave you a tutor in Tilsey to have you near her…"

"Who's told you all this?"

"Uncle Bernard."

"Have you been quizzing that old loafer? All he can do is talk, mainly about himself, or fantastically try to analyse other people like he does his rats and mice. A very unpleasant object is Uncle Bernard. And yet, my mother was truly fond of him. He seemed to be the only relic of her happy childhood. I really think she loved him."

Littlejohn was leaning against the wall by the window as Alec finished his brief meal. Outside, the thin wintry sun was shining. A man up a ladder was erecting a hoarding outside the bank.

SAVINGS WEEK.
BUY SAVINGS BONDS AND CERTIFICATES!

On a smaller board leaning against the wall at the foot of the ladder, another poster in large uneven scrawl:

MYSTERY OF DEAD POLICE OFFICER.

Simpole and Savings Week seemed to have got together!

"Did your mother suffer from some kind of malady, a relic of childhood?"

Alec laid down his cup carefully, like a man slowly and deliberately gathering himself for a fight.

"What did you say?"

"Don't pretend you didn't hear. Did she?"

"Who told you that?"

"Again, Uncle Bernard. It may seem strange to you, but there's been nobody available or willing to tell me anything but your uncle."

"He'd tell you quite a lot. Whether or not it was true didn't matter."

"Was the dancing mania story true?"

"Dancing mania? Is everybody mad, or am I?"

"Let me put it another way then? I'm a bit dubious about the tarantula bite myself..."

"Tarantula? I don't know a thing about tarantulas. What is a tarantula, anyway?"

"Never mind... Did your mother take drugs?"

There was a deathly silence. Alec gulped.

"She's past suffering now... Yes, she did."

"So, that's it. Where did she get them? Uncle Bernard?"

"Yes. She got so she couldn't live without them. Her nerves were shocking. He gave them to her and he also had some way, some mixture or other he gave her, which put her right quickly after she'd had them."

"That explains a lot. A big lot..."

"Yes, it does. It explains the downfall of our family. It seems she started not long after uncle came to live at Beyle. I'm sure he began it all to get her in his power so that he could keep on living at our place. I've heard Elspeth say my father turned him out, but my mother always brought him back. He had her completely in his grip. In the end, father got resigned and lived his own life. Uncle saw to it that she was somehow presentable to the public, if you get what I mean. But morally, it completely undermined her. The queer thing is, nobody had the strength to rescue her, turn out that old sponger, take mother in hand, and save her. We just let it go on. We're like that. It's a weakness in my mother's family... No backbone; just moral jellyfish."

"You were her companion everywhere as a boy?"

"Yes. We went about a lot together..."

"Had she any particular friends?"

Alec hesitated.

"Meaning men, I suppose. Yes, she had. Quite a number."

"Who, for example?"

"There wasn't any particular one. I mean, there was a gang of them, rather a lively lot, cocktails, cards, visits to London, dancing, night clubs..."

"Who was in it?"

"They've most of them gone now, either dead or moved away. Alkenet, our neighbour, was one. Then, Mr and Mrs Trotman were in the gang. The sight of Trotman now wouldn't make you think he was once a bit of a lad, would it? But he was, damn him."

"Why damn him?"

"Nothing. It doesn't concern you, anyway."

"It does very much. I want to know all about everybody in this town who had any connection with your mother or her family. I want to know about Trotman..."

Alec's mouth tightened into a thin line.

"No..."

Littlejohn had been eyeing Alec's profile for some time. He wondered what it reminded him of. Some vague, unformed notion pervaded his mind. The lack of emotion or family bond between Alec and his father. The money saved for Nita alone. Beyle left to Nita and not Alec. The profound air of gloom and secrecy hanging over Beyle. The silence between husband and wife. The wild degradation of Dulcie Crake... He made a blind guess...

Littlejohn walked over to Alec Crake, still sitting at the table with the remnants of the meal before him. He seized him by the shoulders, almost lifted him to his feet, and stared him straight in the eyes.

"Damn Trotman, because he's your father, isn't he?"

Alec flung off Littlejohn's hands in a sudden burst of strength.

"How did you get to know that? From the dead? Or from Uncle Bernard? Nobody's supposed to know except Trotman and me, now that the rest are dead."

"I didn't know; just guessed it on the evidence. But now that I do, will you tell me more? It will help you to talk about it, and help me too, in this case."

"Don't think Trotman killed my mother. He's too big a coward. Soft...Pah! I wish I could wash out of me all the blood, the inheritance he gave me. I feel foul!"

"Pull yourself together! Talk sensibly about it and stop being so damned sorry for yourself. How did you get to know?"

"It was like a cheap drama at a second-rate theatre. Trotman had a daughter by his own wife. We were brought up together. Why, I don't know. It was the foulest thing my mother and Trotman ever did. Worse than having me, between them. Frances Trotman... We called her Frankie. She's married to a fellow in

Kenya; they grow tea or coffee or cocoa or something. What the hell does it matter what they grow? I loved her better than anything in the world, before or since. And she turned out to be my half-sister! Just imagine it. We'd decided to get engaged. She was eighteen and I was twenty. We seemed to have always loved one another. I told my father first. He seemed delighted because he was fond of Frankie. And she told her mother, who was equally pleased. But when it came to telling the other pair, my God! What a shemozzle! I think, somehow, my father and Mrs Trotman expected something of the kind. Past history was remembered. But not quite so bad as that! It all came out. I wasn't Nicholas Crake's son at all; I was Trotman's little by-blow! Do you wonder I took to drink? My father… I mean Nick, was splendid about it and so was Mrs Trotman. No scandal… nothing… Just a sort of terrible heart-breaking silence, a rift in everybody's existence, and they sent Frankie away somewhere. I never saw Frankie again. I got over it, in a way, in time. Then I met Ginette, a model in Paris. I turned over a new leaf. She walked out on me. Now she's back and everything's lovely. How long will it stay so? Since the shock of my parentage, nothing is too big for me in the way of eruptions in my life. I expect them…"

"And the news never leaked out in Tilsey, then?"

"No. There was father's… I mean, Nick's position, and Trotman's. It's a small community, and, had the scandal been made public, it would have ruined Trotman and mother. My… Nick was the sort who always took the broad, kindly view. Mrs Trotman was a quiet little thing who really loved Trotman and didn't want to lose him whatever he did. So it was arranged. They'd no idea that it would have to come out through Frankie and me. I wish I'd never been born, rather than hurt Nick the way it did. Can you imagine it? Living and thinking I was his son for twenty years *and* having a daughter of his own by the woman who'd made him a cuckold… My God! I'd have killed the pair of them! Will you believe me when I tell you that I respected Nick Crake more than any other living creature. And now, he's dead and out of it!"

Alec thereupon broke down, covered his face and sobbed, a harsh, dry, awful weeping. Littlejohn looked through the window until the storm was over. Outside, the man was still struggling with his National Savings advertisement and a small crowd had gathered and was taunting and encouraging him. The board he was erecting was too big for him to manage and he performed like a comic turn in a music hall...

"I'm sorry. I feel better for the talk with you. I guess I'm not much more use to you. I'll be off..."

"Wait! You were in your mother's intimate confidence, weren't you? Was your Uncle once her lover? I mean Arthur Kent... I'm sorry to be so brutal, but it seems quieter ways don't yield any fruits."

"Yes... She and Nick lived separate lives after the Trotman affair. He was the same kind, generous husband to her, but they went their own ways and lived in different parts of the house. Mother just couldn't exist without some man running about after her. She started temporarily painting the town red with Trotman when Nick started his book...his great book... Then, one after another, most of them just came dangling after her without being her lovers. Only Alkenet and Kent, I think, ever went the whole hog..."

"They were lovers when she died?"

"No. I think Kent had cooled off. He was mad about her once. Always at the house when he thought nobody was about. But later he tired. I think Aunt Bee talked of a divorce. That wouldn't have done at all. It would have ruined him..."

"Now another question... Did your mother ever speak of letters...? I mean love letters? Did any of these men write to her and did she keep their letters?"

"Blackmail?"

"I don't know. Were there letters?"

"Yes. She even read some of them to me. They amused her. She kept them all in her desk. I wanted to get them and destroy them, but the policeman on duty won't let me touch a thing. Uncle Arthur was too prudent to write letters; but there were some from Simpole… He was very fond of my mother."

"In love with her?"

"I don't know. A very undemonstrative man, Simpole. But he called a lot and wrote letters to her, letters which, if anybody had got them and made them public, would have shown him in a new and rather ridiculous light. I wondered… I wondered if somebody had got them and tried to blackmail Simpole and driven him to suicide."

"Maybe. Was your mother sympathetic to him?"

"I think he had some hold over mother. She was always kind and polite to him, although she told me she could hardly bear the sight of him."

"Was there something about Uncle Bernard in that?"

"I couldn't say."

"Were there letters from anybody else?"

"Yes. Trotman; written many years ago. They were extraordinary! If Trotman knew they still existed, he'd spend a sleepless night or two."

"Why?"

"There was a letter he wrote after the whole story of my parentage came out. He must have been mad to write it. He says he has told his wife about his being my father and that she has forgiven him. He hopes Nick will take it the same way. He must have been out of his mind to write such a thing. My mother kept it. She kept all her letters…"

"We'd better get along to Beyle at once and see if they're still there. The executors won't be allowed to touch them until matters are cleared up, so the contents of the desk must still be intact. Come along."

They took a waiting police car and went to Beyle.

The constable at the door saluted. He was there alone save for Uncle Bernard who was in his room, silent, presumably engaged in his curious researches.

"Anyone been here, constable?"

"The fingerprint men and Inspector Dyer, who's taken over temporary from Superintendent Simpole..."

Littlejohn had already met Dyer, a rather self-effacing officer, not quite used to his new office, and now busy reading files and trying to take up the threads left by Simpole.

"Did the fingerprint men find anything?"

"No, sir. Whoever hid in the stairs must have been careful. There wasn't a thing 'cept a spot where he swep' off the dust sittin' on a chair there."

"I think I'd better take a look at the hideout."

Alec was eager to show him the place. It was little wonder he and Cromwell had missed it when they made their search after Kent's death. There was no handle to the door and no lock. It simply swivelled when you pressed it in a certain spot and revealed a large, dark cavity. Alec touched a switch and a dim light went on. It was a junk room, used for storing garden odds and ends. Flower baskets, croquet tackle, an old tennis racket with broken strings... Hanging from nails on the walls were one or two antiquated photographs in cheap black frames. Groups taken on the lawn with men and women in old-fashioned summer clothes; a man in legal gown and wig, apparently Nicholas Crake himself; a beautiful woman standing beside an artificial marble pillar with a backcloth in the rear representing a Venetian scene... Dulcie Crake, years ago.

"Now, about the desk. Where is it, Alec?"

Young Crake looked gratefully at Littlejohn for the little touch of friendly familiarity.

"In here..."

A small morning room with a kind of glass terrace or sunroom outside the window. The place was simply furnished with easy chairs, a couch and a table with four chairs round it.

"We used to take meals in here in summer..."

In one corner stood a large mahogany secretaire, more a man's piece than a woman's.

"What about the key, sir?"

"I picked up the keys of the place, which Simpole collected, from the police office..."

Littlejohn paused.

Simpole collected... So the Superintendent had had access to the desk already if he'd wished. His own letters were reputed to be there.

Hastily Littlejohn took the ring from his pocket. It had been Dulcie Crake's and bore a label: Mrs Crake's Keys. Alec looked over the Inspector's shoulder.

"That's the key. The one with the ornamented handle."

Littlejohn selected the one indicated, a fancy object, almost a miniature of a ceremonial key to a cathedral. He inserted it in the top drawer, unlocked it, and tugged.

The whole inside was in a state of utter confusion. Someone had hastily rummaged the drawer, tearing open packets, opening boxes, searching in envelopes. It looked as if the intruder had inverted the drawer on the floor, ransacked it, taken away what he sought if it had been there, and then bundled the rest back, higgledy-piggledy, and locked it up again.

There were three drawers, and each had been treated the same. Systematically looted and the remaining contents shoved in anyhow...

Littlejohn with a sigh decided that he'd better go through the contents of each again and settled down at the table with one after another of the drawers. There were photographs, books, booklets, circulars, pamphlets, ribbons, gloves, chocolates, sweets, lavender sachets, bottles of scent, handkerchiefs... A lot of keepsakes, a photograph album, souvenir pictures of home and foreign places... Nothing of any help in the two top drawers. In the third, bundles of letters, all carefully tied with ribbon. It was a tedious business going through them, especially as there was little hope of anything helpful there, seeing that the drawers had already been rifled. Alec gave a hand in the task, briefly commenting on the writers...

Many of the bundles contained one side of exchanges of correspondence with women friends, school companions, social climbers, members of the same clubs and nursing units, and even scandalmongers in the set which one time, according to Alec, had painted Tilsey red. Here and there, a few letters from an unknown man, letters showing what an impression the lovely Dulcie had made on men whose lives she had entered and then left, like a bright bird of passage. Some tokens of admiring homage, a declaration, a suggestion or two, a hope or a request, and then the letters ended. Littlejohn and Alec looked at each other as they finished reading the final letter in the last bundle.

> *Your callous letter after all that has been between us disgusts me. That after all our love you should simply cast me off like an old shoe, fills me with despair. I shall never write to you again, nor see you again, for next week I leave for Australia. I curse the day I met you and hate all women because of you.*
>
> *ROBIN SCREWSLER.*

"That's all, and a good finish," said Alec, pushing back the final dramatic epistle." I recollect my mother telling me Robin Screwsler married a wealthy heiress a few months after that..."

"Well; that's all. No letters from Trotman or Simpole. It looks as if Simpole got here first... Or could it have been Trotman?"

"The police have been here ever since my mother died, sir. I can't see how Trotman could have got near them. Simpole, on the other hand, could come and go as he liked. It must have been he."

"I'll go through his private things later. Perhaps they will give us some idea."

"Who else could it have been? Kent? He was after something when he called here the day he was killed. I wonder if in some way, Uncle Arthur did get to the desk. On the other hand, it might have been opened and ransacked before mother died."

"That's quite possible. One thing puzzles me. Why, in view of Trotman's affair with your mother and your...Nicholas Crake's... discovery of it, did they both still keep Trotman as their family lawyer?"

"I think it was for Uncle Arthur's sake. He was Trotman's partner, you know. Nick was very fond of Auntie Bee. Besides, Nick had no malice in him. He'd never think of chalking-off Trotman for spite..."

"I'll just go and see Uncle Bernard about all this. Perhaps he knows about the letters..."

Littlejohn smiled to himself at the way he had slipped into the Crake family circle. Alec by his Christian name and Old Doane had become Uncle Bernard to him!

Alec followed him upstairs and there they found Bernard sitting by the large fire reading one of his ancient calf-bound volumes. Whatever went on at Beyle, Uncle Bernard hung on like a faithful dog. Murder, theft, scandal, all passed him by. He was too busy with his own affairs to worry much about other people's. He greeted them calmly and laid his volume aside.

"Still investigating, Inspector?"

"Still investigating..."

"Any nearer a solution?"

"No, sir. You'll have heard of Superintendent Simpole's death?"

"Yes, most unfortunate. A strange man, Inspector, but a sound one."

"Why didn't you tell me, sir, that your sister took drugs and that you supplied them? Instead, you concocted a cock-and-bull story about tarantulas and dancing mania..."

Uncle Bernard looked hastily at Alec who met his glance with a sneer. The old man fumbled about, turned his head as though seeking a solution from different parts of the room, and finally started to blurt excuses.

"She was my sister... I didn't want anyone to know she took morphia...it seemed so disgraceful to the world, whereas to me, it was sad...very sad..."

"I appreciate your sympathy and brotherly solicitude, but they don't come very well from one who started my mother on the road to physical and moral ruin. You made her a drug addict when you arrived here. You wanted to make yourself indispensable to her, so you caught her in the net of your own evil desires..."

"Alec, I am an old man and perhaps not a very good one, but I am hardly as bad as that. Your mother contracted the habit during an illness when a foolish family doctor used a drug which ought never to have been given to a highly-strung, high-spirited woman. I was not responsible. I did all I could. The dancing was to restore the rhythm of her troubled nerves and help her break the habit. After a bout, she was unstrung, and I used the old Spanish cure..."

"I don't want to hear any more of your glib-tongued lies. You have the ability to worm yourself out of anything with your tongue. I despise you; I loathe you... I'll see to it that you get out of Beyle and stay out as soon as things here are settled."

"Nita has already offered me a home with her, Alec. I don't see how you can interfere..."

Old Doane seemed quite unrepentant. Littlejohn got the idea that, like the rest of the family, he lived in a fantastic world of his own creating, a refuge from reality. Uncle Bernard was to stay on at Beyle; that was all that mattered to him. It was all that had ever mattered to him, and he would do anything to remain there.

"Mrs Crake's desk has been rifled and her private papers gone through and many of them stolen. Do you know anything about it, Dr Doane?"

"I…? Why should I? I never interfered in the private affairs of my sister. They were no concern of mine and she had nothing in her desk of the least interest to me."

"You haven't answered the question, sir."

"Very well. I have never interfered with my sister's papers or opened her desk. I hope that suffices."

They were interrupted by the constable on guard. A telephone call from Cromwell at police headquarters in Tilsey. Littlejohn hurried downstairs, leaving Alec and the old man together, silently hating one another.

"Our people have just had a phone call from Spain. Quick work," said Cromwell. "Bernard Doane was a student of medicine at Madrid but left before he qualified. He took up music and made a failure of that too. He was in a mental home for a time. The Spanish police had the news on the files because he tried to kill the conductor of the orchestra which was playing when he forgot his piece. He was in the home for two years; then the family took him out. He disappeared suddenly twenty years ago. They don't know what he did for a living after he left the home. They're still working on it and will let us know more later."

"Thanks, old chap. That's very useful. I wonder how many more theories we'll be able to concoct out of this case. Now it's complicated by homicidal maniacs!"

12
ELSPETH

Littlejohn had to go to Oddington to see Elspeth; she was never at Beyle when he happened to be there but flitted to and fro like a wraith, tidying up the rooms in which anybody was living, laying the table, making a stew or a rice pudding, and then scuttering back to her sister's before anyone could stop her. She was torn between duty to the family and fear of the house and had found a compromise to suit herself. There were four buses a day to Oddington and back from Tilsey and Elspeth was on every one, either rushing into town to buy-in for the family or hurrying to and from the house to do some job or other. She had packed her things, cleared her room, and emigrated from Beyle, but some twitch of conscience impelled her to continue working there.

Oddington is a small place with about a score of cottages, a church, a smithy, Shelldrake's pub, the manor, the vicarage, and about a dozen farms within the rural boundary. Elspeth's sister lived in a tumbledown small-holding, the last in the village. Her husband had been a farm hand, and, after his death, his wife had carried on the house and taken in a marshy field to rear poultry. The gate was falling off and Littlejohn had a struggle to get in.

The path was muddy and a lot of old hens, geese and a solitary turkey were foraging miserably in the wet earth. Half a dozen ducks marched past in single file, a hen cackled and flew out of a dilapidated cote. There was a cart shed and neglected stable as well, with a pair of rotten shafts visible inside.

A large woman with dropsical ankles and red-rimmed eyes emerged from a shed carrying a hen, head downwards, by the legs. She thrust it in a wire coop among a lot of other broody ones and waddled towards Littlejohn. In spite of the cold wind, the sleeves of her rough blue blouse were rolled up to the elbows, revealing swollen, mottled arms, purple with cold. Her hair was rough from the wind and she wore a man's cloth cap.

"Yes?"

She closed her eyes, screwing them up as she did so, as if to clear the vision.

"Is Elspeth in?"

"What do you want?"

It was a flat, stupid, almost animal face, marked with hard work, suffering, greed and bitter disappointment.

"I'm from the police. I want a word with her about Beyle."

The woman shied off. She had all the countrywoman's antipathy for town police. All she asked was to be left alone and sell her eggs at a copper or two more than the regulation price.

"I'll see..."

There was whispering inside and then Elspeth appeared at the door. She was wearing outdoor garments ready for another of her interminable excursions. A little dried-up woman, quite unlike her sister, with a purple birthmark the size of a shilling on her right cheek. She didn't invite Littlejohn in.

"Did you want me?"

Whereas her sister had no religion at all, Elspeth derived great consolation from attending a local spiritualist circle. She frequently participated in séances. She was respected among her intimates. This gave her more self-possession than her sister.

"You'll have to be quick. I've to catch the bus to town."

"I'll drive you there in my car when I've asked you a few questions. You'd better come along and sit inside now while I question you. It's perishing in this wind."

Elspeth gave him a look of triumph. Even the police were not, it seemed, immune from human frailty.

"I'm goin', Mary Ellen," Elspeth shouted indoors. There was no reply, but the curtain of the side window was slightly drawn aside, and the red-rimmed eyes watched them off.

Littlejohn opened the door of the police car and helped the old woman in. She took a long time, fussing and fumbling and settling herself.

"How long have you been at Beyle? By the way, I don't know your second name, Elspeth."

"Elspeth Sly. Mary Ellen's my half-sister. We had the same father but a different mother. I'm a natural child, but father's wife said she'd let me live with the rest. One more among eight didn't matter much, she said."

Funny things happened in the remote country, but Littlejohn wondered why Elspeth had volunteered the information. He soon knew.

"People said my mother was a lady. My father's wife was a hawker, sold clothes-pegs from door to door when he married her. My mother was different."

She was producing her credentials and excusing, maybe, her half-sister for not being quite like she was herself. She wore a moulting fur coat, probably a gift from somebody at Beyle in the dim past, a little black hat and black kid gloves.

"How long have you been at Beyle?"

"Fifty years… More… I went there as kitchen maid at twelve and now I'm sixty-three. I can't get used to not working there. I can't keep away. But I swore I'd not sleep there another night after the master was took and I won't."

She started to weep silently. She seemed utterly bewildered.

Littlejohn waited until she was composed again.

"Mr Crake would be a little boy then."

"Yes. He was about my age. He was away at school. Beyle was a nice place then. Seven servants indoors and four out. The gardens was lovely and the inside spotless. Mr Wanless was butler. We was happy then."

"You remember Mr Nicholas bringing home his wife"

Her face grew like a mask.

"Yes."

"Were they happy?"

"Yes, at first."

"What started all the trouble, Elspeth?"

"She was always a wild one. She couldn't stay at home like other wives, while Mr Nick was at work. She had to be gaddin' about bein' entertained. And she sought some of the worst company in Tilsey to do it with."

"Are there any of the old company left now?"

"That Alkenet… Squire Alkenet. He ought to have died with his broken neck. And the Trotmans. That's all left now."

A woman passing, clad in black from head to foot like a cock-roach, peered in the car, met Elspeth's glaring eyes and recoiled.

"Nosy Parker! That's what she is. Nothin' happens in this village without…"

"Mr and Mrs Crake were estranged. From when?"

"Roughly when Mr Bernard came here for a holiday and stayed for good. I always said nothin' good would come of his bein' there. And I was right."

"Did you know Mrs Crake took drugs?"

"Yes. On and off, she did. She tried hard to stop it. Sometimes she'd go without for months. Then she'd break out again."

"How did you know?"

"There wasn't much I missed. For one thing, I did the

bedrooms and took up the breakfasts when she stayed in bed. My half-sister's husband, Fred Jolly, died of a cancer and was months under morphia. I know drugs when I see 'em."

"When did it start?"

"When Miss Juanita was born. Mrs Crake had a bad time. She never wanted children, specially Miss Juanita. Uncle Bernard was living there then and it's my belief he started her on them. It was him that gave them to her after too, when she wanted them."

"How did he get them?"

"He was a doctor. He'd ways and means. He'd stoop to anythin'."

"And what would you say was his idea in stooping to this?"

"He was a mystery. It's my opinion he was hiding away at Beyle from somebody. He got scared sometimes and got drunk. He talked then and once he said somethin' about their never gettin' him. If he could keep in with his sister — which he did — he was hid safe and sound at Beyle."

"And did Mr Crake stand for all that?"

"Yes. If you'd seen madam in one of her tantrums, you'd soon know why. He was a scholar was Mr Nick. Not used to rowin' and fightin' with women. He just let her have her own way. Then, some years since, there was somethin' up between the master and mistress and the Trotmans. I never got to the bottom of it. Might have been money… I don't know. But after that, the master never bothered much with the mistress again. Spent his time with his books."

"You like Mrs Kent?"

Elspeth gave him a sidelong glance, wondering what he was getting at.

"Of course. She's one of the family. I nursed her when she was little. They were all happy together then."

"What spoiled it?"

"Mr Nick gettin' married. Miss Beatrice…Mrs Kent now…was

sort of struck all of a heap. I think she thought they'd both of them never marry and just go on living happily at Beyle forever and ever. Life ain't like that, though. You're no sooner 'appy then somebody comes and spoils it all."

"Did you like Mr Kent?"

The small mouth grew tight again.

"No."

"Why?"

"Married men haven't no right to be runnin' about after other women, 'specially when they're their own sisters-in-law."

"He ran about, as you call it, after Mrs Crake?"

"It was disgraceful. I couldn't imagine what she saw in him. He was cold, like a fish, and treated us servants awful. No manners. But they do say, 'anythin' in trousers'll do' for some women. I suppose Mrs Crake *had* to have somebody runnin' around after her."

"But couldn't she control herself for her husband's sake?"

"You don't understand, sir. I remember Fred Jolly, my half-brother-in-law, when he was havin' morphia. It made him a totally different man. Only a farm hand, but one of the best was Fred, before he took ill. Kind and gentle. And so he was till the doctor started him on morphia. Then he changed. It made him out of control, full of queer ideas and longin's. The pain went half-way through his illness and the doctor stopped the drugs, but Fred wasn't the same. Now, if you ask me, Mrs Crake was like Fred Jolly. The drug jest took away all her powers of choosing between good and evil."

"Did you ever find her dancing as Mr Bernard played the piano?"

"Yes. She said once that when she was depressed, it always cured her. I think that was right. Mr Bernard had, or did, somethin' that made her look her best even after the drugs. She'd be on the drugs for days and then when it was over, they'd be together, doin' this dancin' and maybe him dosin' her with somethin'. After that, you couldn't tell but that she was like any other woman who didn't take drugs."

"He had some antidote...?"

"Eh?"

"A pick-me-up?"

"That's right."

"You haven't lived at the hall since Mr Crake's funeral?"

"No"

"Why?"

"I don't like it any more. There's evil there. There'll be more evil done there yet and I'm not bein' there at night. I hate the place now."

"You were there the night Mr Crake died?"

"Yes."

"Alone?"

"Yes. I expected Mrs Crake back, but then she telephoned that master was ill at his sister's. Would I send a bag of things along for the night and Mr Kent would call for them...?"

"Did he call?"

"Yes."

"He just called, took the bag, and went?"

"No, he didn't. I hadn't quite got everything, and I told him to wait in the drawin' room. There was a fire there. I was in my carpet slippers, and, when I came down, I was walkin' quiet like, there was Mr Kent, tryin' to open the desk in the mornin' room. Mrs Crake's desk it was. He made an excuse he was wantin' a cigarette. But I knew different. He was nosin' into her affairs. Perhaps after some letters he'd wrote..."

"What makes you think that?"

"Oh, nothin'. She was always gettin' letters from men. They was mad on her. And she didn't try to stop 'em. That was the sin and shame of it. Poor Mr Nick."

"What happened next...?"

"What do you mean?"

"After Mr Kent went."

"I went to bed. Nothin' happened then till after master died. Then, lo and behold! Home comes the mistress and starts her dancin'!"

"Why was that?"

"She always did mad things. You never knew… By the way, I've got shoppin' to do. I'd better be gettin' to town. The family'll want their dinner, you know."

The red-rimmed eyes and flat face of Mrs Jolly were still at the window as they drove off. Littlejohn moved slowly, talking as they went along.

"Did Mr Kent ever try at the desk again?"

"Yes; the night Mrs Crake died, I saw him there. He was that mad at me. 'What, you again!' he says. And he tells me to get on with my work. As I was goin', he calls after me that as executor of the late Mr Crake, he's looking for the grave-papers. He had some packets of letters, all tied up, in his hands and was putting them in his overcoat pocket when I came in."

"He took them away with him?"

"Yes. Must 'ave carried them home because he took the road that leads to where he lives at St Mark's."

"Did anyone else search the desk and drawers at Beyle whilst you were there?"

"Do you mean before or after the people died?"

"At any time you remember…"

Elspeth was a difficult witness. She was bothered by events, confused in her mind, ignorant concerning the relevance or otherwise of all she knew. She was a mine of information about the Crakes, but each crumb of it had to be extracted with tremendous effort. Littlejohn felt exhausted.

"That nasty policeman had them open and searchin' 'em. I watched him a bit and he told me to be about my business. He…"

"Superintendent Simpole, you mean?"

"Yes. I saw the mark o' death on 'im when he came to Beyle. I was right. He died."

If she foretold misfortune for anybody and they escaped it, Elspeth was annoyed with them. When they suffered after her prognostications, she was triumphant!

"Them as treats me bad always suffers..."

She told it to Littlejohn like a warning.

"The Superintendent was searching in the drawers. Did he take anything away?"

"Not that I see. He was more like rummagin' in 'em. As if he might be seekin' somethin' or other."

"Hmm. He didn't find it?"

"I don't think so. That was why he got mad with me, I'm thinkin'. He needn't have... I never touched nothin' that wasn't my business."

They were drawing into Tilsey and Littlejohn decided that he would have to turn over in his mind any further points he wished to talk over with Elspeth. Unless you put them in precise, simple question-and-answer form, you got nowhere with the old woman.

"This is where I got to get out. I've the week's buyin'-in to do for the family. Lucky I got my week's money before the master and missus passed on. Where they're gettin' any more from now's a mystery to me..."

She wriggled herself out of the car and on to the pavement. "Hmm," she said by way of goodbye and vanished into a shop with sausages strung-up in the window. Littlejohn could see the butcher inside rubbing his hands and eyeing Elspeth eagerly.

At the police station there was news from London about the sales of government stock from Nicholas Crake's trust. The Bank of England had, after pressure from influential quarters, lent the transfers to Scotland Yard and they had been tested. The report stated that Arthur Kent had forged Trotman's signature!

Mr Trotman had just got back from court and was warming

himself before the fire of his room when Littlejohn was ushered in by the red-headed boy.

"Good morning, Inspector. Cold weather we're having."

Trotman's huge bulk completely eclipsed the fire. He was deathly pale and there were large dark rings under his eyes. Still rubbing his enormous hindquarters, he moved to his comfortable swivel chair and sagged down in it with a heavy sigh.

"What can I do for you?"

The shifty large eyes with their bilious whites met those of Littlejohn and turned away.

"I've a bit of rather alarming news for you, sir. You were, I believe, co-trustee with Mr Kent in a trust established by the late Mr Crake on behalf of his daughter..."

Trotman reared up on his elbows and his fish-mouth trembled.

"Really! Is nothing sacred in this inquiry? Nothing sacrosanct...? Sacrosanct...? Must you unearth all the secrets of the dead...? Ahem... Who's told you?"

"I can't divulge that. I'd be glad, though, if you'd answer my question, sir."

"The existence of that trust was of the most confidential nature...confidential nature, I say. It was for the protection of Miss Crake..."

He gave Littlejohn a cunning look.

"You know the purpose?" he asked almost out of the side of his mouth.

"Yes, sir. Mr Crake was protecting his *own* child. Need I say more?"

Trotman was now altogether out of countenance, like a naughty boy caught in the act. He tried to bluff it out.

"That has nothing whatever to do with the present circumstances. I warn you, Inspector. Be careful... Be very careful."

"I know my business, Mr Trotman, and I didn't call to wash any dirty linen. I came to tell you that the late Mr Kent, your co-trustee, sold the trust investments on forged transfers and appropriated the funds!"

Trotman didn't make any dramatic gesture. It was as if the last straw found him quite without energy to resist it. He closed his eyes and gripped the bridge of his large nose with his finger and thumb.

"This is amazing," he said at length. "Kent must have gone mad! I shall now have to sort out the whole matter and make the necessary claim under the forged transfers law. As if I hadn't enough worries as it is! I've the whole estate to administer myself and a nice mess it's in, I can assure you."

"What do you mean?"

"What do I mean!"

Mr Trotman suddenly awoke and smote the desk a heavy bang with his hand. Then he nursed his hand.

"I mean, two deaths in the family, the testator and the beneficiary. Two lots of probate, and two lots of death duties. I've the affairs of those two helpless children at Beyle to look after and to crown all, my partner swindles me and gets himself murdered."

"It's not good enough!"

It slipped out before Littlejohn could restrain the thought.

"*What did you say?* I assure you, Inspector, this is not a matter for levity."

Mr Trotman was hurt. He was taking umbrage as an excuse for terminating the interview.

"I don't feel like discussing matters further with you at present. I..."

"Excuse me, sir. You are not compelled to answer my questions, as you know, but I wouldn't obstruct a police inquiry if I were you."

"I... I... Your impertinence, sir!"

"Did you know the funds had gone?"

"Certainly *not*! Certainly *not*! The question is an aspersion against my integrity...my integrity..."

"You never examined the estate accounts?"

"The trust, you mean; the trust. No. Kent did it."

"I see. Was he a wealthy man?"

"Moderately… Yes, moderately. I cannot see why he should steal clients' money… I must investigate this at once. I'm sure it will all turn out to be a mistake."

"I'm afraid not, sir. The transfers were forged. Had it been an honest transaction, Kent, as your co-trustee, would have asked you to join in the transfers. I wonder what he wanted with the money…?"

"I cannot say. I cannot say. I must ask you to leave me now. I am far from well and this has thoroughly upset me. I must think carefully how to act. We will talk another time when I feel more lucid. Now…"

Trotman spread out his white, well-tended hands and shrugged as if his world had ended.

"Very well, sir. I won't trouble you further for the present. Good day…"

"Good day…good day," said Mr Trotman to all and sundry.

With his hand on the doorknob, Littlejohn turned.

"By the way, sir, did you know Mrs Crake was a drug addict?"

"Eh? You what?"

"Mrs Crake was a drug addict…"

"What has that to do with it?"

"Plenty, Mr Trotman. She was morally abnormal through it. I'd say she might be described as *amoral*…"

"I know she took them once through illness. I didn't know…"

"You were a friend…the family lawyer, surely…"

"I didn't… I say, I didn't… Oh, dear, will this never end?"

He thrust his fists under his heavy jowls and rocked his head from side to side.

"You were the family lawyer. Did you ever defend Mr Bernard Doane in court?"

"No. Kent did the court work. He was good at it. Why?"

"I wondered if he'd ever been… You see, Doane isn't a doctor at all. He's a fake. He sponged on his sister and drugged and blackmailed her to hide him at Beyle. What he feared, I don't know, but I shall find out. Do *you* know, sir?"

"Know what?"

"Do you know what Mr Doane is afraid of?"

Trotman rose like a huge fish rearing on its tail.

"No! I don't know. I don't want to know, and I'll bid you good morning for a second time."

"Very well, sir. Small towns like this often have a kind of vicious circle of unsavoury events going on among their principal citizens. I seem to have blundered right in the midst of one here. At present, it's like a maze, but I'll find the way out. I'd hoped you would help me. Well…I'll have to carry on alone… Good morning…"

Mr Trotman sat speechless, looking ahead of him into space. Then suddenly, he awoke, rushed to a cabinet in one corner, took out a bottle of whisky, and filled a glass half full of neat liquor. He drained it eagerly, and, when it was empty, he had another.

Outside, Littlejohn was hardly enjoying a new experience. As he made his way to the police station he encountered Cromwell going the same way with unsteady steps. The sergeant was whistling softly to himself and turned a beaming face on his chief.

"I got what I wanted. Had to drink ole Trumper under his own table to get it, but he told me…"

He smiled with satisfaction and blew a blast of alcohol over Littlejohn.

"Let's get inside, old chap. Hot, strong coffee's what you want. Come on…"

He took Cromwell by the elbow and they made an unsteady line for the police canteen.

"I drunk ole Trumper under his own table and he told me, as one pal to another, it was Arthur Kent set around the tale that Mrs Crake tried to give her husband pneumonia. Excuse my condition, Chief, but there was no other way. Drink for drink, till he spilled the beans, sir. I lef' the ole boy unconscious with his own best tipple... Been lettin' in the New Year two days beforehand..."

It was then that Cromwell discovered he'd lost his hat on the way.

13

CROMWELL STICKS IT OUT

The head postmaster of Tilsey received Cromwell in his office wondering what it was all about. The police didn't often call on him and this morning he was particularly harassed. The season's inundation of mail had fallen away; the post office looked more like itself again; the extra labour had been paid off and had departed; and now it was time to deal with wreckage and casualties. In a large pile next to his cubby hole of a room stood a stack of rubbish which was to tax to the utmost the powers of deduction and imagination of him and his staff for days to come. Parcels from which labels had vanished, packets leaking and broken, articles addressed to places and people who did not, and never had, existed in Tilsey, seasonable gifts for folk who had once lived in the place and vanished without a trace. Some of the packages stank to high heaven; a hare with no address at all, a brace of pheasants with a label which seemed to have been chewed by a dog, a case of three bottles, one of which had broken and completely washed out the name and address of the unhappy recipient-to-be. Handkerchiefs, toys, chocolates, bottles of spirits, and an eau-de-Cologne flask without cork, the contents of which had dried up in a gallant battle with the scents of decomposing carcasses…

"I don't know where to start," the postmaster told Cromwell to whom he gave a cigar with a thick gold band. It was salvage and it was against the regulations, but regarding the pile he had soon to tackle, the postmaster didn't care a damn for regulations and felt, in a brief wild moment, like fortifying himself from one of the orphan bottles on the floor.

"You're on the old hand-exchange for telephones here, sir, aren't you?"

"Yes. We're due to go on automatics when the powers-that-be relax, but meanwhile we've got a very nice lot of girls on the board."

"That suits me," chuckled Cromwell. "I wonder if you'd let me ask them some questions about a certain telephone call I'm interested in."

"By all means. Confidential, of course."

"Of course."

They smiled at one another like old friends. The official was a sandy little man with a bald head, a pink, clean-shaven face, false teeth which glistened as he spoke, and as he worked he wore very large horn-rimmed glasses with deep black rims which almost totally overwhelmed him. You remembered his spectacles long after you'd forgotten everything else about him. His name was Flowerdew and he was due to retire on pension in eleven months. He was ticking off the days to his release on a calendar and, in the little songs with which his staff had merrily and cryptically ticketed the presents on the post office Christmas tree, he had been identified by:

In eleven more months and ten more days,
I'll be out of the calaboose…

"Perhaps I needn't talk to all of them. If you could let me know which girls were on duty on the date I'm interested in..."

"Of course," beamed Mr Flowerdew. "When was it?"

Cromwell told him the time and date of Mr Trumper's call after the episode of the cocktails. Mr Flowerdew consulted a file which he pulled from a drawer.

"Miss Mills and Miss Bligh."

He rang a bell and a smart middle-aged woman entered.

"This is Miss Shepherd, the Supervisor. Detective-Sergeant Cromwell, Miss Shepherd."

"Pleased to meet you."

"Pleased to meet you too, Miss Shepherd."

Mr Flowerdew explained what he wanted, and Miss Shepherd indicated that she could probably help. She left them and soon a young lady with hair of a glorious copper colour, very serious, very self-possessed, wearing a solitaire diamond engagement ring and spectacles with pale green frames of a curious shape which gave her eyes a Chinese slant, appeared.

Mr Flowerdew again explained why Cromwell was there. "Miss Bligh, Mr Cromwell."

Cromwell smiled.

"Not Nelly Bligh?"

"No. Penelope; but my friends call me Penny," said the girl, allowing Cromwell's joke to pass over her shapely head.

"Could you help at all, Penny?"

"Bit difficult, actually."

She spoke affectedly. Subscribers locally, even though they only knew her by her voice, called her The Duchess.

"Bit difficult, actually... We get so many calls, from boxes especially. Still it's registered in my handwriting, so actually..."

She thought hard.

"It was to Trotman & Co, remember, Penny?"

Light began to dawn on Miss Bligh's unusually pretty but solemn face. She resembled a Rossetti model and her lover had told her she was a second Elizabeth Siddal. This honour accounted for her grave bearing.

"I do remember, actually… There was some trouble on the line. The caller hadn't two pence to pay for his call but was so eager that he offered to put in sixpence. I agreed, actually."

"What was it all about, Penny?"

"We aren't supposed to listen to calls, sir."

Penny looked very virtuous and her Rossetti mouth and nose added to her angelic efforts.

Mr Flowerdew tactfully rose and left the room with a smile. They could see him through the glass partition helping his staff with the Christmas salvage.

"Now, Penny," smiled Cromwell." This is strictly between you and me. If you did hear anything, say so. It's very important. May help us catch a murderer before he can kill anybody else."

Miss Bligh did not change her angelic look, but you knew that she was coming out on the side of law and right.

"Actually, I did hear. I didn't listen in, not deliberately, actually. But the man making the call kept flashing… I mean, he couldn't get through at first. There was a private switchboard at the place he was calling. Trotman & Co, actually."

"What did he say?"

"He wanted Mr… Mr… The man who was killed… Mr Kent."

Red spots of excitement at the thought of murder flared up on the graceful curves of Miss Bligh's cheeks.

"Yes, Mr Kent. The switch at Trotman's seemed to be trying to get Mr Kent and couldn't. Of course, the caller couldn't hear, actually. I had him on the 'hold line' key. I remember they seemed to be ringing Mr Kent and he wasn't in and then Mr Trotman — I know his voice — Mr Trotman answered. I put them through and I just listened to see if all was right."

"What did they say, Penny?"

"As far as I remember, it was Mr Trumper, the grocer, and he wanted Mr Kent. Actually, Mr Trotman said he *was* Mr Kent. Now why should he do that?"

The innocent eyes behind the butterfly spectacles searched Cromwell's own for an answer. They were steady, eloquent eyes, and Cromwell felt they were quietly challenging him to be gallant and even suggest a rendezvous sometime, somewhere. He grew a bit hot under the collar.

"I really can't say, Penny. What happened?"

"All Mr Trumper said was that a detective had called to question him about what happened at the Kents' window when they sang carols. He said he hadn't told anything, but he was a bit scared about it. Mr Trotman said there was nothing in it. The police were just making random guesses, actually, and if Trumper kept cool and stuck to his tale, he'd be all right. Mr Trumper then said that if there was any trouble he'd expect to be supported... stood by... I think the word he used was, actually..."

"And that was all, Penny?"

"Yes. Should there have been more?"

She stared Cromwell out of countenance again.

"No. That's all, thanks. I'm much obliged for your help, Penny."

Miss Bligh pursed her Rossetti mouth.

"You'll not tell anybody?" she whispered conspiratorially. "It's our secret...actually..."

"Yes, actually, Penny."

She turned on her heel and left him, made stately progress through the office and vanished without looking back.

"Phew! That's a tasty dish," said Cromwell to himself.

"Isn't she?" said Flowerdew, who had quietly returned. "A kind of deep ocean in which men drown themselves."

Mr Flowerdew wrote poetry under a pseudonym from time to time for the local paper and Penny had figured occasionally in outpourings about Circe and La Belle Dame sans Merci...

It was half-closing day when Cromwell arrived at Trumper's

shop and the shutters were up and the place deserted. Mr Trumper, a widower, lived, however, in rooms over the premises and Cromwell, by pressing a button labelled "House" on the jamb of the shop-door, brought down Mr Trumper looking very suspicious and bothered.

"Good afternoon," said Mr Trumper coldly. It was hardly afternoon, but Mr Trumper always called it that to justify early closing. "Wot can I do for you? The shop's shut."

Cromwell smiled benevolently.

"I'd like a chat with you, Mr Trumper. I'm afraid I was a bit irritable with you last time we met. I quite appreciate it was a joke you played, and I ought to have been more sporty. I'd been up late the night before, so I must ask you to excuse me."

Mr Trumper beamed all over his face and his precariously balanced pince-nez twitched on their perch as he smiled.

"No h'ill feelin's, I'm sure. Come h'up..."

He indicated a flight of stairs leading to his upper quarters and they ascended together. Mr Trumper even placed his arm protectively round Cromwell's shoulders to intimate that they were pals again.

They entered a cosy room full of sofas and armchairs, as though Mr Trumper sought extreme comfort wherever he might wish to sit. There were knickknacks; presents from Brighton, Southport, Cleethorpes, John o' Groats and Margate, boldly endorsed to that effect in gilt script; family groups and framed reproductions from Christmas almanacs all over the walls. The sideboard and mantelpiece were filled with recent Christmas greeting cards. In the middle of the room stood a dining table decked in a red plush tablecloth. This cloth held a pot of paste, a huge scrapbook — formerly a greeting card sample book with the samples removed — scissors, pens and ink.

Mr Trumper beamed and indicated the tackle on the table.

"My 'obby," he said.

"Scrapbook?"

"Not h'exackly... Poetry."

"You collect poetry cuttings?"

Mr Trumper tried to look austere.

"Yes; of a certing sort. In Memoriums..."

"Funeral rhymes, you mean?"

"Well...yes...you might call them such. There's a lot of good poetry h'inspired by death, Mr Cromwell. F'r instance, I wrote quite a lot myself under the h'inspiration of sorrow when my wife passed over."

Mr Trumper sniffed to indicate he still sorrowed. His moustache drooped.

"Best poetry comes from a sorrowful 'eart, Mr Cromwell. Look at this one out of last week's *Tilsey Trumpet*... It's beeootiful..."

He wrung his hands in an ecstasy of appreciation.

He took the clipping between his large finger and thumb, cleared his voice and intoned:

"When Willie breathed his last farewell,
It shocked me more than words can tell.
This world seems quite a different place,
Without the smile on Willie's face."

"Lovely, ain't it?"

"Very touching."

Cromwell sniffed to hide the twitch of his upper lip.

"Or this, Mr Cromwell, cut out jest before you rang the bell:

"We think of you, dear Rupert,
We call you by your name,
But there's nothin' left to answer,
But your photo in the frame..."

Mr Trumper looked at all the photos in the frames on the walls and sighed. One of them showed Mr Trumper himself in his

Volunteers' uniform, fifty years ago. He paused as his eye caught it. It seemed to make him think.

"Let's 'ave a drink to cheer us h'up," he shouted. "An' this time it'll be a proper one, Mr Cromwell. No joke, I assure you. Proper ole meller whisky. Wot say?"

He produced the bottle and they had a tot together.

"Your werry good health, Mr Cromwell."

"Here's to you."

Mr Trumper had already had one or two beforehand. He always warmed himself up to his poetical horrors with his best whisky.

"Like to see a few more?"

"Not just now, if you don't mind. They upset me, Mr Trumper, I must confess. Life's full of sorrow, isn't it?"

"You never said a more truer word, sir. Let's have another… Jest a little one to drown our sorrow and celebrate our new friendship. Say when…"

"When… Your very good health, sir…"

"And yours, Mr Cromwell, I'm sure. Any relation of Oliver Cromwell, Mr Cromwell?

"I believe I am. A long way back, but all the same…"

"Yes… Yes…"

Mr Trumper brooded as he refilled the glasses.

"I always envied people like you, as has 'igh-soundin' and honourable names…names that rings with 'istory, sir. Names like Cromwell and Montmorency and Plantagenet…My own name makes me shame… I blush to h'utter it, sir… I blush…"

He blew out his moustache and beat the table top.

"It's short for Trumpeter…and 'oo wants to be a trumpeter? I ask you, 'oo wants to be…? Have another drink, sir, to drown my sorrow at me name…"

They drank each other's health again.

"Why fret about a name, Mr Trumper? Besides, what would all the pomp of great names be without a herald to announce them on ceremonial occasions? The herald or trumpeter's just as important as the Cromwells and the Montmorencies, if you look at it in the right way..."

Mr Trumper raised his sad eyes to Cromwell's. They were, by now, so watery that they looked ready at any moment to float out of their sockets and glide down his cheeks.

"That's right. You've give me a lot of comfort puttin' it that way, Mr Cromwell. Necessary part of regal ceremonial is the Trumper. I'll remember that..."

The whisky was certainly potent and pre-war. Cromwell knew that unless he transacted the business he'd come for and in aid of which he'd broken his rule of never drinking on duty, not only would he, but Trumper also, be incapable of dealing with it. In fact, Mr Trumper was rapidly growing incoherent, and that wouldn't do. Cromwell eyed him critically and decided the time was ripe.

"You've got your own sorrows and problems, I know, Mr Trumper. You must be terribly worried in your mind about the lie Mr Kent told you to tell the police and set around the town..."

Mr Trumper's caution had gone under the whisky. He again turned his swimming eyes on Cromwell.

"It's nearly more than I can bear, Mr Cromwell. I've kep' it locked up in me breast till I can't sleep o' nights nor do me work proper by day..."

Two large tears detached themselves from the copious reservoir surrounding his eyes, ran down his cheeks, and vanished in his moustache. His pince-nez trembled precariously on the end of his nose as his mouth trembled.

"Suppose you tell me. It'll relieve you, my friend." Mr Trumper revealed his last vestige of caution.

"Promise it won't be used against me. Then I'll confess. I 'aven't done anythin' wrong really, but I never was good as a liar, and God 'elp me, that's wot I am now."

"I'll see you right."

"That's a pal..."

He solemnly wobbled to his feet and wrung Cromwell's hand heartily.

"It was this way. On the night Mr Crake tuck ill, me and my men, eight of us all told, went round carollin' in the cause o' charity, like we always did for last thirty years. We called at the Kents' pretty near the end...must a' been about three."

A marble clock on the mantelpiece struck one, and Mr Trumper looked at it bewildered as though it were contradicting him.

"Three!" he said. "We'd just started to sing when the curtain of the window above where we was moved aside, an' there stood a man in dressin' gown and pyjamas. He looked down at us, sort of surprised, and then a woman, Mrs Crake, come beside 'im, pulled him away and closed the curtings..."

Cromwell's head was beginning to swim and he fought down the feeling of drunkenness which he marvelled, in view of the whisky, wasn't even more overwhelming.

"Who was the man, Mr Trumper?"

"Not oo' you think. It was Mr Arthur Kent. Of course, you might 'ave expected to see 'im looking down from 'is own house, but with Mrs Crake in what you might call her dishevell, her negligy, her dressin' gown and nightie, so to speak, it struck me as proper improper..."

"Quite right."

"Glad you agree, Mr Cromwell. No sooner 'ad the curtings closed than out comes Mrs Kent all upset. Her brother's in the room above where we was singin' and he's werry ill. She's sorry not to give us the usual 'ospitality, but could we go away? That seemed to explain the seein' of Mrs Crake and Mr Kent in the room. Quite nacherall if they was sick-watchin'. But... But..."

Mr Trumper paused for effect and drank the remnants of his glass.

"But... As we left the grounds of St Mark's and was passin' the

tradesmen's entrance down a little lane aside the 'ouse out comes Mr Kent and takes me by the arm. He draws me away from the rest an' says, 'Tom, I want a word with you'. He then says he don't want it known that he was in that room when he was. 'I know you saw me, Tom, because you reckenised me, didn't you?' I said I did. 'Did anybody else see me?' he asks. Now Mr Cromwell, we was all standin' in a ring, some with their backs to the 'ouse. On'y me and Willie Kneeshaw was facin' full on and, as like as not, didn't see plain 'oo opened the curtings..."

"I see. And he asked you...?"

"He asked me to see that it didn't get any further. But, I told 'im, there was certainly some who knew the curtings parted whoever there might be behind 'em... 'In that case, Tom,' he sez, 'In that case, say Mr Crake was tryin' to get out and Mrs Crake was a-restrainin' of him.' I was sort of surprised. Mr Kent to want such a thing! Askin' me to tell a deliberate untruth about his sick brother-in-law. It looked to me as if Kent 'ad even been carryin' on with Mrs Crake in the werry sick room itself..."

Mr Trumper paused and snorted. He looked ready to doze off and Cromwell gave him a good shake to keep him going. He mistook the gesture for one of reassurance and resumed confidently.

"I told 'im I didn't like it. Not only that. I was surprised at Mr Kent askin' such a thing. And him bein' proposed as next Member of Parliament for Tilsey. If it 'ad got out, his chances would 'ave been poor. They're particular in Tilsey, you know."

"Member of Parliament... Well, well..."

"Yes. I told 'im so. Then he got nasty. He threatened me, Mr Cromwell. He threatened me with ruin, if I didn't do wot he wanted."

Mr Trumper started to sob in self-pity.

"Never mind. He's dead now and past harming you, Mr Trumper."

"Yes... Makes it easy now to tell you. You see, Kent holds, or rather he held while livin', a large mortgage over my shop. Things 'aven't been so good since my daughter got married and left me alone…"

Cromwell eyed the whisky and the state of his new friend and understood.

"So, Kent lent me three thousand on the property. He said if I didn't oblige 'im, he'd call in the loan an' sell me up. What could I do, Mr Cromwell? I jest 'ad to do as he said."

"What about the rest of the singers?"

"Only Kneeshaw and one other saw Mr Kent plain. And Willie's not right in his head…sort of soft. All the same, I 'ad a proper job with 'im, makin' him see his mistake and agree that it was Mr Crake, not Mr Kent, at the winder. I offered 'im money, but he said it was no use to 'im. Do you know what he wanted, to agree with me? Two Christmas puddin's and a bottle of Cocky Dick, free! I gave 'em to him with pleasure. As for the other who thought he saw Mr Crake…well… I sort of overwhelmed 'im with argument. I talked 'im out of it. In the end, Docker…that was his name… Docker was spreadin' the news about Crake and his missus strugglin' at the winder, jest as Mr Kent had said. Docker did more than me in spreadin' the scandal."

"Didn't the others get suspicious about your long talk in the dark with Kent?"

"No. I told 'em he was apologisin' for not askin' them in, and I also said he'd give me a pound to stand 'em some drinks, which I then 'ad to pay for at me own expense…"

"And that's all there is to it?"

"Yes. It's a great relief to get it off my conscience. You'll stand by me, now?"

His swimming eyes were a bit doubtful.

"Of course…"

"Let's 'ave a drink on it, then."

"I think I've had enough, Mr Trumper. That's strong stuff. I'll bet it's pre-war…"

Mr Trumper touched the side of his nose and his glasses fell off. He started to fumble about for them.

"I must be going. It's Mr Kent's inquest this afternoon and I've got to be there, you know."

"I'm sorry 'e got himself killed, but he shouldn't have done it to me. I suppose Mrs Kent'll come into my mortgage now. She'll deal better by me. She's a good sort..."

They parted like old friends, Mr Trumper sentimentally pumping Cromwell's arm up and down until it ached.

After the door of the flat had closed, Cromwell paused to gather himself together. The keen air increased his sense of bad balance. Also, he felt full of mirth. He remembered the man with his photo in the frame and wanted to recite the poem to someone and laugh about it. Suddenly, he saw Littlejohn across the way and, walking unsteadily, hailed him and clung to him like a drowning man to a spar.

"You're drunk!" said Littlejohn.

14
BEATRICE

The inquest on Arthur Kent was adjourned. Mr Gladstone simply took the testimonies of those who had discovered the body and of the doctor who examined it. Death had been due to a violent blow on the back of the head by a heavy instrument. A certificate of interment was granted and the funeral, fixed for the following day, was thus confirmed.

Mr Gladstone then went on to inquire into the death of Superintendent Simpole. Ample evidence of a discreet nature was produced to prove that his behaviour previous to his suicide had been eccentric and depressed. He had something on his mind. His landlady, a pathetic, hungry-looking woman with a goitre, who had once been financially comfortable on what her father left her and had since, through increased living costs and the political fury of those who had no mercy on her class, had to scratch around taking lodgers and sewing to make ends meet, testified that for nights on end, she had heard the Superintendent pacing the floor almost till dawn.

"If he'd only told somebody his troubles, Mr Coroner, or even got drunk for a change, it might have done him good."

Both inquests were crowded. The townsfolk were out to enjoy

a perfect orgy of crime and sordid testimony. But they were disappointed. The official damper had fallen upon the Coroner and his court. The police would be much obliged by a mere formal taking of evidence and an adjournment pending further inquiries. Mr Gladstone's reputation suffered in clubs and in the local library where a forum gathered on cold days instead of in the small rectangle of seats around the flowerbeds in the town square.

"He's keeping something up his sleeve the public ought to know. One law for the rich and another for the poor. It's not good enough hushing things up like this."

Littlejohn called at St Mark's to see Mrs Kent after the inquest at which she had given evidence of identification and an account of Kent's movements leading up to his disappearance into Beyle House just before he died.

She received the Inspector in a calm and collected manner. She had testified in court in the same way. She was widely respected locally, but everybody was surprised at her lack of emotion.

"She mustn't have loved him…and no wonder!" someone said.

Beatrice Kent ordered tea and took a long tune pouring it out and settling down.

"I shall not be at the funeral tomorrow. Our family don't believe in women going to funerals. It will be all men."

She reminded Littlejohn of a card player, shuffling and sorting ready for the fray. She seemed to sense that his visit was ominous, perhaps fatal for her and persisted in performing trifling courtesies and keeping conversation trivial whilst she prepared for the first onset.

Littlejohn took his first sip of tea and carefully put down his cup on the table by his chair.

"Did you know, Mrs Kent, that your husband killed Mrs Crake?" he asked quietly.

Beatrice did not turn a hair. She had her cup to her lips when he said it, and many in such circumstances would have spluttered and choked. She finished her drink and nodded.

"Yes."

"You approved, I suppose, seeing you didn't inform the police or alter your way of life together."

"The way I felt when she died, I would have killed her myself had Arthur not done so. Now, I have my doubts."

"Because you discovered that Mrs Crake did not cause her husband's death, as rumour had it? Because the man at the window was your husband, not your brother?"

"Yes."

"How did you know?"

"Arthur told me."

There was silence, broken only by the roaring of the gale. Outside, the snow had turned to rain and the water lashed and splattered the windows, driven almost horizontal by the cutting wind.

"Did he tell you everything?"

"I think so."

"He and Mrs Crake had been in love and carried on a clandestine affair together. Then your husband cooled off. He was, I suppose, normally a conventional type bothered by his conscience which gave him no peace during the infatuation he couldn't throw off."

"He was a victim of Dulcie, just like the rest. On some men, she seemed to exert a peculiar magnetism. They could not resist; particularly if she singled them out. She had no morals and no scruples, Inspector."

"She had lost them through addiction to drugs, fostered by her brother."

"I know. I've known it for years. Nick used to tell me most of his troubles. I knew about Alec's parentage. But the last straw was Arthur falling for her. Not that I was jealous. Such feelings had been frozen out of me years ago. But Nick's wife...and my husband... It was unthinkable."

"Mr Kent cooled off. His conscience got the better of the struggle, assisted by the fact that his fellow townsmen wanted him to stand as their candidate for Parliament at the next election. He had managed to keep the liaison secret except from his intimates, but with political honours, and all they might lead to, in sight, he realised he couldn't afford to risk his reputation any longer. He told her so, and she refused to give him up."

"You have learned quite a lot in a few days, Inspector!"

"It is my business, Mrs Kent. Your brother had made provision for his only child in the shape of a trust. Trotman and your husband were trustees. There is a gap in my knowledge of what happened, but I make a guess... I guess that Mrs Crake found out the existence of this trust, resented it and, being short of money, coveted the funds. Your husband — involved right to the hilt in his affair with Mrs Crake and fascinated by her and by a situation which he had never before experienced — ultimately weakened to the extent of realising the assets of the trust, forging documents, and appropriating the funds. She must have had a firm grip on him and his emotions at one tune."

"She had. He was like one possessed. He even wrote poetry! It was quite good poetry such as I had never inspired in him."

She laughed harshly at the thought of such a cold fish suddenly thawing and bursting into amorous rhymes.

"What you guessed is quite true. She wormed the money out of him, and then, when he had given it to her, he realised what he had done and set out to put it right. He even tried to borrow five thousand pounds from me. Said it was to buy a larger share in the partnership. I discreetly sounded Trotman and found he was deceiving me. I suspected it was for Dulcie, and I refused. He thereupon started to save furiously. Poor Arthur, he'd accumulated seven of the ten thousand when Nick died."

"Your brother died too soon; another year or two and your

husband would have been safe. As it was, Mr Crake's death brought matters to a head. Your husband had to have the money at once."

"Yes."

"On the night your brother was brought here to die, your husband feared he wouldn't survive and, in the small hours, went to the bedroom where Mrs Crake was alone and sick-watching to plead with her to find the balance of the trust. Or at least to help him, by her influence over his co-trustee, Trotman, to hush the matter up till he could straighten it out. As they were arguing, Trumper and his troupe started to sing carols under the window. Impulsively, your husband went to close the window which had been opened…"

"That's it! It had been opened…!"

"He was afraid the noise would awake Crake. As it was, he revealed himself to Trumper and others. Not only that, Mrs Crake, in dishabille, appeared behind him, pulling him away. What a tasty bit for the gossips! It seems that only Trumper, a half-wit, and one other saw your husband well enough to identify him. Mr Kent used blackmail and money on Trumper and silenced him. To satisfy the third looker-on, a tale was told about Mrs Crake exposing her husband to the wind."

"I know… Arthur told me everything. I hated him for it, but somehow, I pitied him. He was like a small boy in trouble. I told him I would lend him the money to put the trust right. After all, he had killed Dulcie; I had done the same thing in my heart many and many a time for what she'd done to Nick. And when Nick died I blamed her, even after Arthur had explained away the gossip about the open window."

She automatically poured out two more cups of cold tea, meticulously adding sugar and milk and passing biscuits. She was like one in a dream.

"He went to Beyle for Mrs Crake's things on the night she stayed watching her husband, didn't he?"

She nodded.

"What else did he bring back? Letters? Papers?"

"He tried to find out from her papers in the desk how much of the trust money was intact and where it was. He didn't find what he wanted, but he took other things."

"Letters from Trotman and Simpole to Mrs Crake?"

"Yes. Terrible, damning letters for both of them. They would have ruined both or either of them if they'd been made public."

"When did he tell you all this; after he'd killed Mrs Crake?"

"Yes. He came home like a naughty boy...terrified. 'I've just killed Dulcie,' he said. 'It was an accident.'"

"He went to Beyle after Mr Crake's death to resume the argument interrupted in the sick room. He wanted the trust matter putting right. Mrs Crake refused. Or what is more likely, offered to do it at a price, the resumption of the old affair. They quarrelled. She, in fury, attacked him with a knife. In defending himself, he killed her, Mrs Kent."

"That's just what he said. She flew at him like a wild cat; he merely tried to twist the knife out of her hand, and she seemed to *thrust* herself on it. He left by the back stairs after wiping away his prints. In any case, he could have explained being in the room. He'd been there the night before, getting her things. Nobody knew..."

"You're wrong there. One person saw him leave; another was on his track like a hound. Uncle Bernard saw him go, but he didn't tell anyone. Now that Crake and his wife were dead, Uncle Bernard was without means of support. He didn't want to leave Beyle a beggar. He chose your husband as his victim for more money. But his luck was out. Before he could apply the screw, someone killed Mr Kent."

"Was it Doane?"

"No. I was with Uncle Bernard when it happened."

Funny how Littlejohn kept calling the old reprobate Uncle Bernard in a semi-affectionate way! It seemed somehow to fit him.

"Who did it then?"

"It might have been Alec, or Nita…or you, yourself, Mrs Kent…"

"I swear I had nothing to do with it."

"Uncle Bernard did, I fancy, try to pin his sister's death on someone else. He tried to implicate Simpole who had been madly in love with Mrs Crake and had been repulsed. She had his letters, remember, and Simpole wanted them back. Uncle Bernard knew that. He tried to protect Mr Kent from any suspicion by saying his sister said 'Police' as she died. Uncle Bernard dearly wants me to ask him what 'Police' meant. He will then say, 'Perhaps she wanted to tell me the police had done it; in other words, Simpole.' But I won't ask him. I prefer to wait for him to tell me. Then I shall know what he's at. Mrs Crake could never have spoken after that vicious blow. She died even before it ended."

Beatrice winced and covered her face with her hands.

"The other person who knew was Simpole. He was clever, very clever. We asked him to trace a call from Trumper to some third party about the rumour of the open window. He did that successfully but didn't tell us his own theory. He simply laughed and said Trumper had been scared into taking legal advice because the call was to Trotman. But Simpole didn't let it rest at that. He got on the trail of Trotman and your husband, found out about the defalcations and was on the verge of solving the case. Then his suspect was killed. So, you see, he'd to start all over again."

"He was behind us in a police car the day I took my husband to Beyle for the last time. I saw him through the driving mirror. He must have been shadowing Arthur!"

"You're sure?"

"Quite sure. I'd know Simpole anywhere. His wasn't what you would call an ordinary face."

"But when you stopped at Beyle and dropped your husband, Simpole wasn't there then?"

"No. He seemed to vanish at some distance away… Let me think! Yes, he might have taken the old road. It passes the other side of Beyle and you get to Beyle from it by crossing a paddock in a ring of trees."

"So, Simpole might actually have turned up on the scene of the crime and spotted the murderer leaving or hanging about?"

"It takes just as long on the old road as by the new, so Simpole was probably crossing the paddock as Arthur was going up the drive. He was perhaps keeping an eye on Arthur, if what you say is true."

"The letters you say your husband took from Mrs Crake's desk. They involved Trotman and Simpole?"

"Yes."

"Not your husband, then?"

"I don't know. It's very likely. As I said, he took to writing poems in the heat of his infatuation for Dulcie. He might have sent some, and even incriminating letters. Perhaps that's what he was after in the desk."

"Very likely. Did he bring all the letters home?"

"Yes. He had them in the pocket of his overcoat. He put them in the little wall-safe in his room. I saw him do it. He alone had the key. I guess if Trotman's letters were in among them, Arthur wouldn't take them to the office safe. At any rate, they aren't there now. I got the key and looked after Arthur died."

"Did your husband show you the letters then?"

"Yes. He told me everything. He was begging me on his knees to find the money to put the trust right. He was terribly afraid of being found out as a murderer and embezzler. In spite of his cold surface and apparent phlegmatic way, he was highly strung…"

"I know that. Otherwise he wouldn't have attracted Dulcie Crake. She must have brought out the nervous and emotional side of him."

"And when he was scared, he came to me! Do you know, he

had one funny failing. He was afraid of the dark. He always had an electric night-light on in the room where he slept."

"The letters; did he say anything?"

"He didn't mention Trotman's, but he gloated over Simpole's. He said if Simpole got on his track, he had a lever in them to silence him."

"He'd blackmail Simpole?"

"That, at least, provides one solution, Inspector. Simpole killed him for the letters, destroyed them and then killed himself."

"But why kill himself, if he was safe from the letters being made public? Remorse, maybe. We know he was behaving strangely. He must have loved Mrs Crake in spite of everything and her death unhinged him. He couldn't conscientiously continue, a murderer, in his position with the police..."

"But *was* he conscientious. Remember, for Dulcie's sake he hushed up Uncle Bernard's cruelty-to-animals affair."

"Are you sure it *was* cruelty to animals, Mrs Kent? It seems such a silly petty affair to cause so much fuss about. Are you sure it wasn't more serious than that?"

"What do you mean?"

"Uncle Bernard is bogus, you know. He's not a qualified doctor. He's just a fake. He provided Dulcie with drugs. Why couldn't he do it for others, too? Dope peddling. Simpole got on his track and his infatuation for Mrs Crake sealed his lips."

"I don't know... The whole affair is bewildering..."

Quite right, thought Littlejohn. Here he was discussing the case with the wife of one of the murdered victims. He was theorising with her like a colleague and she was as calm about it as if no dead husband or family scandals concerned her at all. A very cool, clever and charming woman. Far more clever than Kent, Dulcie Crake...yes, and maybe than Simpole.

"There is another theory, you know, Mrs Kent."

"What is it?

She raised her head and looked him in the eyes steadily.

"Let's assume that after he stopped trailing you on the main road, Simpole turned off to go the other way to Beyle. Why? They were there, Uncle Bernard and Nita. Alec was drinking at the airport and has an alibi. Did he wish to see one of them? We don't know. Probably we never will. He may just have been revisiting the scene of the crime. But when he got there, something happened. Your husband was murdered and perhaps Simpole saw the murderer. And then…what followed? Simpole committed suicide. Why?"

"The letters again?"

"Exactly. The murderer had taken the letters from your husband's body. In fact, he or she may have killed Arthur Kent to get them. Simpole was given his choice. To keep silent or have his letters published. He took an unusual way out. He killed himself. He was overwrought. He couldn't take one course, because as a conscientious officer of the law it was against his principles. The other course meant the end of his career which was his very life. He left no suicide note, but, in his diary, he left clues which any self-respecting detective could read like a book."

"But who could have wished to kill my husband…?"

She was showing signs of strain. She clenched her hands until the knuckles showed white through the skin.

"There are plenty… For example, where were you when the crime was committed, Mrs Kent?"

"Am I suspect, then?"

"No. I shall have to ask everyone who could have killed Mr Kent. You had good reasons for doing it, you know."

"I have no alibi. I could have returned and done it. I could have blackmailed Simpole to death. But I didn't. I was going to divorce Arthur when all this was over and cite Dulcie, alive or dead! Elspeth had promised to give evidence. That would have been my revenge on Arthur Kent for all he did to me and mine."

Her eyes were blazing, and her voice was harsh and loud. It startled Littlejohn.

"Elspeth promised? Then who might she not have told? Knowing what was to happen, Alec, or even Nita might have killed Kent to protect Mrs Crake's name. Only Bernard has an alibi. He was with me. Nita was downstairs, alone. She wasn't fond of Dulcie, but the thought of what Arthur Kent had done to her father…well…"

"You don't suspect me any longer, do you? I wanted him to live. That's why I didn't betray him. They would have hanged him. I wanted him alive. I wanted him to eat the fruit of humiliation before everybody in this town. I wanted to ruin him and make him pay to the last farthing… I wanted…"

She pulled herself together.

"I hated him too much to wish him dead."

15

JULIUS SIMPOLE CLAIMS THE BODY

Superintendent Simpole had, it appeared, an only brother Julius whom he had made sole beneficiary and executor in a sixpenny will form, executed two years before his death. Julius resembled his brother only in the bright glistening eyes and long nose. Otherwise, he was small and fat. Julius had read the news of his brother Henry's death whilst travelling for breakfast cereals and had hurried to Tilsey post-haste.

"What have they been doin' to 'Arry?" he asked, indicating nobody in particular but presumably suspicious of the Mayor and Corporation of the town.

"Pleased to meet you," he said to Littlejohn. "Bein' like 'Arry, one of the police, you'll understand. He was worked to death... No mercy on the police these days, 'ave they? More crime than they can manage..."

He was a timid, bewildered little man with a shiny bald head and he expressed a wish to take his brother's body away as soon as possible and bury it in the family grave at a place called Heckmondwike, somewhere in the North.

The presence of Julius made the examination of Simpole's effects much easier. Littlejohn accompanied him to the late

Superintendent's lodgings in the upper part of the town. Since his mother's death, Simpole had lived in a long road of semi-detached Victorian houses, once homes of the fairly well-to-do now dilapidated and badly in need of paint. Many of them had been converted into seedy-looking flats.

The woman Littlejohn had seen at the inquest admitted them. Her name was Miss Gill, a faded middle-aged lady with a goitre and the obsequious manners of one who must please to survive. She had lost the lodger with whose help she managed to live and support a sick sister. She thought, at first, that Littlejohn and Julius were applicants for the now spare rooms she had advertised, and her face fell when she learned their business.

"I would be grateful if you could get his things away. Not that I'm hurrying you, but there are others who want the rooms."

She smiled wanly and apologetically and bade them follow her. The hall was covered in old linoleum with a threadbare strip of carpet running down the centre of it. You could hear someone coughing in an upper room; otherwise the house was strangely still.

Julius eagerly pranced into the room as soon as Miss Gill opened the door. He looked round like a valuer sizing up the contents.

"Quite cosy!"

Simpole must have furnished it with odds and ends from the former home he had sold. Comfortable armchairs, a sofa, a round table and a large desk. It was just as he had left it, even to his pipe half-filled on the mantelpiece. Over the fireplace was a portrait of a young, dark, intense-looking woman.

"That's a good one of mother when she was in 'er twenties," commented Julius and started to examine the books in shelves on each side of the fireplace.

"He was a bit religious at one time," he said, as though excusing a Bible and some devotional books in Moroccan leather standing in a prominent place. "I'll get a bookseller in an' see if he'll buy the lot, as they stand."

On the mantelpiece, a photograph of Simpole and his mother, standing rather woodenly under a back-porch. There were framed photographs of groups of policemen on the walls and one of Simpole, strangely incongruous, in flannels and a cricket cap. He was holding a bat.

"'Arry was one of the best medium-pace bowlers I ever see," explained Mr Julius Simpole, like a guide. "Perhaps we'd better open his desk. 'Ave you the key?"

Miss Gill was fluttering anxiously around.

"Ahem. I hope you don't mind my mentioning it, but Superintendent Simpole… I mean, he really owes me a fortnight's rent. You see… I mean…he took the rooms by the month and as this is only month-end and they ran from the fifteenth of each month…well…I…"

She wasn't used to such situations.

Mr Julius looked horrified.

"Reely. I hardly think this is the place or time…"

He bent again to open the desk.

Miss Gill turned red.

Littlejohn opened his notecase and gave her five pounds.

"Will that…?"

"I'll just get you the sixteen shillings…"

"Don't bother. I know you've had a lot of trouble, Miss Gill."

Miss Gill burst into tears and ran from the room.

Julius had opened the top drawer and was greedily fingering a large gold coin he had taken out.

"Whew! That'll be worth a packet at the present price o' gold."

Littlejohn took it from him.

It was an old Spanish gold coin.

"I shall want to keep this," he said.

"But why? This ain't good enough. What use is it to the police? And when do I get it back?"

"Mr Simpole, you owe me five pounds for your brother's back-rent which I've just paid. You can call that in part payment, but I want the coin. It's connected with your brother's death, if you want to know."

Julius Simpole's thin eyebrows rose.

"So there was dirty work, eh?"

"And now, please, let me do the searching of the desk. You can stand by to see I don't take what I shouldn't..."

"Oh, Inspector, please don't think..."

But Littlejohn was examining a newspaper cutting which presumably had been with the coin. It was taken from a *Police Gazette* of twenty years earlier.

A valuable collection of coins was removed in the coolest manner from the Museum at Toledo on the 24th of this month. It had been bequeathed to the city by Don Pedro Guzman, an eminent collector, and was valued in intrinsic worth alone at over five thousand pounds. The caretaker testified that on the day in question, two men, one scholarly-looking middle-aged and the other of a rough working-class type, entered the museum and pretended to examine the furniture which was in the same room. On returning, he discovered that the glass in the coin case had been skilfully cut and the contents removed. The men had disappeared. The police are making inquiries.

Attached to this was another cutting, dated a fortnight later.

A notorious local thief, Juan Casado, was arrested on the 3rd instant in connection with the Toledo museum robbery. He resisted arrest and stabbed a policeman in the course of a scuffle. He was found to have in his possession a diamond glass-cutter...

And then another:

Juan Casado, arrested in connection with the Toledo museum robbery, was yesterday sentenced to twenty years' imprisonment. The police officer whom he wounded in the scuffle on his arrest, died two days ago. None of the gold and silver coins have been recovered. Casado confessed that he had an accomplice, whose name he said he did not know. The man had disappeared with the booty whilst Casado was finding a cab to take them from the city...

Littlejohn whistled. No wonder Uncle Bernard was desperate to keep in his hiding place, with Casado hunting for him after his release! And his so-called inheritance of coins was really the Toledo loot.

Littlejohn pocketed the papers and went on with his searching, Julius watching him closely and breathing hard by his side.

"What was that?"

"Some important papers connected with police work."

The rest of the contents of the desk were trivial; family souvenirs, bills, keepsakes, and, in the bottom drawer, a violin and bow without a case.

"'Arry did a bit of playin' when we were all at home. We had a little quartet, mother on the piano, dad on the 'cello, 'Arry the violin, and me on the flute an' piccolo."

Superintendent Simpole, the real Simpole, was gradually coming to life as a warm-blooded man, in spite of his frosty manner.

In the top of the desk were Henry Simpole's bank book, showing a very tidy balance, a notebook with a substantial list of investments, a cheque-book, and various police documents, certificates of merit, a letter from the Lord Lieutenant of a county congratulating Simpole on his gallantry during air-raids in the war, and then, the Police Medal, for distinguished service.

The piccolo player wasn't interested in his brother's fine record. He was totting-up the notebook and bank balance.

"Six thousand! Phew! I never knew..."

He rubbed his hands and seemed to grow inches taller. Then

greed came in his eyes, he gave Littlejohn a queer look and pocketed the lot as if the police were going to impound it as well.

It was evident that Simpole had tidied up his affairs before killing himself. There were no letters; no evidence of his connection with Dulcie Crake; nothing…except the coin and the news-cuttings. Again, it seemed that Simpole had left for Littlejohn just the necessary clues to guide him, like a thread through the maze of Beyle. The coin and the cuttings must have been a powerful weapon in Simpole's hands against Uncle Bernard and Dulcie had he cared to use them. Instead, he had stuffed them away in a drawer.

"Funny, he never got married. I don't believe 'e ever had a girl. Didn't seem to appeal to 'im at all. His job was all 'Arry lived for…"

Julius was looking round for anything else of value. He eyed two silver cups on the sideboard.

"I wonder if he won these two outright…"

"I imagine so," said Littlejohn sharply. "They were for the long-jump in 1921!"

He wished the piccolo player would himself take a long-jump and leave him to think about the new Superintendent Simpole he was getting to know.

Littlejohn stopped and picked a scrap of paper from the carpet. It must have fallen from the news-clippings. It bore in pencil a name and address.

WJ EARP

Gallowgate. 22.4.1948.

The Inspector slipped it in his wallet.

"What's that?"

"Nothing of value…"

Littlejohn took up the directory beside the telephone on the top of the desk and thumbed the pages.

WJ EARP
Jeweller and Watchmaker
12 Gallowgate. Tilsey 5657.

Miss Gill had returned, rather red about the eyes and pale in the cheeks.

"Is there anything I can do, gentlemen?"

"No," said the piccolo player.

"His bedroom, Miss Gill?"

"It's in the next room. He was so kind. He asked if he could have it there instead of upstairs. Then, if he were called out in the night, he could go quietly or return quietly and not disturb us. He was the kindest of paying guests I ever…"

She began to weep again.

"I'll see these things cleared out as soon as I can…"

Julius indicated the contents with a sweep of his hand. With his new fortune he had grown masterful and aggressive. "What the Inspector gave you will cover it meantime."

"No, it won't," said Littlejohn. "Miss Gill needs this room for letting."

There was some loose money from the desk which Julius had been counting when Miss Gill interrupted. About a dozen pound notes. Littlejohn took five more and gave them to the woman.

"'Ere… What you doin'? Those are mine now."

"I don't care whose they are, Mr Simpole. You owe Miss Gill for the rooms until you clear them, and this is the least you can give her for all the trouble she's had."

"I shall report you for this."

"By all means do so…"

Miss Gill stood clutching the money eagerly.

"That will be all right, Miss Gill."

The bedroom was completely barren of anything useful in the case. Simpole's clothes, all neatly brushed, pressed and hung in the wardrobe; his underclothing and shirts in the drawers; his shoes in a row under the window; his shaving and toilet tackle in a cupboard over the washstand.

"So kind... He paid himself for the hot and cold basin..."

"I'll 'ave to see about somebody coming to buy all the clothes..."

The dead Superintendent had made a clean sweep of all the clues to his life in Tilsey.

"Did he ever have visitors, Miss Gill?"

"Never. I don't remember anybody since he came here eighteen months ago."

"I think that will be all, then, for the time being. You haven't anything more to tell me about his way of life before he died? Anything you didn't say at the inquest?"

The woman pondered.

"I think not. A very tidy man, he was. No trouble. Never complained. A day or so before he...he died...he burned a lot of papers. So kind... He cleaned all the ash from the grate and put it in the dustbin."

"Is it still there?"

"No. The men called yesterday. They were earlier this week! I think they were after their Christmas boxes, you know."

"Do you know what he burned, Miss Gill?"

"They seemed to be letters. He was busy when I came in with his supper."

"Did you see any of them?"

"Yes, I did. He had them on the rug. He was kneeling before the fire and seeing they burned to the end. There was a little pile of them... I saw one envelope on the top. Funnily enough, it did seem to me to be in his own hand as though he'd got some letters back he had sent to...somebody dead..."

Her voice was almost a whisper.

"Somebody dead? What do you mean?"

"The letter was, I think, addressed to Mrs Crake, Beyle House... Shouldn't I be talking like this?"

"Of course. Are you sure of this?"

"My eyesight is very good for one of sixty. I could see it quite plainly. As a matter of fact, had it been on the table and not on the rug, I couldn't have read it because my near sight is defective..."

Julius was standing with goggling eyes.

"You don't mean to say that after all, 'Arry was..."

"Harry wasn't!" snapped Littlejohn.

Miss Gill looked gratefully up at him.

"Shall we go, then?"

On the way out, Miss Gill took Littlejohn aside.

"One thing rather worries me, Inspector. About six months ago, Superintendent Simpole bought new carpets for his bedroom and living room. He said, if ever... They would be mine, if ever..."

"Then for goodness' sake, Miss Gill, don't tell the flutist..."

"I beg your pardon."

"Don't tell Mr Julius. He'll have them up and sold. If that's what the Superintendent said, take it as right. They're yours, Miss Gill. Not a word."

"He was so kind..."

Littlejohn asked Julius which way he was going and then said he was taking the other. The little bald-headed man was beside himself with his legacy.

"At least, let's 'ave a drink together. *On me.* I feel I want to celebrate."

"I'm sorry, sir. Never do it on duty. I'll probably be seeing you later."

"I'll be back next week for my brother's things. I'm off tonight. Takin' the body to 'Eckmondwike. Family grave, you know. I never thought 'Arry was such a warm man. Must have had a good screw to save so much..."

He tripped off lightly to the nearest pub.

Littlejohn soon found Earp's shop. Mr Earp was in attendance himself, selling a lady a cameo.

"They're antiques as well as fashionable jewellery, you see. Nine pound's my price an' I'd be losing if I let it go cheaper."

An oily little man with a big head and shifty eyes which he hid behind large black-rimmed glasses. He kept putting the spectacles on and off nervously, tapping his even, white dentures with them, chewing the sidepieces, waving them about.

"Right. I'll keep it a day or two, till your husband can call. Good morning..."

Then he saw Littlejohn. It was obvious he knew the Inspector either from pictures in the local paper or having him pointed out. He looked scared.

"Good morning." He rubbed his hands and tried to look as if Littlejohn wanted a cameo as well. "And what can I do for you, sir?"

"Good morning. Did you ever have any dealings with my late colleague, Simpole?"

Littlejohn handed the jeweller his card. Mr Earp read it upside down and placed it on the counter with trembling fingers.

"Can't say I had the pleasure."

His teeth evidently didn't fit properly, and he cast up a spray of saliva as he spoke. It reminded Littlejohn of a fizzing soda-water syphon.

"Sure, sir? In 1948?"

"Let me see... Maybe. It's so long ago."

"A Spanish gold coin."

Mr Earp jumped. He licked his lips.

"I think I do. That's nearly four years, though," he fizzed.

"You bought a Spanish gold coin from Mr Doane, of Beyle, didn't you? Superintendent Simpole had evidently been trying to trace it and found it here. Now do you remember?"

Earp was still trying to look as if he didn't remember.

"Would you mind turning things over in your mind then, sir, and then you'll be able to tell a proper tale at the resumed inquest on Superintendent Simpole...?"

"Wait!"

Littlejohn halted half-way to the door. Mr Earp was chewing his spectacle frames furiously.

"I remember. I did buy it from Mr Doane and the Superintendent did take it. I never got it back nor heard a thing about it after, and I never got the money for it either."

"How did you come to buy it?"

"I bought quite a number from Mr Doane. His father was a collector, he said. They were all different, some large, some small," he hissed and splashed. Littlejohn stood back a pace.

"What did you do with them, sir?"

"They were only valuable to me for the gold content, of course. I am licensed to deal in bullion and am allowed a certain amount for use in my workshop."

"Have you had any more from the same source of late?"

"No, sir. They ceased after Superintendent Simpole took the one you mention."

"Is that it?"

Littlejohn handed over the large gold coin.

Mr Earp carefully examined it, even screwing a jeweller's glass in his eye to make it look professional.

"I think so. It's very like it. Spanish, you know. Old Spanish."

"And that was the last you heard of them?"

"Yes... Except..."

"Yes?"

"Except, funnily enough, not Mr Doane but Mrs Crake came in with about half a dozen of them. She said she had some in a collection from her late father. Could I take them, assay them, and melt them down into gold bars for her...?"

"Gold bars? Whatever for?"

"She said she thought it as well to hold on to gold now, in view of inflation and all that... She wanted to put the bars in the bank."

"And what did you say?"

"I wouldn't touch them. I'm not a dealer in a big way. Just for my own requirements or for passing on to larger firms. I didn't like the idea of handling so much gold. It's against the national interest, if you gather what I mean, sir."

"I do…"

Had it been a question of buying the gold at a good profit the little fizzer would have dealt, Littlejohn was sure.

"Thank you, sir. That's all for the moment."

"Will I get the money for the coin you showed me? The inquest, will I…?"

"I'll let you know if you're needed. Good day, sir."

At the bank, Mr Shotter was very pleased to see Littlejohn and told him so.

"I hope you're making progress, Inspector. It's not nice, a killer in our midst, is it?"

"We're getting along nicely, sir. I came to ask if you had a strong box belonging to the late Mrs Crake?"

"Why, yes. It isn't exactly a strong box. It is a wooden one with a lock. It reminds me of those things they used in the army in my day. I was in the Royal Artillery in the first war, you know. A strong wooden box with rope handles. Know the kind? I think she must have kept bricks or shot in it. It took two of my men to carry it in when she brought it…"

"How long ago?"

"Not long before she died. I could get the exact date…"

"That will be near enough, sir. You still have it?"

"I think so. It's awaiting probate, then the executor will presumably take it away."

Mr Shotter rang a bell and a clerk appeared.

"Snellgrove, have we still got Mrs Crake's wooden box in the strong room?"

"Yes, sir."

"May I see it?" asked Littlejohn.

"A bit unusual, sir, but…in the public interest, yes. You can't, of course, take it away."

Two clerks then brought in the box and it took them all their time to carry it. Littlejohn found himself wondering how Uncle Bernard got it all out of Spain...and in a hurry at that, with the police on his heels.

"It is like one of the old ammo boxes, isn't it?"

"It certainly is."

Littlejohn took out the keys which belonged to Mrs Crake and which he had held pending the closing of the inquiry.

"Mind if I open it?"

"I really ought not, you know. All the same, if you do it before witnesses...Just a matter of form in case the executors..."

"Of course."

Two clerks were again sent for and Littlejohn, after trying a few keys on the ring, found the right one. He turned the lock and flung back the lid. The little party circling the box gasped like one man.

It was like Kidd's treasure itself. The case was half full of gold coins of all sizes and, on top of the lot, lay a magnificent golden jewelled crucifix with a ruby in the centre which, catching the light from the pendant overhead, shone like blood.

16
THREE COFFINS

Littlejohn and Cromwell were the only two who said a silent farewell to Superintendent Simpole as he left on his last journey to Heckmondwike. It was cheaper to take the body by train than by road, so Mr Julius Simpole saw the coffin to the station and set out on a long and rather tiresome trip north. The local police had, of course, paid their respects and bade a formal farewell to all that was left of their old chief. This had been done at the police station and then the undertaker's men had assumed charge and borne it off in a hearse to the platform. Official wreaths had been sent to the North ready for the funeral. Littlejohn who, thanks to his investigations, knew more about Simpole than those who had served with him all the time he had been in Tilsey, felt impelled to see the train off. He and Cromwell, therefore, stood bareheaded as the coffin was placed in a compartment reserved for it and for Mr Julius. There was a solitary wreath on it: "From his colleagues of New Scotland Yard." Mr Julius, temporarily insane through the discovery of his large inheritance, had substantially fortified himself for the cold journey and followed the obsequies with unsteady feet. As the train left, the flutist leaned from the window and waved a cheerful bowler hat at the two detectives...

Next day, it was different. The funerals of Arthur Kent and Dulcie Crake were each splendid in different ways. They were held two hours apart because many of the mourners of one were due to appear at the other, like theatregoers who rush from a matinée to an evening performance with hardly a break for breath.

The day was sunny and cold as the first cortège began to move from the funeral parlour where, strange to say, the two one-time lovers, principal characters in the tragedy of Beyle, had occupied separate rooms in the stillness of death. Dulcie Crake was the first to leave. She was a Catholic and went to her own church for requiem.

"Never miss a funeral," was a saying of Cromwell's and it was wise of its kind. In the course of an investigation such a function assembles a strange panorama of principals and supers of the case and sometimes brings to light some trifle which adds to the whole of the solution.

The church was almost full when the procession arrived. There had been no previous selection and arrangement as at Nicholas Crake's funeral service and as the party mounted the steps, they trod on the confetti of a wedding which had taken place only half an hour before. The body of the church was filled with lower-class women, some with children, drawn there by the sensation of the murder. Dulcie Crake's two children by different fathers followed the coffin and Uncle Bernard brought up the rear. He was wearing his coat with the astrakhan collar and his silk hat of ancient vintage. His features were pinched and his nose red and he kept sniffing the air like a hound on the trail. The pealing of the organ, the chanting of the choir, the intoning of the priests, and the censer and aspergillum had no effect on him; he stared into space like one in a dream. Beatrice Kent was absent, but both the Trotmans were there. This was the first time Littlejohn had seen Mrs Trotman. She was a little, thin, modest woman with a strange dignity in her bearing. Now and then, she glanced at her husband affectionately, as if she might be proud of him. Trotman seemed oblivious of all this, pacing the aisle to his seat on ponderous flat feet and barely seeing that his companion had a place for herself.

At the cemetery, a new grave had been made on the Catholic side and there Littlejohn was surprised to see how many of the rather shabby people from the church had followed the coffin. Most of them were obviously not mere sightseers but were visibly moved. Several were weeping and had put on seedy black for the occasion.

"She got in some queer places in her time," whispered a threadbare man at Littlejohn's elbow. "Look at all that lot..."

His eyes indicated the lower orders, more so in contrast with Trotman and his party.

"She gave a lot of money away," said the man. "Anybody with a sorry tale could touch her for a quid or two. Reason I'm 'ere is because of the way she treated my dead wife when she was ill. She was in the nursin' corps then and stopped up night after night with 'er. I'll never ferget it and nobody can talk to me about Mrs Crake bein' a bit of a wrong 'un. That don't matter to me."

He sniffed, put on his hat and melted away like someone with a brief walk-on part to play. The priests had said their say, the last earth had been flung on the coffin, the notables were hurrying off to the next funeral, and the gravediggers were coming along with their shovels ready to fill in the grave. It was then that Littlejohn noticed that Uncle Bernard and Trotman were in trouble. Uncle Bernard had come to life and was apparently denouncing Trotman for something. He was pointing to the grave and raising his hands aloft like somebody demented. Trotman was trying to hold the old man at arm's length. Mrs Trotman drew him away to their waiting car.

Uncle Bernard was still pointing an accusing finger at the retreating back of the lawyer.

"Never came near her when she was in trouble. What's he come gloating here for...?"

They persuaded him at length to enter his taxi and he was driven off too.

Kent's funeral was more ceremonial, and the town officials, including the Mayor and the legal faculty, turned out. Mr Huxtable, the Mayor, was still coughing in hollow fashion and wondering if he'd be the next. The Rev Joshua Roebuck officiated like one of the deadly sins in appearance, his gluttonous mouth rolling out the beautiful phrases of the burial service. They did not go to church. Mrs Kent had shown singular indifference to ceremonial and the funeral service was held in the mortuary chapel at the cemetery. It was like trying to get a quart in a pint pot for the chapel held only a hundred people and there were two hundred there. A huge crowd gathered outside. The building was cold and damp and the breath of those present rose like a large cloud of steam heavenwards. Those outside, including Littlejohn, stamped their feet and beat their hands to keep warm. Above all could be heard the Mayor's hollow coughing...

Uncle Bernard, Nita and Alec were present, this time as equals, and formed a trio together. People remarked about the absence of the widow and many made excuses for her on health grounds. She had taken the whole business badly. At length, preceded by the swollen shape of Mr Roebuck, they carried Arthur Kent to his family vault and interred him with his father and mother and a sister who had been killed in a car accident. The crowd melted away again just as it had done from the other part of the cemetery two hours earlier. A few hangers-on started to read the cards on the wreaths. And then Littlejohn saw something which gave him a thrill he always felt when light suddenly dawned on a case for the first time.

Uncle Bernard was putting on his top hat!

And, keeping his distance from the old man this time, Mr Trotman was also covering his large head with his black homburg. Littlejohn felt like rushing to where they stood, swopping their hats, and putting the silk one on Trotman and the homburg on Uncle Bernard. He remembered his feeling of mirth on the night they had found Kent dead at Beyle and how he had sympathetically handed Uncle Bernard a soft hat as he left the house. The hat had almost suffocated the old man! At least, it had fallen over his ears and Uncle Bernard had said, "Give me my own hat; this isn't mine." Whose had the hat been? Had it belonged to the man Alec had surmised was hiding in the cubby hole under the stairs when they found Kent's murdered body? Had he hidden himself and, in his haste, left his hat on the hall table where Littlejohn had found it and handed it to Uncle Bernard?

"Are you ready, sir?"

Littlejohn awoke from his reverie with a start and realised that the funeral party had broken up and gone… The spectators were still reading the cards on the flowers…

"Let's go to Beyle. I want a word with Uncle Bernard…"

The constable on duty at the door of Beyle saluted as the two detectives entered.

"All the family are at home, sir…"

Littlejohn and Cromwell didn't need telling. Loud voices raised in angry altercation could be heard in Uncle Bernard's room.

"I don't care what's my duty. Whatever it is, it's not to you. You've sponged on us long enough. I'm leaving tonight."

Nita's voice was high and determined.

You could just hear Uncle Bernard rumbling an answer in plaintive tones.

Then it was Alec's turn.

"I'm leaving for Paris the day after tomorrow. If you can't persuade Elspeth to come back, you'll have to look after yourself.

The house will be all yours till Nita decides to sell. I never want to see the place again..."

Littlejohn and Cromwell stood in the doorway of Uncle Bernard's room. The family formed a little trio, gesticulating, leaving the group one after another, and then moving back.

"Elspeth's promised to stay the night and help with the packing, but she insists on sleeping in the other bed in my room..."

Nita turned and saw the new arrivals. She halted.

"You two again? Is this investigation never going to finish?"

Alec nodded to them jauntily.

"I'd like a word with Mr Doane in private, please."

Nita and Alec exchanged glances.

"Don't let us intrude..." Nita sounded annoyed.

Brother and sister left the room together.

"By the way, Mr Alec..."

Alec turned on his heel to face the Inspector.

"How many croquet mallets did you keep in the room under the stairs?"

"There were two left... Why?"

"There was only one when you showed the place to me. When did you last open it?"

"The day before Uncle Arthur was killed. I was just wandering round and looked in... Both mallets were there."

"Have any of you seen the other one?"

Littlejohn looked from one to the other and then the three relatives looked at one another, too. Their faces were blank.

"I'm not suggesting a game. I'm suggesting that Mr Kent was killed with a blunt instrument. I can't think of anything better than a croquet mallet..."

"Very easily disposed of... Burned, for example..."

"But who could have...?"

"There was only one fire in the house as far as I recollect. Elspeth was out, and the kitchen fire was dead. There was an electric stove going in the room where you were sitting, Miss Nita. The only fire was…there…"

He pointed to the hearth of Uncle Bernard's room in which a log fire was blazing.

Nobody spoke.

"And now, if you don't mind, I'd like to speak to Mr Doane."

This time Nita and Alec made a hasty retreat. They were ready to compare notes and discuss what Littlejohn had just said.

Uncle Bernard looked all in. Wearily, he indicated two chairs by the fire and himself sat down in another.

"I wonder when all this is going to end?"

He got up again, went to the cupboard, and brought out the sherry and glasses. Removing a large paraffin lamp with an elaborate reservoir and green shade, he spread the glasses and decanter on a small table.

"Will you join me?"

"No thanks, sir."

Cromwell shook his head.

"No, thanks."

Uncle Bernard helped himself liberally, gulped down the drink and filled up again.

"This is my food and drink these days."

"I'm afraid what I have to say, sir, is not very pleasant. First of all, why did you pose as a doctor when you never graduated?"

It didn't seem to disturb old Doane at all. He shrugged his shoulders.

"I never said I was qualified. People persisted in calling me doctor. I didn't ask them. I studied medicine but gave it up for music."

"And attacked the conductor at your first concert…"

Uncle Bernard rose to his feet in rage.

"The fool! The fool! He ruined my concert. He got the orchestra in such confusion that I lost my memory… I couldn't remember…"

He started to tear his hair.

"After which, did you spend some time in a nursing home for nervous cases?"

"Who has been spreading slander about me? I resent your intrusion on my past life, which doesn't concern you… Who told you?"

"The Spanish police, Mr Doane."

"The…"

His long hand clawed at his lips and he stepped back a pace, caught the edge of his chair on the back of his knee, and fell into a sitting posture.

"The police…?"

"Does the name of Juan Casado mean anything to you…?"

A look of fear crossed Uncle Bernard's face and then vanished.

"No!"

"He was arrested, I believe, in Toledo for stealing a collection of coins. The coins were never recovered. His accomplice escaped."

"Indeed. And where do I come in, sir?"

"The coins are now in the bank in a box lodged by your late sister."

Doane was on his feet again.

"This is ridiculous…"

He hung over Littlejohn like a bird of prey.

"You're trying to trap me… I won't have it. I know nothing about the stolen coins…"

"Yet you sold several of them to Earp, the jeweller, until Superintendent Simpole found out what you were doing. He had previously encountered you and met your sister in connection with your unlicensed vivisection. He fell in love with Mrs Crake and lost his sense of proportion. She persuaded him to keep quiet about the coins although he discovered that you held the stolen Toledo collection."

"It was…it would…"

Doane seemed to be choking.

"Go on, sir."

"It would only have fallen in the hands of the republicans… those anti-royalists I hated. I was justified in taking it."

"You simply stole them, ran out on your accomplice with the booty, left him to take the medicine of twenty years in jail… And then you came here and hid from justice and Casado. You made up your mind that nobody was going to make you leave here. You made your sister into a drug addict, broke down her resistance every time she tried to cure herself, undermined her morals and health, and made a wreck of her. You broke up Nicholas Crake's home and happiness…"

"Dulcie was never stable. It didn't need me to assist her. You know, of course, who was Alec's father. You seem to know far too much. I didn't cause that…"

"They were living happily…as happily as two such incompatibles could live. You were responsible for all the tragedy of Beyle, and you did it to save your own beastly skin and for your own crazy comfort."

"The coins were Dulcie's…"

"I wouldn't lie any more if I were you. You sold the coins to your sister. After Simpole found out about them, you sought ways to be rid of them. How did you persuade her to buy them? Did you talk economics to her? Did you tell her that gold was better than depreciating paper money; that the best way to invest the cash she wrung from her other crazy lover, Kent, was to put it in gold in the bank?"

"The cash she got from Kent was her own by rights. What business had Nicholas Crake hoarding money to leave away from his wife? What did Nita ever do to deserve such a fortune? When Kent told Dulcie of it, she never rested until she got it for herself. It was hers by right. She was his wife, wasn't she?"

"Is that the way you put it to your sister? Whenever you

wanted anything, you drugged her until she couldn't think for herself and then forced your will on her…"

"I always looked after her. Even when she was a child…"

"Please, don't let us have any more sentimental scenes, Mr Doane. I only wish I could arrest you for the murders in this house. They all lie at your door and are you're doing, indirectly. As it is, I have seen to it that the Spanish government are informed where the Toledo treasure is hidden. That, I'm afraid, is now a matter for diplomats. Extradition is a bit difficult in present circumstances, but I hope you end in some foul Spanish jail or other for all you've done. Meanwhile, I'm going to hold you on a charge of receiving stolen goods. That sounds funny, but I'm stretching my technical conscience a bit. You will not leave this house until I say you may."

Doane, limp and dishevelled, had listened to all this and then, in a sudden spasm of energy, began to flail his arms about like drumsticks.

"This is outrageous! It's all lies and fantastic nonsense, just to implicate me. My sister needed a helper and adviser…"

"Her husband was eminently qualified for that role. Had you not arrived here and started your devilry, the victims of these foul attacks would have been alive now. After your sister died, how did you get the letters Simpole wrote to her?"

"I didn't… I never saw the letters…"

"I don't believe you. Kent stole them from Mrs Crake's desk. You knew that, with your sister dead, Simpole's promise of silence to her was finished. You had to find another way of keeping him quiet. You got another promise from him by dangling the letters which you got from Kent. Did you threaten Kent as well? Threaten to make known the fact that he'd embezzled the trust monies invested by Crake for Nita?"

"All lies… You're trying to implicate me in…!"

"You know it's the truth. You knew of the money Kent gave your sister. He gave you the letters for your promise of silence and you, in turn, handed them to poor Simpole in exchange for *his* promise. Simpole was a gallant officer, torn between duty and disgrace. He broke down and took his own life. Another score against you..."

There was a knock on the door and Elspeth entered bearing a tray.

"Here's your tea," she said with a baleful glare at Bernard Doane. "I'm leaving tomorrow..."

She had avenged herself as best she could against the man she always hated. The tray bore a shrivelled chop, a couple of greasy potatoes, a hunk of bread, and a glass of water.

"I haven't time to do a sweet. I'm packin' for Miss Nita."

And she left the room.

Uncle Bernard regarded the contents of the tray critically and then, with an angry gesture, swept the lot in the fireplace. There was a crash of glass and crockery and the water began to hiss on the tiles.

"If my sister had been alive, this wouldn't have happened!"

"And now, sir, would you mind telling me what size you take in hats?"

Cromwell looked anxiously at Littlejohn, wondering if the scene just passed had unhinged him a bit.

"My what?"

Uncle Bernard couldn't believe his ears either.

"Your size in hats..."

"Six and a half..."

Littlejohn looked at the small head on top of the thin, sloping shoulders. He wondered what the anthropometric men at Scotland Yard would make of it!

"Cromwell, do you mind going down and asking for one of Mr Nicholas Crake's hats and also ask Alec what size he takes?"

Cromwell gave Littlejohn another queer look and slowly went on his business.

"Will you be all right?" he asked his chief as he turned at the door.

"Why not?"

Uncle Bernard's eyes glinted.

"What is this new idea…? Hats, hats, hats… What are you doing? Trying to drive me mad?"

"Mr Alec takes six and seven-eighths… And here's one of Mr Crake's…"

He handed over an old fishing hat with flies still stuck through the band. There was no ticket in it.

"Try it, Cromwell…"

Cromwell dubiously put on the hat. It fitted him exactly and gave him a raffish look. Littlejohn could not resist a grin. Cromwell, faithful under any strain and stress, returned a sickly smile.

"What size do you take, Cromwell?"

"Sevens…"

"Quite a variety of sizes. Now, who would take, say, seven and a quarter?"

"What *is* all this?"

Littlejohn turned angrily on Uncle Bernard.

"You know what it's all about! On the night Kent was killed, as I saw you off to your temporary lodgings, I handed you a soft homburg hat. It fell over your ears. It was neither yours, nor Crake's, nor Alec's. It belonged to whoever was hiding in the hole under the stairs. It belonged to somebody who killed Kent, or else saw who killed him. It belonged, unless I'm very much mistaken, to Mr Trotman!"

"It's a lie! I don't remember anything about a hat. How did Trotman get away if he was hidden there? The place was full of police!"

"Patience, Mr Doane. Just patience. He just needed to sit and wait until the constable went off to make some tea, say, and then he bolted through the front door. It was dark then. Why did Trotman kill Kent? Do you know?"

"How should I know? I don't believe he did. I believe it was Simpole did it. I believe he killed my sister, too."

"Why?"

"She said 'Police' with her last breath. She didn't want me to *call* the police. She knew I'd do that. She tried to convey with her last breath that the police had killed her…"

"Rubbish! You know as well as I that the wound she got killed her outright. She never spoke at all. You knew who killed her. You saw him. But you didn't tell me because you wanted someone with influence in the family on your side; someone you could blackmail by your knowledge into seeing you kept your nice comfortable little hideout here. You're a low-down swine, Mr Doane, and nothing would please me better than to hand you over to the hangman, or better still, the Spanish police. They aren't so humane."

"I don't know what you're talking about. I shall report this bullying to the proper quarter. You've no right…"

"But, unluckily for you, Kent was murdered in turn. So, you got Trotman. What is Trotman going to do for you? Buy you this house; cheat Miss Nita out of it; settle it on you; become your new protector? Because I'll see that he doesn't. We're going to have a thorough cleaning up at Lepers' Hollow if it's the last thing I do."

"I can assure you, it *will* be the last thing you do. When I've finished with you, you'll wish you'd never been born. I'll…I'll… I have powers beyond the law and the police… I have read and experimented and dug into the records of the past…I have secret drugs, powders, and potions that will make you die in torment. And you'll never know when the food you eat or the beer you drink holds your doom. I have… I have…"

He rose and pointed a skinny hand at Littlejohn, foam flecked his lips, and his hair grew more dishevelled without his even touching it. Like Hitler raving over his secret weapons!

"You cannot conceive the power I have over those who try to do me ill... I have secret..."

The door opened, and anti-climax entered in the shape of Elspeth again. This time she carried a piece of solid, soggy Bakewell tart with a streak of cold yellow custard slopped over it.

"I found this in the refrigerator... It's still fit to eat. If you want it, you can have it... Well! I never did!! Oo's thrown that chop in the 'earth and broke the pots? Was it you?"

Uncle Bernard descended from his pedestal of supreme power, gazed at her as if he'd never seen her before.

Elspeth's patience was at an end. She deliberately laid the tart and custard on the table, placed her hands on her hips, and faced the old man.

"You threw my good food on the fire. Well, you can starve for what I care, now. Yore a wicked old man, if ever there was one. Wicked and devilish and crool... You ruined Mrs Crake, but, what's worse, you made my poor Mr Nick's life into one long 'ell. You deserve to rot in hell, you blasted ole sinner, and rot you will. Well...you can stop in this 'ouse all yourself after tomorrow. You can sit an' brood an' get cold and starve. Nobody's goin' to raise a hand to help you... Thief, liar, devil, 'ypocrite, murderer..."

She cast around for other epithets to fling at his head and, finding none, looked for other means of damaging him. Her eyes fell on the Bakewell tart. With aim quite deadly for one so old, she swept it from its plate, palmed it, and swung it at Uncle Bernard, who took it full in the face and collapsed.

17
THE SORROWS OF MR SKRIKE

Mr Caleb Skrike was a qualified solicitor who, in his early days, had shown great promise. Then he took to drink. This may have been due to the fact that he got little peace at home for, almost as soon as he had settled down to married life, his wife had started to present him with children. Boy, girl, boy, girl; until there were seven of them. Life became monotonous, so the father of this little flock took to staying at the club until late; sometimes he slept on the couch in the billiards room. His wife had a professed preference for infants; after they reached the age of one she lost interest in them and wanted another suckling. At the seventh accouchement, Providence seemed to intervene; there were no more to follow, and the ordeal came to an end. But not Mr Skrike's drinking. He was too far in the toils.

After thirty years with the firm of Trotman, this little lawyer with the misty eyes, the little grey beard, and suits which always seemed a size too large for him, and who, by the way, conducted a ladies' choir when he was not drinking or doing his children's homework, turned awkward. He handed Mr Trotman his resignation from the blue. Trotman spent a few sleepless nights as a result. Arthur Kent was a good court man, but someone always had to prepare his briefs; Trotman made a song of specialising in common law and conveyancing but Skrike did the work. It looked as if the firm would have to shut up shop! Skrike then said he would stay on as a partner, and, in spite of all the tut-tutting of Kent and Trotman, he stuck to his guns. When he felt himself weakening, he crossed to the club and got drunk.

"I've got my family to think of," he kept repeating.

At last he won the day, his name went on the plate and notepaper, and he received one-fifth of the net profits of the partnership. Having done this, he drank himself under the billiards table at the club and slept the night on the front lawn of his house. Fortunately, it was midsummer! The Skrikes lived in a semi-detached house not far from the centre of the town. On leaving Beyle, Littlejohn called there and found Mr Skrike just about to go out to choir practice.

"I haven't much time," he told Littlejohn." But come inside for a minute."

Inside, in the badly lighted hall, it looked like a boarding school. A lot of little hats and school caps hanging on pegs in the lobby, appropriate top-coats under them, and a heap of school bags on the floor. It was the hour of homework and the silent brood were working hard in the dining room at anything from illustrating nursery rhymes in coloured chalks to differential calculus. They were extremely well brought up, the lot of them, for Mr Skrike did not hesitate to administer corporal punishment when necessary. This he invariably did with a cane on bending and tight hindquarters, and, when they were all good, he chastised the worst of them nevertheless, to keep up morale. When he was absent, his wife took on the task of monitor. The children dreaded her punishments more than their father's for these consisted of smacks on the head which almost rendered the recipients unconscious; she used her left hand on the finger of which a large wedding ring, symbol of their legitimacy, acted as a knuckle-duster.

Upstairs in the nursery, two little girls who had finished their exercises were quietly playing with dolls. They were putting them to bed and singing soft little lullabies.

Mr Skrike was a well-bred man in spite of his short-comings.

"Pray, step in, Inspector," he said, and opened the door of the parlour. A blast of cold damp air rushed from the little-used room and Mr Skrike hastened to dispel it by lighting a large old-fashioned gas fire which roared and plopped throughout the interview. A solitary electric lamp with a shade made of little beads, strung together by the eldest daughter, illuminated the room. Mr Skrike's law books and a lot of cheap editions of the classics stood in rows on shelves on each side of the fireplace over which hung a framed photograph of the Skrike family, Mrs Skrike sitting with two children on each side of her, a child in arms on her knee, two sitting tailor-wise at her feet, and Mr Skrike behind with a protective hand on her shoulder. Other photographs on the walls and mantelpiece showed the children in various stages of development from naked and lying on their bellies to prize-winning at fancy-dress balls as pirates, page-boys, Pierrots, Pierrettes, and admirals. Splendid and outshining the rest, a large picture of Mr Skrike sitting among forty women, with a label on the frame: "Tilsey Festival Choir. Winners 1946."

"Please sit down."

Mr Skrike indicated an old-fashioned armchair, the springs of which were visible and uninviting through the plush. He didn't ask Littlejohn if he would drink. He half-filled two tumblers with whisky, added the same amount of soda, and handed one to the Inspector.

"Your very good health, Inspector, and success to your cause."

"Thank you, sir. Good health. I came to ask you a few questions about the case."

"Fire away..."

The gas fire thereupon exploded, put itself out, and Mr Skrike had to fiddle with the air vent and relight it. The room grew heavy with the smell of gas.

"May I ask you what you think, sir, of the murders at Beyle House? Your firm were the family lawyers and one of your partners was a victim. Have you formed any views?"

Mr Skrike took out a large, curved pipe, lit it, and seemed to derive great comfort from puffing it. He invited Littlejohn to take a pipeful of shag from his pouch.

"This is a bit awkward," he said at length, rubbing his fingers in his short beard. "Private views of a case like this are dangerous, especially when one's own colleagues are concerned."

"I don't need to tell you, sir, I shall use with the greatest discretion any information you may care to give."

"I don't doubt it for a moment, Inspector. I've watched you at work, I like you, and I wish you success. Good health and good luck!"

He drank off his whisky with the skill of long practice. Then he laid down his glass and put the tips of his fingers together.

"We have here a case of very tangled family relations. That old reprobate, Doane, has brought nothing but unhappiness to that house. In fact, I don't think I exaggerate when I say he's brought about its downfall."

"I agree."

"I thought you would. Now, as far as I can see, the untimely death of Mr Crake brought to a head a lot of very dangerous situations. I suppose you know the relations which once existed between the late Kent and Mrs Crake... I needn't dwell on it."

"Yes, I know, sir."

"I have seen her in the office...not long ago at that...and I knew that she either still loved him or else, as he cooled off, womanlike, she refused to be scorned. And I have not worked with the firm of Trotman & Co for over thirty-five years without knowing my principal partner's secret which, unless you know it, I shall not divulge."

"Mr Alec?"

"Right again. You amaze me. Yes, Alec. A closely guarded secret which was only brought to light fortuitously and with strange irony. I will confess to you, Inspector, that I rather went out of the way to acquaint myself with the secrets of my partners. You see, it made my position with them secure. I was indispensable, the confidential man they could not afford to dismiss. They took me in the firm to ensure my silence. I admit it freely. I trusted neither of them. In the game we were playing, I had to fortify myself with some trump cards and use them with skill. I have a large family dependent on me. I was not going to allow myself to be at the mercy of a pair of rascals at an age when it is difficult to change jobs. You follow?"

"Very clearly. I don't blame you."

"I thought you wouldn't. I will now tell you something else. I think Kent killed Mrs Crake. I think, with her husband dead, she was very dangerous to Kent. She must have had incriminating evidence…letters, photographs, what-not…and she may have pressed Kent, crowded him too hard and made him lose his head. He was ambitious of late. He aspired to be our next MP in Tilsey and even talked of taking silk…he was a barrister…with a view to parliamentary honours. He grew rotten with ambition and neither his wife, his ex-mistress, nor anybody else was going to spoil his chances. I would hesitate to say it publicly and I would deny it if you said I said it, but now you know my views."

"And very useful. I'm afraid you've almost hit the bull's-eye with your conjectures…"

"Inspector, although I do not vulgarly advertise the fact on the firm's notepaper and brass plate, I am an MA of Oxford and I specialised in logic. Most of Kent's brilliant court work was *mine*."

"What about Simpole?"

"Ah… I'm afraid I'm going to keep my ladies waiting for their choir practice, but this is too good to miss. I knew Simpole well. I played chess with him. I also had another thing in common which will astonish you…"

"You were both musicians…?"

"Is there anything you don't know?"

"Not very difficult, sir. I examined his effects after he died."

"A very sensitive man, Simpole, and of great integrity. Somebody tried to silence him by threatening his disgrace. He killed himself out of very shame. I knew of his infatuation for Mrs Crake. I believe Simpole was on someone's track about these murders. I know his mental acumen as a chess player; he was a stern, clever, but strictly honest adversary. It's funny that after Mrs Crake's death he should suddenly go to pieces. Why? Because someone found in her effects the means of blackmailing him… disgracing him…"

"Good! Good! You're doing well, sir."

"Look here, Inspector. Why call on me if you know all the answers? Do you know who killed Kent?"

"No, sir. I thought you might help me there."

"I don't know. I could mention several people. What about old Doane? If Kent killed Dulcie Crake, the old man might have sought revenge. Or did Kent get from Mrs Crake some evidence against the old man?"

"I think we can put him out of court. I was with Doane when Kent met his death."

"Ah… That narrows the field. It leaves Beatrice Kent, his wife, who hated him for his infidelity…"

"She was seen dropping Kent at Beyle in their car and then driving away."

"By whom?"

"Nita."

"Bah! Those two are in league. Both very deeply fond of Nick Crake. But why should Beatrice go to Beyle to kill him? She could easily have done it at home."

"I think we might leave her for the present. Let's say Nita told the truth."

"Very well. Alec, then? Revenge on his mother's betrayer. Or did he hate his uncle for some other reason? Money, for example."

"Now, sir. What do you know?"

"I know that the Nicholas Crake trust funds were violated, and that Kent got the money for Mrs Crake because she thought it was hers by right. I know that Kent was mad about her at the time and was persuaded to betray the trust, that he repented and tried to make it good. Perhaps he even killed Dulcie when she refused to hand over the balance of the funds, if any, because, owing to the death of Nick Crake, the whole matter might come to a head."

"*Might*. Wasn't it sure to?"

"No. The trustees were Kent and Trotman. Dulcie Crake got the money from Kent. Her will left all she had to Alec, her favourite. Does that give you any ideas?"

"Trotman! His son would get it! Do you mean he still felt like a father towards that young man?"

"Trotman had a daughter who loved Alec Crake madly. They arranged to get married. Then, along comes Trotman and just has to tell them both that they are half-brother and half-sister and the whole thing's impossible. Frankie Trotman went almost off her head. After all, it is rather a terrible thing…like the tales of the mad and gothic novelists. She was six months in a home for nervous cases then she married and left the country. She never spoke to her father from the day she learned his secret. Mrs Trotman forgave her husband. A splendid little woman that! But Frankie, no. Now…on the other hand, Alec Crake got over it better. After the first blow, he took to drink, but he never treated Trotman like Frankie did. I think, somehow, he felt a bit filial towards him. After all, he was his mother's boy… Trotman was crazy about Alec. He was his son, remember, and Trotman couldn't get it out of his blood. When Crake stopped subsidising young Alec's wastrel career, Trotman stepped in and, through Mrs Crake, made Alec an allowance. *I know.* Nothing that passes in that office evades me. I will tell you this without shame. I have seven children. I intend they shall all grow up disciplined, courteous and, if they show promise, clever. They shall all have their chance. I have no intention of having my plans thwarted by men like Kent and Trotman. If they had shown the least inclination to edge me out of the job on which I depend for my plans, I would have blackmailed them just as mercilessly and much more cleverly, I can assure you, than the dirty little parasites you are accustomed to bring to justice, Inspector. I even, when all the staff had gone, went through the wastepaper baskets in their private rooms and pieced together the minute scraps into which they reduced some of the very important secrets they wrote. Luckily, the place is central-heated and they rarely have fires to destroy their handiwork. Blame me, if you like. I'm not ashamed. Was it Buffon who said: This animal is dangerous; when he is attacked, he defends himself!"

"I appreciate that, and I appreciate your confidences, which I'll respect."

"I'll deny I ever said 'em, if you don't."

There was a tap on the door and a large Juno of a woman entered. She looked under forty, had golden hair, blue eyes and a formidable forehead. An ex-mistress of physical culture in a girls' school, Mrs Skrike was several inches taller than her husband and looked quite capable of tying him in knots. She carefully eyed Littlejohn and seemed to approve of him. She did not fancy many of the strange characters who called on her husband for cheap legal advice and to drink his whisky.

"This is Inspector Littlejohn... You've doubtless read of him in the papers, my dear Isabel... My wife, Inspector..."

Mrs Skrike took Littlejohn's hand in a grip of iron and pumped it up and down.

"I hope you're getting near the end of the case, Inspector."

Grimly she slipped the glass stopper on the whisky bottle, locked it in the tantalus, and kept the key in the palm of her hand.

"You won't forget the rehearsal, Caleb," she said. "It's well past seven..."

"I'll remember... I'm just off..."

An outbreak of scuffling in the next room reminded her that her brood were unattended, and she left them with an apology.

"Fine woman, my wife, though I say it myself. I was saying, I have many responsibilities and I shall take care that nobody injures my family if I can prevent it. Where were we?"

"We were discussing the affection of Trotman for Alec..."

"That's right. Our firm is a queer set-up. The principal partners had been Dulcie Crake's lovers. One was the father of her son though the other didn't, or wasn't supposed, shall we say, to know it. At the time of her death, both had tired of her, but Trotman was fond of her son for obvious reasons. Now, what do we find? We find not that they were antagonists for her love. That had died in them. Dulcie Crake was so intense that she burned out her lovers and lost them. The quarrel between these two partners was about money. Ten thousand pounds. Dulcie Crake had wormed it out of Kent when he was madly in love with her. He repented and wanted it back. What would have happened if he'd got it? Kent himself would have restored it to the trust and saved his reputation for the polling-booths. *But*...on Nick's death the trust money would have gone to Nita, his daughter, to whom he bequeathed it. If Kent didn't get it, he thought he was ruined. Trotman, his co-trustee, would surely take the matter to court and get him jailed. He forgot or didn't know that Trotman, however, wanted that money keeping *out* of the trust. He didn't want Kent to put it back. He wanted it to belong to Dulcie so that, dead, she could pass it on to his son, Alec, whom he loved but couldn't keep subsidising. Trotman is not a wealthy man; he lives too well...much above his present income. How does that sound to you?"

"Very reasonable. You remember the day and time Kent was killed?"

"Very well."

"Where was Trotman at the time?"

"Out. He left the office just before Kent did."

"Do you know where he went?"

"To Beyle, Inspector. Are you surprised?"

"No... But how do you know?"

"It was all arranged... By Doane."

"You mean, he planned for one of them to kill the other?"

"I do. For some reason, greed or fear, he must stay in Beyle. With Dulcie alive he was safe. With her dead and Nita the owner, he wasn't sure when he'd be on the street. I think he planned to seize power himself..."

"Isn't that a bit absurd? How could he?"

"He is trustee for Alec under his sister's will. You know Alec's temperament. Let him get hold of his mother's money and he'd go through it in twelve months. Dulcie seems to have trusted her brother...or else he had some hold over her..."

"Maybe it was both. He fed drugs to her when he wanted her to give him his own way."

"So that was it! Well...with Kent out of the way and the trust money willed to Alec, he'd charge of over twenty thousand pounds. How better invest it than buying Beyle for a mere song from Nita who hated it...?"

"That's a theory. But how did he induce Trotman to kill Kent?"

"I'll tell you. He rang up Trotman first and told him that Kent had discovered where Dulcie had hidden the gold... Now what that meant, I don't know. It sounds like a pirate tale to me. But it was enough to send Trotman pell-mell to Beyle."

"It's quite true. I told Trotman that the trust had been robbed and he pretended to pooh-pooh the idea, but he must have known. It suited his purpose for it to *be* robbed, provided the loot was intact for Alec. It was. It was in the form of gold in the bank.

Dulcie spent the money Kent handed over in buying a large collection of gold coins from her brother."

"Doane must have told Trotman that and that Kent had found them hidden in Beyle."

"That's it. But what got Kent down to Beyle?"

"The same thing. Doane telephoned him to say that he had found the trust money in Dulcie's hiding place. That got Kent to Beyle in a hurry."

"Trotman got there first, hid under the stairs when Kent arrived but forgot his hat when he hid. He left it on the table in the hall and I found it there."

"Did you, by gad!"

"But first tell me, how did you know of those phone calls, sir?"

"I listened in. You will doubtless have seen my quarters in the office. There are only two private rooms and the lowly third partner therefore was relegated to a small glass pen in the main office. Just outside that greenhouse stands the main switchboard. The girl answers it as a rule, and, as the caller mentions his or her name, she writes it on a pad for filing. Believe me, in my own interest, I keep an eye on that pad. As I work, it is an automatic reaction with me to glance at the pad as she writes names down. That day when I saw Doane written, I took the earpiece from her and I listened. I'm not ashamed of it. I've already told you why."

"So Trotman went to Beyle first, and no sooner arrived than his partner turned up. They fought, or else Trotman took Kent unawares and brained him with a croquet mallet…"

"Oh, Lord! A croquet mallet!! Why, Trotman was quite a champion in his day at that genteel game! What irony. His last shot…!"

"Where is Trotman now, sir?"

"Most likely at home. His doctor has told him to take things easy and he spends many of his evenings resting by the fire or in bed."

"I must go to see him at once…"

"I must go to rehearsal, too. My women will tear me in pieces.

We are practising *Belshazzar's Feast* and next week the local men's choir is joining them. They are naturally all of a twitter about being the best of the united party..."

He saw Littlejohn to the gate and there they parted, Littlejohn to the right and Trotman's home, Skrike to the public rooms where the rehearsals were held. On his way Littlejohn puzzled over what he had just heard. Skrike was evidently all out to become sole partner of Trotman & Co by bowling down his associates like ninepins.

The family man, fighting for his brood!

Skrike too was excited. He rubbed his hands and chuckled on his way.

"That's about cooked Monsieur Trotman's goose," he said to himself. "Half fact and the rest damn good theory. Took him in properly..."

He rehearsed his ladies like one possessed for the rest of the evening and then, still beside himself, went to his club, broke all his solemn oaths to his wife, and there slept a drunken sleep on the billiards table. Next day he did not turn up at the office. His wife, at the end of her patience, chastised him herself when he returned home at dawn, and gave him two black eyes which kept him indoors for several days.

"I fell in the bathroom," he told his children when he paraded them that evening and marched them, in strict order of age, into the dining room for dinner.

18
THE FRIGHTENED MAN

Littlejohn might have been expected by the glib lawyer, Skrike, to run all the way to Trotman's and arrest him at once. In fact, Mr Skrike half thought to find his partner in jail the next day. But Littlejohn was too old a dog for that. Mr Skrike's nicely conceived solution of the case aroused in the Inspector's mind a feeling akin to sales resistance. The whole thing was too easy and, to his feeling, too malevolent. With Trotman in jail, or perhaps executed for murder, the field would be open for Skrike. He would become Trotman & Co. Littlejohn called at the police station on his way. There he found Cromwell enjoying a cup of tea with another detective-sergeant of the local force.

"We're terribly pulled-out at present with men and lads stealing lead off buildings," the Tilsey officer was saying, and Cromwell, in his customary modest and patient way, was open to learn how they laid the criminals by the heels.

"I've another job for you, old man," said Littlejohn, "and don't get drunk this time. It concerns the bar of the airport..."

They parted at the door of the police office. It was raining hard and the asphalt of the town square shone like glass with the sodium lights turning it to amber and making passers-by look like corpses.

"Better take a taxi, Cromwell. It's at least a couple of miles out..."

They parted. Littlejohn turned up his coat collar and crossed to the official park for the police car. The journey was a short one. The Trotmans occupied a large old house not far out of town. Mr Trotman disliked the trouble of a garden. He had not even the patience to instruct a hired man how to arrange and fill a plot of ground. He had, therefore, had the old lawn and beds at the front of the house paved over to form a kind of courtyard with a solitary willow and a sundial breaking the monotony. The former iron railings and gate had been sacrificed to the wartime scrap-iron drive, and Mr Trotman had now had these replaced by expensive wrought-ironwork which gave a new and attractive appearance to the whole place.

Littlejohn rang the bell and an elderly maid in cap and apron answered the door. She seemed surprised to see a caller on such a night and at such an hour. Lights glowed behind the curtains of one of the rooms to the right of the door and in one of the bedrooms above.

"Mr Trotman can't see anybody. He's retired to bed."

"Is Mrs Trotman in?"

"I'll see..."

She took the Inspector's card and soon returned.

"Come in, please."

He followed her along the deeply carpeted hall, illuminated by a lustre chandelier and furnished in heavy mahogany. She opened a door to the right and bade him enter.

Mrs Trotman rose to meet him. She had been playing patience and the cards were spread out on a little card table by the fire, which burned in a large open grate with iron dogs and a stone surround with a crest in the middle of it. Over the fire, a portrait of Mrs Trotman in oils, evidently done when she was young. She met Littlejohn as he entered and shook hands with him.

"Good evening, Inspector. I'm sorry my husband isn't well. He's in bed… Can I do anything?"

Littlejohn's first impression of the woman was of her absolute integrity. Somehow the idea of her sitting quietly alone in the great house playing patience with the stew pond of murder and her husband's guilt so close impressed him. She was small, slightly built, and the fair hair shown on the portrait had now changed to snow white, still worn long and neatly braided. The fine lines of her face remained, but the firm cheeks of the picture and the pink complexion had given place to the looseness of later middle age and the yellow tint of declining health. Her hands were fragile. A comparison between the painting and the woman before him filled Littlejohn with melancholy at the thought of the ravages of time and experience.

"Please sit down…"

She indicated an armchair on the opposite side of the fire from her own. Probably Trotman occupied it when they spent a quiet evening at home.

"I'm sorry your husband isn't well, Mrs Trotman…"

"His blood pressure troubles him from time to time and he has to ease off. He retired with a book immediately after dinner."

She seemed resigned and quite in repose. The type of woman to whom the adventurous, flamboyant Trotman would be unfaithful from time to time but to whom he would always return. The kind too who would make the best of a situation like the birth of Alec and not create melodrama out of it or think herself a public martyr on account of it. A woman too good for Trotman but in whose mind such a thought would never enter.

"I wished to see him very urgently…but it can wait. Perhaps you can help me…?"

"If I can…"

She looked anxious, but it was on Trotman's behalf. She didn't want his peace disturbing.

"I realise, madam, that this might seem like taking advantage of the situation... In other words, I ought not to ask you questions concerning your husband. I also warn you that anything you say about him cannot be used in evidence for you cannot testify against him..."

"But, surely, he is not suspected of any of these dreadful crimes at Beyle! He is the last man to use violence. He absolutely abhors it. Why! I even have to kill the mice we catch in traps. Last week, in this very room, a mouse appeared whilst we were sitting by the fire. It would have been so easy for him to kill it with the fire tongs. Instead, he opened the door and chased it into the hall and left it there for Daisy, the maid, to scream about... When it comes to violence, I'm afraid he's a terrible coward. He could never kill anybody..."

"Not even in panic?"

"He would run..."

She stopped.

"Please, don't think he has no moral courage. He is full of it. Once his mind is made up, he will see things through stubbornly. But violence..."

She shrugged her shoulders.

The room seemed cut off from life except that outside you could hear vehicles passing now and then, or the footsteps of some hurrying passer-by. The heavy curtains and the circle of light from the reading lamp made a little circumscribed world of its own. Here it was that Trotman and his wife spent their evenings. Littlejohn wondered what they did. Talk? Read? Play cards? They didn't seem to have much in common, but it was certain that here the ageing and bombastic lawyer sought shelter in a good woman's love and admiration for him.

"Do you mind if I mention a rather painful subject...? That of Alec Crake...?"

"Not at all. Any pain…as you call it…is of the past and, I hope, is done with."

If she felt unhappy about it, she showed no sign. She calmly gathered her cards from the fireside table with steady hands and shuffled them automatically.

"Has Mr Trotman any great affection for Alec?"

"None whatever. Alec's conduct of late has considerably distressed him. All this drinking and idleness… One would feel it about any young man of one's intimate acquaintance. But if you are referring to any paternal feelings… I fear there were none."

"Who provided the money for this young man's so-called studies which, I believe, were really a long holiday in Paris…?"

"His mother. She did it with difficulty for Nicholas Crake refused to increase the reasonable allowance he was giving the boy. My husband made her a number of advances against the life policies in her favour on Mr Crake's life. It was not good security and my husband was very worried about it, but, he felt if he didn't help, Mrs Crake might make a fuss which wouldn't sound very well to the public…"

"Mild blackmail?"

"I'm afraid so. Anything of the kind worries my husband terribly. He bears it so far and then confides in me. I can do that for him, at least…listen to his troubles and comfort him."

"It is as well you did, Mrs Trotman. You have probably saved him from very serious complications in connection with matters at Beyle. If he is not well and police inquisition will greatly upset him, you can save him a lot of trouble. Do you know his partner, Skrike, very well?"

"Yes. He was once chief clerk and a very good one too, but he drank heavily and was unreliable. Such a shame with a nice wife and family. But somehow Mr Skrike seems to think life has not given him his dues. Drink and malice have been the cause of that. He talks too much, too bitterly, and too publicly. Nobody would trust such a man."

"Yet your husband made him his partner?"

"You have, of course, read *David Copperfield,* Inspector. You remember how Uriah Heep got his master in his power. There are many things in a lawyer's office which lend themselves to such tactics. My husband and Mr Kent came to an arrangement to suit all parties..."

"Are Skrike and your husband on good terms?"

"I'm afraid not. He resents my husband's manner, I gather. But really, I don't think one ought to be called upon to fraternise with one's business associates in private life if one doesn't want to do so. Mrs Skrike is a very nice woman, but I don't want her and the family calling here. Mr Skrike seems to think we ought to throw the house open to them."

"I see..."

So that explained a lot of the little lawyer's venom and spite against Trotman. But it didn't solve the case...

"Your husband didn't find it difficult to subsidise Alec Crake, then? I mean, the drain on his own resources...?"

"I can help him there. My father was a local brewer and I was his only child... I have an income... It is a nice help..."

She rose and took a log between a large pair of tongs and threw it on the fire. Then she turned to Littlejohn.

"And now, Inspector, will you please tell me what we are getting at? Your questions are not put out of idle curiosity. There is some underlying purpose. What is it?"

She asked it quite calmly, but firmly. He could decline to reply and probably miss several important links in the case because, short of some explanation, she was not going to answer any further questions about her husband.

"I will tell you, Mrs Trotman. We have a list of suspects in this case. Each one has to be questioned. It is your husband's turn. He has motives. He did not kill Mrs Crake, but we have not yet discovered the murderer of Arthur Kent. Kent killed Mrs Crake but..."

"Kent! Never!!"

She looked more moved than she had shown before.

"Yes. Kent and your husband were trustees for Mr Crake of a sum of about ten thousand pounds and infatuated, temporarily it seems, by Mrs Crake, Kent stole the trust funds and gave them to her. Then, when he cooled off and wanted to keep his good name, he asked for them back. She refused. She attacked him, and, in the scuffle, he stabbed her."

"But I knew about the money and the trust, Inspector. My husband was helping Kent to recover it. After all, they have their firm to think of… Imagine too, Dulcie getting all that money for Alec and leaving little Nita with nothing but that ruin of a house at Beyle. It was monstrous. Arthur Kent confessed the crime to my husband and said he would do his best to recover it. If not, he could make part of it good from his own money. That was why Mr Trotman told me. I said I would lend the firm the balance…"

So easy! And yet here had a complicated web of intrigue and suspicion been spun around the coward, Trotman. It was as well he was in bed and his fine wife acting as his deputy. Trotman left to himself would never have told a straight tale out of very fear and thus have involved himself to the hilt.

"I quite understand, Mrs Trotman. And now, may I digress a minute? Do you know Mr Trotman's staff…the little red-headed office-boy and the telephone girl?"

"Yes. The telephone girl, Maud Hankey, is really their typist. She and the boy answer the telephone… Why?"

"I wish to see them…"

In Littlejohn's mind rose the scene when the boy had asked him for his autograph. The office… Mr Skrike in his glass pen… The girl typing and rubbing out. Then the buzz of the telephone… Mr Skrike had calmly gone on reading a document… Yet Skrike had said he was interested in the telephone. Perhaps he had contained his curiosity on account of Littlejohn's visit. On the other hand…

"The girl attends our church. Her mother asked me if I could ask Mr Trotman for a job for her. They wanted a girl fortunately, because the old one was getting married. She would have stayed on, but we felt that her interest would go... Besides, she wasn't first-class... Miss Hankey, the present girl, lives with her mother in Church Lane just at the bottom of the hill as you leave here..."

"Thank you. And the boy, if we need him?"

"Gerald Shipperton? He is the park keeper's son and lives in the lodge at the gates of Central Park, on the other side of town. An impertinent little boy, my husband calls him, but he does his work well and, I expect, will soon be leaving for more money. They all do."

"Thank you."

"What have they to do with this?"

"I want to check certain happenings in the office... I will tell you another thing too. I know he has a nice family, but, at the first opportunity, your husband ought to get rid of his junior partner. He is too indiscreet. He has been questioned by the police and, candidly, his talk has done no good to Mr Trotman. I..."

She interrupted with some spirit.

"You are not telling me anything new... But after Arthur's death and all this trouble, my husband is going to retire. I have told him, and the doctor has told him that at the rate he is going on my husband won't live another year. And with Kent dead, it's just too much for him. If Skrike cannot raise the money for the whole of the firm, he will have to be sold with it or leave. That's already one problem settled."

"I'm very glad to hear it."

"Thank you for your confidence, Inspector. And now, tell me plainly, is my husband suspected of killing Arthur Kent?"

"He was. You see, we gathered that he was opposed to Kent in the matter of the trust. In other words, he was interested in Kent failing to replace the funds and their being left in the name of Mrs Crake to become Alec's inheritance..."

"Meaning, he was working to get the money for his illegal son?"

"Frankly, yes."

"It is not true. I hope I have convinced you of that. How else should I know…? I was asked to lend the money to restore the trust funds."

"I am glad I mentioned it to you. There is one other matter though. I will be candid. It is serious. After the death of Kent by violence, we found what we thought was Mr Trotman's hat on the table in the hall at Beyle. In his agitation, he must have left it there after following Kent. It was a damning piece of evidence and, whatever the motive, will need a lot of explaining away if it *was* his hat. Process of elimination seems to lead us to such a surmise."

Mrs Trotman rose and went to the door of the room.

"Come here, Inspector…"

He followed her. She indicated the hat-stand in the hall. There were two hats, alike, hanging from pegs. One was a bit shabbier than the other, that was all.

"Is one of those the hat?"

Littlejohn crossed and examined them. The newer one had 7¼ on a ticket in the brim.

"Yes. I think so. I handled it, and this is the size."

She took the two hats in her hand.

"That would be the one you handled," she said quietly. "My husband has not worn it for some time. It has frayed in the band. On the day Kent died, it disappeared until next day."

"You mean…?"

"It was taken to put you on the wrong track… The track of my poor husband."

"But how…?"

"It is strange how your mentioning all this has brought back an incident which I didn't really heed. Alec Crake called in the morning of the day of Kent's death. He asked for my husband. Alec was slightly drunk…or seemed so. He never wore a hat."

"Well?"

"He must have taken that hat as he left. I didn't see him do it, but he took it."

"If you didn't see him…"

"Yes…but the following day he called again. He wished to apologise for his condition the day before. The maid let him in, but, hearing his voice, I went right into the hall. I'd no intention, if he were drunk, of allowing him to come farther in. *He was hanging up his hat.* Now, if he never wore a hat…? I have kept a kind of mental picture of the incident and have never noticed the peculiarity of it till you mentioned the hat…"

"Good! I'm very glad I found you in and didn't have to disturb your husband with all this…"

But, as if the patient upstairs had overheard, there was a clanging of a bell in the kitchen, behind. The maid appeared and ran upstairs.

"He's wantin' somethin'," she said as she mounted.

She was down in a minute.

"Mr Trotman asks if there's callers, madam, and wants to see you at once."

"Don't go, Inspector. I'll be down in a moment."

It took longer than that. Littlejohn could hear Trotman's rumbling voice raised in one of the upper rooms. Then his wife appeared.

"Please come up, Inspector. My husband insists on seeing you."

He entered a large room with thick red carpet on the floor and expensive furniture. Trotman was sitting up in a large bed. He wore blue silk pyjamas and had a travelling rug round his shoulders. His hair was a bit dishevelled, but the situation of being in bed for a police interview didn't at all put him out of countenance.

"What is all this?" he thundered, ignoring the Inspector's polite greeting.

"I called to ask you a few questions to help in the case, sir. Mrs Trotman has been able to answer them so I didn't disturb you."

Mr Trotman reared in his bed.

"How dare you, sir! How dare you! How dare you, I say, badger my wife? I shall complain…complain in the proper quarter. I never…never, in the whole of my extensive experience, heard of such an outrage."

"Now, dear, don't get excited. The doctor said, you know…"

Mr Trotman emerged still further from beneath the eiderdown, waving his arms and the travelling rug, beating the bedclothes with his clenched fist.

"To hell with the doctor… I won't have my wife bullied. Are you aware, sir…are you aware that you have exceeded, far exceeded, the rules of police inquiry and of decency…inquiry and decency, I say…?"

There had been two books and a newspaper on the bed, but, in his rage, Mr Trotman swept them into the air and they crashed on the floor.

Littlejohn stood quiet, unperturbed, smiling at the angry lawyer. Mrs Trotman was smiling too. It enraged him more.

"And, may I ask, what is the joke? WHAT IS THE JOKE…?"

"There is no joke, my dear. On the contrary, it is very serious, but it has a happy ending…"

"Don't talk in riddles… I insist on knowing all he has asked you. Why…without me there to guide you, you might have said terrible things…! AWFUL things…!"

"I'm afraid they *were* awful, but they've cleared you, my dear, of suspicion of killing Arthur Kent…"

"What?"

He pounded the bed again.

Mrs Trotman had had enough.

"Be quiet!" she said, like a schoolmistress entering a room of unruly scholars.

Mr Trotman looked amazed at such a change of front. It affected him so much that he slid down in the bed.

"Take the electric blanket out, dear," he whimpered. "It's burning me..."

She dealt with him like a spoiled child.

Then she told him all she and Littlejohn had been saying.

"Come here," said Trotman to his wife, when it was all over. He had been all eyes for her as she told the tale and now it was as if Littlejohn were not there at all.

"Come here..."

"Excuse me, sir... May I ask where you were at the time Mr Kent was murdered?"

Trotman looked at him blankly.

"I was at Beyle. I was in the room under the stairs. Skrike was right. Doane did ring me up..."

"Are you sure it was Doane?"

"I think so..."

"Are you sure it was his voice?"

"He said it was Doane..."

"But otherwise you weren't sure?"

"How could I be?"

"What happened?"

"He said Kent had found the money, would I come? I went. When I got there, the front door was open. I entered. I heard voices upstairs with Doane. I recognised yours, Inspector. I didn't want to meet you... I resented your intrusion... I admit it. I was afraid you'd stumble across the violation of the trust. You couldn't have annoyed me more at that time...just when I was hoping to come upon the funds. Kent wasn't there. I hesitated about leaving. Then I saw the little panelled door below the stairs was open. I went in there...shut myself in and listened for you leaving..."

"Right into the trap, like a mouse after the cheese. He'd worked out everything... The open front door, the panel ajar... Did you see your hat on the hall table?"

"No… Why? I'd got my hat on my head… Oh, you mean the one Alec took… I can't believe it… He wouldn't do that to me…"

"What happened next…?"

"The catch on the door clicked and I found I was locked in. I didn't want to make a row by beating on the door with you there. I sat and waited, and, as I waited, I heard the horrible truth. I heard you find the body of Kent, I heard the police come… I hardly dared breathe. How long I was there I don't know. It seemed hours. I heard them post a constable on the door and leave the place with the body. I was cold with fear. I knew that nothing would save me if anybody learned I'd been where I was when Kent was killed. I could form no theory; I daren't tell you. And there I was… I daren't even tell my wife…"

His fleshy lips began to tremble, and his hands shook like those of one with the palsy.

"Then?"

"Suddenly I found the door loose… I gently opened it. It was dark and there was nobody there. I could hear the constable fumbling in the kitchen, running water in a pan. He had called there to make tea, I suppose… I crept out… I ran…I ran all the way home. I don't know how I got here. My wife was out… I drank a glass of whisky… I…"

He began to sob, caressing his wife's hand, clinging to it with both his own.

"I'm terribly sorry, Kate…terribly sorry. Sorry about this and everything…all the misery…all your unhappiness…terribly sorry…"

His habit of repeating himself was no longer funny.

Littlejohn quietly withdrew and left him to be comforted.

19

THE BAR AT THE AIRPORT

Mrs Trotman descended on his heels.

"I'm so grateful to you for calling, Inspector. It might have been very serious for my husband if we hadn't talked together. He would never have survived the shame if..."

Littlejohn had intended to arrest Trotman if necessary. Now it was all different.

"I wonder if you could tell me, Mrs Trotman, the Paris address of Alec Crake? I may need it..."

"Why? Has he left already?"

"No. He leaves in the morning."

She returned to the dining room for a moment and brought back a dog-eared address book. She turned the leaves.

"12 bis, Impasse Auguste-Comte, Paris, 12."

Littlejohn returned to the police station. They were surprised to see him back again.

"He certainly works for his living..."

The Inspector rang up the Yard.

"Give me Sergeant Mullet, please."

A cheerful voice answered almost at once. It was so full of

vigour that Littlejohn held the receiver about three inches from his ear and yet could hear plainly.

"Mullet, I want you to do something for me, quickly, please. Ring the police in Paris. Ask for Commissaire Claparède, if he's in. Tell him it's for me, urgently. Inquire if there's an Alec Crake, a young Englishman, known at 12 bis, Impasse Auguste-Comte in the 12th arrondissement. Ask what he does when he's in Paris. Also, if there's a girl called Ginette connected with him…"

"His amie?"

"Fiancée, he says. Ginette sent him a telegram the other day. Check what the telegram was about and then please ring me back here. As quickly as you can…"

Then he dialled Beyle.

The constable on duty answered the telephone as instructed.

"PC 54, sir. Harkuss…"

"Who of the family is at home, Harkuss?"

"All three. The young lady and gent are packin' and the old 'un's followin' 'em around lamentin'…"

"See to it that none of them leaves on any pretext. I'll send you some help."

After arranging for another policeman to stand by at Beyle with Harkuss, Littlejohn strolled into the rain again.

Church Lane was just behind the police station, a narrow, cobbled street with iron posts across each end to keep out wheeled traffic and which climbed out of the square to the church on the hill above the town.

The Hankeys occupied a house which had been a fashionable shop in days when Church Lane was the little Bond Street of Tilsey. Now the buildings were mostly humble dwelling-houses or tenements. Children were playing under the gas lamps which shed pools of pale green light in the dark. The bow window of the one-time hat shop had been covered with gauze curtains. Mrs Hankey, a little, dark, thick-set woman like a peasant, with a lisp, rather hesitated before asking the Inspector in. Then she led him through the dark front room to the living quarters behind.

Maud was there busy with an electric iron on a frilly dance frock. She gave a little shriek of surprise on seeing Littlejohn. Sitting in an armchair by the fire, his pipe in his mouth and an empty bottle of beer on the floor beside him, was a small, grey-haired, refined-looking man with a little pointed beard. He waved a friendly hand, but, before he could speak, his two women had started to bicker.

"You shouldn't have brought him in here, mother. The front room's the place. You must excuse the untidiness, sir. I'm going to the farmers' ball tomorrow night."

"I hope you enjoy yourself, Miss Hankey."

Mrs Hankey was annoyed at her daughter's rebuke. She stood defiantly at the door looking angrily at the evening frock.

"Don't you give me impertinence in front of strangers, miss. I'm your mother, remember..."

The girl flushed.

"Were you wanting something, sir?"

She was a tall, thin, delicate girl with a flat bust and a frail, pink tuberculous look which was very attractive and made men feel protective. You noticed, after her delicate features, her neatness. Hair, hands, nails, eyebrows...all well cared for. Her speech was quiet and careful. She switched off the iron.

"Do you take all the telephone calls at the office, Miss Hankey?

"Yes. Except at lunch time. My machine's just near the board."

"Is Mr Skrike particularly interested in the calls?"

"Why, sir, I don't know. Sometimes he is. It all depends."

"On what?"

"Lately, since Mr Crake died, he seems to have been expecting some news to come through."

"Why?"

"He keeps looking up from his work and saying, 'Who's that?'"

"Do you remember the day Mr Kent died?"

"Rather. I'll never forget it as long as I live."

"You remember the calls that came in?"

"I can't say I do without looking at the record pad and that's at the office."

Mrs Hankey seemed to scent a plot against her daughter's virtue.

"And you're not goin' out at this time o' night for anybody, miss."

"Really, mother, nobody suggests I should."

"Let me try to help you, Miss Hankey. Did Mr Bernard Doane, of Beyle, ring up that day?"

"I think he did..."

"Whom did he ring?"

"Both Mr Kent and Mr Trotman, one after the other, just before Mr Kent went off for the last time."

Mrs Hankey still wasn't comfortable.

"Our Maudie's got a good job and it's confidential, bein' a lawyer's. I think you ought to be careful, Maudie, what you say. Good jobs are hard to come by if you get sacked for talkin'..."

"But this is police, ma. I've got to tell them what they ask."

Mrs Hankey sniffed and took up the smoothing iron, spat on it to test the heat, and then switched it on and set about the frock with great vigour.

"I'll finish this. I never saw sich a gel for wastin' time."

"I won't detain you, Miss Hankey. Are you sure it *was* Mr Doane's voice?"

"No, I'm not. He said it was Mr Doane, but I remember quite well, now you remind me, it was different some way. I recollect saying to Gerald, that's the office-boy...that Mr Doane was different. Sort of knew his own mind for a change. As a rule, he waffles and wambles over the phone...keeps forgetting what he's talking about."

"Stammers?"

"Hardly that. Sort of can't collect his thoughts and can't tell plainly what he wants."

"Did you listen to what he said?"

"No, sir. This time Mr Skrike asked who it was and listened himself. Please don't tell him or I'll get into trouble."

"I won't. But who could it have been if not Mr Doane?"

"You think it was somebody else, sir?"

She started to blush and, to hide her confusion, pretended to interest herself in what her mother was doing. It gave Littlejohn his answer. He knew how young girls get "sweet" on attractive men like Alec Crake. Here was something of the kind.

"Could it have been Mr Alec Crake?"

"It could... But what did he want ringing...? I don't know..."

She grew confused under her mother's eagle eye.

The little grey man by the fire who had hitherto listened carefully without speaking hereupon raised himself.

"You will see, sir," he said, in a very refined, dramatic tone," You will see, sir, I'm not the master in my own house. My women run it for me. I am a silent spectator...a sleeping partner. May I offer you a drink, sir?"

He looked appealingly at Littlejohn. If he could persuade him to drink, his women could not refuse him too and would have to increase his nightly ration of a pint.

Mr Hankey was an artist who couldn't sell any of his masterpieces. He had seduced his housekeeper in a moment of despair and, finding what later turned out to be Maud on the way, had had to make an honest woman of her for she had a brother who was a boxer in a travelling circus and took on all corners for five pounds a knock-out. Now, Mr Hankey's two women kept him, one as a seamstress, the other as a typist. Not that he didn't try. The upper rooms were littered with his unsold efforts to earn his bit. Heavy oils, small watercolours, calendars, Christmas cards, plaster models of horses and naked women, and even grotesque birds carved out of knots of wood.

"May I offer you…?"

"I'm afraid I must be off. Thank you all the same, sir."

Mr Hankey was in the habit of secretly reinforcing his beer with uncoloured methylated spirit which he ostensibly bought for his works of art. Beneath his white crown of venerable hair his face glowed purple.

"A very good night to you, sir. A very good night. Phoebe, my dear, show our guest to the door." He waved a dismissing hand and sank back in his chair.

Maud had grown very quiet. Two hectic spots appeared on her cheekbones and she pretended to concentrate on the dress on the ironing board.

"Good night," she said stiffly without looking up.

"Who did you say he was?"

Littlejohn could hear the old man asking his daughter as Mrs Hankey led him to the door. Littlejohn found himself in the gaslit alley among the ragamuffin children and stray cats.

Cromwell was at the airport about the same time.

"Huh!" said the bartender to him. He was a tall man in a spotless white coat. The skin hung in folds on his face and furrows of care crossed and ran down it. He was politically minded and was worried about the direction the world was taking. He also had aching flat feet due to days of standing at the bar and shaking drinks.

"Huh? Beer? Only bottled. Two shillin's…"

Cromwell took a sip, made an entry in the little book from which he transcribed his expenses sheet and then took another good swig.

"Ah… That's good."

"'Ave a good time while you can, mister. There's 'orrible things comin'. I was readin' in a book the other day…"

The place was quiet. The last plane had left, and all the airport offices were closed. Only the light in the control tower and those in the bar and restaurant still shone. A few half-intoxicated young bloods and their girls sat in the well-carpeted, chromium-fitted lounge. They were getting fresh…almost indecent…

"Bellowin' and purrin'… I'm sick of it. I was readin' in a book the other day…"

"Young Crake about?"

"Eh? No. Hasn't been 'ere since 'is mother's funeral. Sobered him up if you ask me. Always could down his drinks, could Crake. Recent 'appenin's has cured 'im. I read in a book last week… 'Ho, eloquent, just, an' mighty Death…' It's right, you know. We all come to it."

He had been drinking his own wares and had grown owlish in his cups.

"You're right. Crake was here after his mother's death, though?"

"Huhu. 'E was. But a changed man, you know. Death made a bit of an 'ypocrite of him."

"A what?"

"Look 'ere! Wot's all this, eh? Wot you after? Does he owe you money, or are you out to save his soul?"

He grinned at this thrust aimed at Cromwell's look of muscular evangelism, black suit, black tie, black bowler and black boots.

"No… Police…"

"Wot!! Well, you ain't got nothin' on us. Licence quite clean and hours kept to."

"I never said they weren't. I'm just checking the movements of the family, that's all."

There was a stir among the gay party under the large palms in pots which decorated the place.

"Hi, Joe. More pink gins all round. Five…"

Joe sighed and started to pour the spirit and sprinkle drops of colour in it.

"Won't be a tick…"

He dispensed the order and rattled the money in the cash register.

"That'll be all this time, ladies and gents," he called out.

"Here… What…?"

"I said no more."

"Awri'. Keep your shirt on…"

The girls squealed and one good-looking one announced her intention of being sick.

"Out you go…"

Joe steered her through the door into the open air.

"*Leave* me alone…"

He returned to Cromwell.

"Wot things are comin' to. Her ma oughter slap her behind… Too much o' that round 'ere. Other day, young Crake was sick as well. T'aint everybody's got the stomach for gin."

"When was he sick?"

"You ask so many questions, you muddle me. Let's begin at the beginning… After his mother died…shook him. He'd had a right old binge from comin' home from Paris till the day his mother got murdered. Tight day and night, he was. Then, sudden like, he sobered. I h'actually saw 'im pour good whisky, bought for him by consoling friends, poured it over the palms there when they wasn't lookin'. Whisky ain't good for palms, but I didn't mention it on account of him bein' bereaved."

The folds of his face sagged more, making him look like a doleful spaniel.

"Went steady, did he?"

"Yep."

"Remember the day his uncle, Kent, was killed at Beyle?"

"I should think I did. Was the talk of the place."

He mopped the counter and looked at Cromwell's glass.

"No? Right. Crake was here that afternoon."

"How long?"

"From lunch till they fetched him to tell him of the murder."

"Right in this room, was he?"

"Yes, except, as I was tellin' you, when we got mixed up, except when he was sick. Like that young no-good girl as just went out. Young Crake 'ad been pretendin' to drink hard. Hypocrite, pretendin' to drown his sorrow to get sympathy, I reckon. But drownin' the palms with whisky instead. I saw 'im. Then he was sick..."

"What time would that be?"

"Around four-thirty to five. I know because I rushed 'im out. Afternoon teas was on...a plane-load of people just in...nice people. No place for soaks to be sick."

"Was he out long?"

"Oh, half an hour. Then he came an' asked for a peppermint."

"Sure he stayed around here whilst he was sick?"

"I never saw him go. I told the other police that. They wanted alibis. 'He was 'ere,' I says. Where else could 'e have been?"

"Where's the carpark?"

"Across the tarmac by the airport entrance..."

"You can't see it from here?"

"You can, but I never do. Too busy in the day with comin's and goin's."

"So Crake might have gone off for a run in his car for some air for half an hour and then come back?"

"And 'im sick and unsteady? Besides where would he want to go? His gang was here. He came back when he was better. They welcomed him like a lost brother an' made a fuss of 'im. Some of 'em said the same that I did to the police. 'Oh, yes. 'E was 'ere,' they said. Nothin' wrong with that, uh?"

"No... Except that he might not have been here that half-hour. You didn't go after him, did you?"

"Why should I? And me busy with the passengers."

"All eyes on the plane, then?"

"Yes. That's what they come for. Drink and watch the planes. Very nice entertainment for them as likes it. Specially the last one that was goin' as Crake came back. A bit of a sight. Flarepath lit up…"

"Thanks. That's all. Good night…"

"Uh?"

"Good night."

"S'long…"

Cromwell found Littlejohn standing with his back to the charge room fire waiting for the telephone. Someone had run over a dog and the sergeant was taking down a statement.

"…the first intimation was a bump…then another bump… Was it a big bump or a little bump…?"

Littlejohn and Cromwell compared notes.

"Looks as if poor Simpole was on the wrong track and killed himself on a wrong theory, Cromwell…"

"Damned shame…"

The telephone rang, and the cheerful voice of Mullet had a lot to say.

Alec Crake lodged at the address given. The police of the district, after questioning the neighbours, said his life was riotous to say the least. Women couldn't resist him. He drank a lot. Seemed a man of means…always paid for what he got. There had been several girls. Ginette… Mullet laughed. Ginette was the concierge of the flats, an old woman with bronchitis and bad feet. The Paris police had been quite colourful about the telegram. Ginette had sent it…that was right. It was in English, sent from the post office in the rue de Clichy. A little joke on somebody. Old Ginette says Alec Crake telephoned another Englishman early on the day she sent it. He asked him to wire it as a joke and dictated it over the phone. Ginette paid for the wire. She kept the message to prove what it cost…"

"Thanks, Mullet."

Littlejohn lit his pipe and puffed it gently.

"Funny! That young man is too thorough. He overdid it. Trying to prove and more than prove that he'd turned over a new leaf. If he'd only been content to say that his mother's death did it. But he had to pile it on...to try to put on an act with me. He just had to be dead sober to kill Kent and to keep his wits clear whilst he framed Trotman. He overdid it. Now, we'd better go to Beyle and ask him some questions right away. Our men have the family safely cooped-up there. I'd better get a warrant. Somebody's going to get annoyed about warrants at this hour of night...."

The sergeant-in-charge was getting red.

"Applied brakes...skidded... Got away! Why didn't you say so at first that the dog ran off? What's the use of makin' a long ramblin' deposition like this if there ain't no dog's body...no corpus dee...licktie..."

20
THE BELL AT BEYLE

They couldn't have sent a more unsuitable relief man to Beyle than PC Wigg to help PC Harkuss. From behind they were as alike as two peas in a pod but face-on they were complete opposites. Harkuss was a profound thinker, very concerned with the world and where it had come from and where it was going. He pondered the problems of anatomy and physiology and how to keep in good health. He was worried about eating animals for food and, now and then, as his meditations on the matter reached a climax, he became a vegetarian and lived on fruit and nuts. His open, homely, moustached face wore an eternally troubled look, as though all the cares of the world rested upon him. Wigg, on the other hand, never read a book, never brooded on a problem, didn't care a damn. Now and then Harkuss would revolt against Wigg's carefree acceptance of existence. He would doubt the virtue of a democracy which allowed the Wiggs of life to vote at all or, turning to a colleague, would say, indicating Wigg, "There 'e goes... Nice, intellekchule specimen, ain't 'e?" And Wigg, taking this as a compliment, would flush with pleasure and tell people that Harkuss was "a cut above an ordinary constable."

When Wigg cheerfully arrived at Beyle, Harkuss groaned. He

liked night-watching alone; he pondered life's problems very deeply in the still, small hours. Now…

Wigg removed his helmet, hung it on the hat-stand and joined his colleague in the kitchen. He carried a small fibre case in his hand and immediately opened it, revealing a large packet of beef sandwiches at which Harkuss glared for it was one of his fruit and nut periods. Furthermore, Wigg had been a father for three months and, to his adoring parent, little Albert Wigg was a phenomenal baby…a comedian too.

"Is there any tea brewed?" asked Wigg, looking anxiously round for the jug.

"No," said Harkuss, who thought tea was slow poison. He drank a beverage called Strength-Oh and had brought a tin with him.

"Never drink tea. Rots your guts. Like to try some o' my Strength-Oh?"

"No, thanks. I think I'll make a brew. Know where there's the needful…?"

Harkuss passed a huge paw airily over a shelf which contained the tinned milk and dry tea as well as a jug and a mug left there by a previous constable on duty.

"Kettle?"

"On the 'ob there… Can't you see it?"

Wigg still smiled broadly, presumably at his own thoughts. He poured the boiling water over his mixture, drew a chair beside that from which Harkuss was keeping an eye on the hall through the open kitchen door and settled himself.

"I laughed…" said Wigg.

It was coming! Every fresh episode in young Albert Wigg's life was prefaced by his father's mirth. "I laughed…" It was the overture to more long tales of infantile wonder.

"I laughed…when I got 'ome last night, there was young Albert sleepin' the sleep o' the just and my wife wet-through. He'd pulled a pint o' milk all over her… She was bending down, like, with him in 'er arms and he…"

PC Harkuss groaned.

"I'd better take a look round," he said and took himself off. He wished the high-ups had left him alone on the job. Now… Well… It looked as if he'd have to wander all over the place all night avoiding Wigg and Albert instead of reading his nature cure papers by the kitchen fire. He couldn't abide the thought of a whole night of Albert's humorous carryings-on; it would drive him off his nut. He paused at the foot of the stairs. The young lady and gent still seemed to be packing. They were hurrying from room to room gathering things… And the old man…he sounded very quiet. Harkuss shuddered as he thought of Uncle Bernard and his rats and bottles. He breathed deeply, counted ten as he did so, held his breath as he counted out fifteen more, and then breathed out in ten jerks. It was the method advocated in "Breath is Life", to which he was addicted. It made him feel buoyant and light-headed.

The telephone rang in the hall. Wigg came from the kitchen at the double.

"All right, all right. I'm 'ere," said Harkuss.

"'Ello… 'ello. Who? Oh, yes… He's in… Jest a minute…"

He carefully laid down the instrument as if it might be brittle and tiptoed up the stairs. The place filled him with a certain amount of awe and he moved here and there reverently.

Alec was strapping up a bag in his room with the door open.

"Wanted on the phone, sir…"

"Who is it? I'm busy…"

PC Harkuss looked coy.

"Young lady, sir."

Alec impatiently got to his feet and ran downstairs.

"Yes…?"

He listened with indifference.

"Is that you, Mr Crake…? Alec…?"

"Yes..."

"Maudie Hankey... You remember me, Alec? The airport bar last September and in your car...?"

Alec took a cigarette from his pocket with one hand and lit it by a similar feat. He looked bored. Maudie Hankey! What a name! She talked as if she had been the only woman in his life.

"I'm engaged, now, Alec..."

"My congratulations... What do you want?"

"You don't sound glad to hear me. And after all that went..."

"I'm busy packing, Maudie. I'm leaving tomorrow."

"Oh, very well. I'll ring off."

"Look here, Maudie. Tell me what it is, that's a good girl. I'm sorry I was a bit rude. I've been through a lot, you know."

He couldn't resist a conquest even over the telephone!

"I've got to go. I managed to slip out... I just wanted to tell you the police have been round at our place askin' questions about *you*..."

Crake turned white and gripped the instrument spasmodically.

"What's that?"

"The police. Mr Doane rang up Mr Kent and Mr Trotman on the day Mr Kent was killed. A policeman... Littlejohn, I think he's called...was here tonight. He knew I was in Trotman & Co's office and wanted to know if the call was from you or Mr Doane. I didn't say anything, Alec. You know me better than that. But as it was about a very good friend of mine, I thought I ought to ring him up and tell him..."

Alec hung up the telephone on her as she spoke. Panic seized him. His head began to throb, and he could not gather his thoughts.

"All right, sir?"

Alec looked blankly at PC Harkuss, rather deflated without his helmet.

"Yes..."

He slowly climbed upstairs, his face growing more evil with each step.

Uncle Bernard was sitting in his room reading a book on salamanders. The fire crackled on the hearth and the soft glow from the oil lamp, which he preferred to electric because it added a touch of shaded mystery to his retreat, fell across his book. Now and then, as some passage pleased him, he grunted with satisfaction and from time to time took a pencil from his pocket and marked it or made a note in a margin.

Suddenly Alec Crake entered. He closed the door after him, turned the key, and stood over his uncle. It was then that Uncle Bernard observed that Alec had a revolver in his hand and that his eyes were wild.

"What is it, Alec?"

"I have no time to talk now. Listen. One cry and I'll shoot. I want the ten thousand in cash my mother gave you for your beastly gold coins…"

"I haven't got it. Shoot away, Alec. Those men downstairs, they'll get you before you reach the door. Shoot, I say…"

"The money! You don't keep a banking account. It's hidden away somewhere here. Tell me, or I'll shoot. I must have it. I've got to go away at once…"

"The police?"

"Yes. Give me the cash and you can have your gold back."

"Never! I'd enough trouble getting rid of that as it was. I had to throw in the ruby crucifix as well…"

"That will do. No more of your talk."

The old man cackled and rubbed his long hands together.

"Shoot, Alec. Your bullets can't hurt me. I'm impregnable."

"I'll give you till I count five. Then I'll shoot and ransack the place for the money."

Alec's eyes were bright and shifty. Drops of sweat shone on his forehead and upper lip.

The old man was enjoying himself. He'd expected this. One by one they would all go. Nick, Dulcie, now Alec, and then Nita. Beyle would be his...

"SHOOT!"

Alec's revolver went off with a roar, and then again until he had emptied the magazine.

Uncle Bernard still sat laughing.

"I knew you for a murderer, Alec. If Kent hadn't killed your mother, you would have done. You killed your uncle. Nita saw you crossing the park at the back, dodging from tree to tree...and she was in the morning room off the hall when it all happened. She's your friend, Alec. She never betrayed you to anyone but me. And I bluffed her into thinking it wasn't you, but Trotman. Do you think I haven't seen you rifling your mother's papers...and then ringing up Kent and Trotman and setting them against one another? I was here when you killed Kent. I found him, my boy. I knew Trotman was hidden somewhere and I knew who killed Kent. And now I'll give you twenty pounds and you can be off."

"Twenty!"

Alec's mouth fell open and then he sprang at the old man and clawed for his neck. Uncle Bernard, wonderfully wiry, rose from his chair with Alec still clinging to him, like an old stag at bay with hounds at his throat. They rocked to and fro, finally stumbled over the rug, fell and overturned the table. The lamp rolled across the floor, struck the wall and exploded into sheets of flame which spread to the curtains and the bed. Soon the room was a holocaust.

"Let me go..."

Uncle Bernard was anxious to be free to save not only his money but the strange paraphernalia in the next room, the purpose of which nobody knew but himself.

The policemen were busy drinking tea and Strength-Oh in the kitchen. The shots had not disturbed them, muffled by the thick walls and distance.

"Sound to be 'ammerin' somethin' up," said Wigg.

"Packin'-case, as likely as not," replied his colleague, carefully measuring out a tablespoonful of his cure-all.

They were quite surprised when, a few minutes later, Nita appeared at the kitchen door, a slight figure in nightdress and dressing gown, with little red slippers on her feet.

"Uncle... His room's on fire. He and Alec are in there and sound to be fighting. The door's locked and I can't make them hear..."

Her dark eyes had grown larger and her black hair, flying, loose and a bit dishevelled, combined with the pure whiteness of her skin and the simple elfin look of her attire gave her a wild beauty and a look of helpless childishness which caused both the bobbies to goggle in astonished admiration.

"Well... *Do* something. The place is burning down, and Uncle and Alec will be burned to death..."

"Come on, Wigg..."

Harkuss rose with a melodramatic gesture like an officer leading a cavalry charge.

The two policemen lumbered out and up the stairs.

The original founder of Beyle had a terror of fire and, to call as much help as possible from the surrounding country to his isolated home in case of an outbreak, he constructed a bell tower on the east gable. The old bell still hung there, rusty and stiff, with a frayed rope hanging from it. It had been restored during the war as an air-raid signal.

Nita, in her little red slippers, ran to the tower and frantically tugged the rope. Littlejohn and Cromwell, speeding to Beyle in the black police car, heard it.

"Sounds like a fire... I'll bet it's at Beyle," said Cromwell. "It only needs the place and all of 'em to go up in smoke and make a spectacular finish..."

"It *is* Beyle..."

They could see the upper storey of the mansion now fully alight. There was mist in the valley again...in Lepers' Hollow...

and the glare of the fire tinged it with red like the demon king's abode in a pantomime.

As the two officers arrived, the wing occupied by Uncle Bernard was fully ablaze and in the distance the bell of the Tilsey fire engine, hurling its way through twisting country roads, could be heard answering the bell at Beyle. Littlejohn and Cromwell met Nita at the front door.

"Uncle and Alec…upstairs, locked in uncle's room…"

They ran aloft side by side. The two constables were struggling to open the door, which resisted their weight. "We can't make it budge. Where's a h'axe…?"

Littlejohn turned to Nita.

"The linen room key?"

She hurried and brought it.

"In panic, I forgot it…"

It was as if the two men inside had been waiting under pressure for release, for, as Littlejohn inserted the key and opened the door, they both ran out. Alec was desperately anxious to kill his uncle on whom, once dead, he might have put the blame for the murders. Furthermore, Alec was now too frenzied to care for anything but the destruction of his antagonist.

Uncle Bernard, hair flying, eyes protruding, was holding in his arms a large glass vessel, clear and iridescent, apparently empty, a kind of retort the shape of a face with inflated cheeks with a spout like an elephant's trunk, protruding from it.

Like two running a race, Alec and Uncle Bernard pattered past the astonished new arrivals, ran up the servants' staircase and could be heard careering through the corridor above. Uncle Bernard's breath came and went in little screams; Alec was grim and silent, intent on his purpose.

Cromwell hurried inside the old man's room as the others followed the two madmen on their wild chase. Five shots sounded from Cromwell's revolver and he reappeared muttering to himself. "Better that than fry…poor little devils." He had shot

Uncle Bernard's menagerie of rats and guinea-pigs. The firemen were below, unrolling hoses, seeking water, getting out their fire-fighting tackle.

Cromwell ran up the further flight of stairs which Littlejohn, the policemen and the two demented men had followed. On the way he met Wigg returning.

"Inspector sent me down to tell the firemen to 'old one of their jump-sheets ready… They gone on the roof… Trapdoor at the top of the ladder at the end of the corridor…"

He cluttered noisily downstairs.

Cromwell followed the directions. Down below you could hear the firemen bringing up their apparatus to the burning wing. The fire had by now burned its way through the ceiling of Uncle Bernard's room and was breaking out in the attic. The glare lit up the sky and as Cromwell reached the roof a strange sight met him.

Uncle Bernard and Alec had crossed the flat gutter which led between the two pepper pot towers and Uncle Bernard, now faced with jumping over the gable end, climbing the slates of the pepper pot, or crawling over the sloping roof into the next gully by a fixed cat-ladder over the slates, had chosen the latter. He was slowly creeping upwards on his hands and knees, followed by Alec.

"Come down, you pair of fools," yelled Littlejohn on their heels. Uncle Bernard seemed inclined to follow the advice but finding his retreat cut off by Alec, kept grimly on…

Cromwell had merely to cross to the next gully by way of the parapet which ran round the building and wait there in the dark for Uncle Bernard to descend. It was easier mounting the high pitch of the roof than descending it and half-way Uncle Bernard missed his footing and slid down the slates into Cromwell's arms.

"Got you!"

Uncle Bernard fought like a tiger for he had not recognised his antagonist. He seemed to think that somehow Alec had taken a short cut…

"Mercy… Mercy…" he breathed hoarsely.

"Come on, now, Mr Doane. That's enough of it. Come down quietly. It's dangerous up here…"

The old man grew limp, and gave in.

"Is it Mr Cromwell…?"

"Yes…"

"I'll come down, but I want my globe. I put it at the corner of the roof for safety. It contains an invisible essence which I have distilled…a food for the sylphs, the spirits of the air, which visit me… My globe…"

Cromwell had no time for Doane's fantastic talk; he could hear scuffling on the other side of the roof. The old man was docile enough and seeking his glass bottle; Cromwell again hurried to the first ridge. Alec, finding his own way barred and Uncle Bernard in safe hands, now turned to his own escape. He stood silhouetted by the firelight high on the sharp edge of the roof, took a few desperate paces along the top and balanced at length, after sliding down the tiles, on the two-foot coping which ran round the house. There, with space before him and Littlejohn and a constable behind, he swayed a minute and then leapt. He gave a wild cry as he fell… The firemen below, breathlessly directed by PC Wigg, caught him in their safety sheet, lowered him to the ground and PC Wigg had him by the collar before he could recover himself. Then Alec raged and tore about like a lunatic. It took Wigg and two firemen to hold him.

"Where's Doane?" asked Littlejohn as Cromwell joined him.

"Hunting for his sprites or something. He says he's got them in a bottle. I left him… He must have gone down."

Uncle Bernard had gone downstairs and, pushing aside the firemen at the door of his room, entered. It was like a furnace.

"My books… My papers… My essences… My rocket…"

"Your what?"

The firemen had followed him and were dragging him out by force.

"Half my life I have fashioned a rocket which would fly out of our tainted atmosphere and return with refined sun essences on which the nymphs and sylphs feed and on which I shall feed myself when I de-materialise…"

The three of them, Uncle Bernard and his fire-fighting captors, were smoke-grimed and sweating. All the first fireman could do was to tap his forehead significantly and look at his pal. Then the pyrotechnics began.

The furnace of flames reached the chemicals of the inner room and one by one ignited them…

Those below were amazed to hear a mighty rushing noise and see, propelled from the window, a large white-hot rocket which swished its way ponderously across the park and into the spinney where it vanished, only to start a fresh conflagration among the dry pine trees which ignited and threw great flames and showers of sparks to heaven. In the alchemist's room wonders had not ceased. Red, green and blue masses of fire, like Bengal lights, began to glow, violent explosions occurred as, one by one, the sealed bottles containing his essences and brews burst, and finally when all had died away, there rose a mighty, dreadful, unbearable heat and a glow like that of a thousand Roman candles. The light grew, seemed to penetrate to the very centre of the house, the floor crashed into the storey below, and the staircase collapsed just as Littlejohn and Cromwell with the firemen reached safety.

"What the 'ell was that?"

"That rocket thing looked like a buzz-bomb to me," said PC Harkuss. "As fer the rest… It's jest past me…"

Uncle Bernard wrung his hands and wept.

"All my apparatus gone…all my chemicals…my spagiric equipment…"

"Your wot?"

"The rocket… The thermite…"

"Thermite?" said Littlejohn.

"I had a large stock for use. I could not afford a furnace… I made diamonds, transmuted base metals into gold… I needed it to get the heat… Where shall I…?"

The police van had arrived, and Littlejohn ordered the prisoner, Uncle Bernard, and Nita to get in. Then, leaving the firemen to the burning shell of Beyle, he steered Cromwell to the little black police car and they followed the van to Tilsey.

Littlejohn and Cromwell laughed at each other in spite of their weariness as, in the wash house at the police station, they stood, a couple of dirty dishevelled wrecks from their roof-climbing adventure.

"They were like a couple of cats," said Littlejohn, vigorously towelling himself. "Before I got on the roof they were climbing about on the slates. Uncle Bernard was terrified to death. Alec must have tried to kill him… Well, let's hear what they've got to say."

Alec, Nita and Doane were waiting, grim and silent, in the office once occupied by Superintendent Simpole. Littlejohn had a strange feeling that something of the dead officer remained there. Simpole's belongings were still in their old places and there was the shortened cord of the window which had not yet been replaced, a grim souvenir of the Superintendent's last act.

Alec and Doane were dirty still from their struggles. Nita, over whose shoulders Littlejohn had flung his overcoat in the grounds at Beyle, was still wearing it. All her clothes were lost in the fire, and someone had gone to try to find her a change from her night attire, her dressing gown and her little red shoes.

"Well…?" said Littlejohn sitting at the desk.

"He tried to kill me. He shot at me with a revolver, but knowing him as a murderer, I took out the bullets and put in blanks this afternoon…"

Uncle Bernard couldn't wait. He wanted Alec putting safely away.

"Why did he want to kill you…?"

Alec remained silent, glaring wildly at his uncle.

"He wanted money from me. He was fleeing from you."

"Why? Why from us?"

"Excuse me, sir," said PC Harkuss. "A young woman rung him up just before all this 'appened."

"Maud, what's her name...Hankey was it, Crake?"

No answer from Alec.

"He killed Kent... Nita knows that," went on Doane eagerly.

Alec at last spoke.

"Liar! You know you killed him yourself. He did it. He wanted my mother's money for himself."

"What do you know about your mother's money?" asked Littlejohn.

"He knows everything. He's been through her papers."

Uncle Bernard was almost dancing with eagerness to convince.

"I heard him telephoning to Trotman and Kent the day Kent died. Just as Maudie whoever-she-is said. Nita knows Alec came creeping home just before Kent was killed and he tried to frame it on Trotman because he hated Trotman for being his father and making him illegitimate... For causing all his troubles and depriving him of Frankie..."

"Frankie!!"

Alec Crake uttered it in a long wail, like the cry of a wounded animal.

"Frankie...! Oh, curse them all. Curse my mother, Trotman... eternal damnation to them all..."

"You killed Kent?" asked Littlejohn.

It was Nita who answered.

"Yes, he did. I saw him cross the park, creeping on all fours like an animal, so that he should not be seen. He went in by the back. I was lying resting on the couch in the morning room. He thought there was nobody about. I wondered what he was doing because from where I lay, looking out of the French window over the spinney, I could see he had a hat in his hand and he never wore a hat himself. Funny what one notices..."

"And then...?"

"Auntie Bee dropped Uncle Arthur at the gate and drove off. Uncle Arthur came in and... He mustn't have given him a chance. He hit him... A little while before I saw Mr Trotman coming over the lawn... I daren't even get up to see what was going on. I was terribly afraid... The house seemed full of evil. Just outside the door...evil going on..."

She began to weep hysterically at her own imaginings.

But Nita had not finished. She looked the same pathetic, childish figure she had seemed to the bobbies at Beyle. Her voice, clear and musical at the best of times, was now hoarse and ominous.

"I kept quiet... Then I told Uncle Bernard. He said what had happened. He said how Alec had tried to rob me of all I had. How he hated my mother in his heart and would have killed her himself in course of time, if she hadn't died before... I still kept silent. He is still my brother...or rather part-brother. Uncle Bernard told me that as well. But when he tried to kill Uncle Bernard tonight, I decided to tell what I knew. You are a murderer, Alec, a cold, heartless, dangerous, crazy murderer... I hope they put you away for life where you can do no more harm..."

"My little Nita..."

Uncle Bernard, apparently overcome by Nita's devotion, was now approaching her in tears, wanting to embrace her.

"Get away! It wasn't because I love you that I hated Alec's trying to kill you. I almost wish he had done. It was because if he had killed you, I would have been the next. I am telling what I know for my own safety..."

She pointed an accusing finger at Uncle Bernard.

"You have caused all the unhappiness in our family. Whenever a spark of trouble appeared, you fanned it into flame. You came between my father and mother. You caused my father's death if the truth were only known. All you wanted was Beyle to hide in. What you hid from I don't know. But you spared nothing to get your way. I despise you. Alec ought to have killed you…"

"Have you all finished now?" asked Littlejohn patiently. "Better take Mr Doane and give him a place to wash, and some tea. Miss Crake needs some clothes… She'll get her death in those night things… Leave Mr Alec… I want him…"

At length they were alone… Littlejohn, Cromwell and Alec.

"Well?" said Littlejohn.

"What do you expect me to say?"

"Nothing, if you don't wish. I must put that formally…Alec Crake…Alexander Crake…I arrest you for the murder of Arthur Kent. You need not make a statement and I warn you that anything you may say…"

"Cut it out… You can't pin this on me… It was Trotman…"

"I warn you that anything you say will be taken down and may be used in evidence…" Littlejohn continued inexorably.

"Could I have a drink?" asked Alec. "I've nothing else to say."

At the next magistrates' court Alec Crake was found guilty of wilful murder and committed to the assizes. There too he was found guilty. During the strain of the trial he broke down completely.

When the clerk at length asked him if he had anything to say before sentence, Alec Crake addressed the judge.

"Of course I'm guilty… What's all the fuss about?"

And he went on to denounce his mother, Trotman and many others, until they led him raving below. He was ordered to be detained during Her Majesty's pleasure by the Home Office, and, whilst the inmate of an asylum for criminal lunatics, he confessed again and again, each time giving the same minute details, which tallied for the most part with those of Littlejohn's report.

Before Littlejohn finally left Tilsey after winding up the case, he was surprised to receive a visit from Mrs Trotman.

"I called to thank you for all you've done," said that pleasant little woman. "But for your understanding and skill, I'm afraid things could have gone hard with my husband."

"Someone else would have found it out, Mrs Trotman. If your husband was innocent, no harm would have come to him."

"You're wrong. Had he been arrested, even to be proved innocent later, it would have killed him. It would have ruined him in Tilsey, and, after all, Tilsey is his life."

Littlejohn knew that. The regard and adulation of Tilsey folk was meat and drink to the vain, pompous lawyer.

"He is very grateful, I can assure you. He couldn't come himself. So I just came..."

That was right too. Trotman would never come and eat humble pie and express gratitude for his safe delivery from disgrace. He'd left it to his gallant little wife to do. "Since this thing was cleared up, my husband has been a new man. Beyle has worried him terribly for years. Kent's disgrace and death and then...the finger of suspicion pointed at him... Now, as I say, he has taken a new lease of life. I wish you could see him now. He is being Father Christmas at a children's party. The annual party for the poor. The Mayor usually takes it, but he's ill with bronchitis. He specially asked my husband and to my surprise he accepted..."

Littlejohn smiled; not, as Mrs Trotman thought, out of joy at Trotman's conversion, but, at the very idea of Mr Scrooge, Trotman suddenly becoming an elephantine Santa Claus for the youngsters.

"He is more like his old self again..."

Remembering Trotman and Dulcie Crake and all the havoc they had caused between them, Littlejohn hoped not!

Uncle Bernard was charged with unlawful vivisection again — a technical charge to hold him pending news from the Spanish police and further inquiries concerning his other mysterious carryings-on. He was granted bail and took rooms in a hotel with Nita, who was very troubled concerning his disposal.

Three days after the fire, PC Harkuss, patrolling the grounds of Beyle, stopped what he thought was a trespassing tramp. The man got violent and Harkuss had to use his truncheon. Later, at the police station, the vagrant turned out to be a sailor, a Spaniard, whose papers were in the name of Juan Casado. A tin box he carried contained over nine thousand pounds in notes.

Casado was unable to explain himself but finally broke down under the ordeal of police questioning through the Spanish master at the local grammar school. He confessed that he had taken the money from the cellars of Beyle. He said it was his own money, stolen from him years before. It seemed he had been travelling between English and South American ports and every time he landed here, he had searched without success for the accomplice who had robbed him more than twenty years ago. Finally, he had seen Bernard Doane's name in a national newspaper in a report on Dulcie Crake's inquest. Casado could read a bit of English, he said, and soon found his way to Tilsey. He had been there three days and let his ship sail without him in his excitement.

As he spoke, the patrol sent to Beyle returned. They had found the body of Uncle Bernard buried in the ruins with a sailor's knife in his back. He must have been rescuing his money from its hiding place in the house and had been followed and set upon by the man he dreaded most.

Casado, his life's ambition to get even with Uncle Bernard fulfilled, seemed quite content, even when they hanged him.

Dulcie, Kent, Simpole, Alec, Uncle Bernard, Casado.

Nicholas Crake, a just man who loved his fellows, would have been dumbfounded by the overwhelming way in which the gods avenged him!

A KNIFE FOR HARRY DODD

GEORGE BELLAIRS

1

TROUBLE AT MON ABRI

Two women were sitting in the drawing room of *Mon Abri,* a small bungalow on the main road between Helstonbury and Brande. The lights were on and you could see inside. They never drew the curtains, thus giving a peep-show for passers-by.

They were obviously mother and daughter. By looking at the old one you could tell what the young one would be like in twenty years' time. They sat there among a lot of modern furniture, pink silk cushions with pink parchment lampshades to match, illuminated by a lot of little lamps instead of one from the ceiling. The old woman was knitting, her back straight, her lips moving, counting the stitches. The younger one was reading a novelette. She had her legs tucked under her in the large chair, and from time to time she helped herself from a box of chocolates on a little table nearby. In the hearth an electric fire glowed; two hot bars and beneath them a lot of illuminated cardboard coal and a fan revolving to make it flicker.

The younger of the two still bore traces of good looks in a lush kind of way. She was small, with large eyes and yellow dyed hair. Her face was round, good-natured and self-indulgent, her figure full and rather attractive for those who liked them that way. A smell of cheap powder hung around her. The way she was sitting showed a good five inches of pink flesh above the top of her stocking. The old woman leaned forward and, with a tightening of the lips, decently adjusted her daughter's dress.

Mrs Nicholls, the old one, was the thinner of the two, a worried-looking woman with a mass of white bobbed hair and always dressed in black. She wore rimless spectacles and seemed to be ever on the alert, as though expecting something to happen at any minute. She knitted interminably. Scarves, jumpers, stockings, gloves, caps. It kept her arthritic finger-joints from stiffening and found her something to do to while away the time.

The radio was going at full blast. A smart comedian cracking jokes and pausing for laughter, which came regularly like a roar created by some monotonous machine. Neither woman heeded the wireless. It provided a background of noise; otherwise it might just as well not have been on.

'Is that the telephone?'

The old woman cocked an ear in the direction of the door. Above the chatter of the comic they could just hear the rhythmic noise of the bell.

'Shut that thing off…'

The younger woman lazily turned and flicked up the knob. The bell kept ringing.

'Hello…'

The old woman's voice grew affected.

'Hello…'

She listened, gingerly laid down the instrument, and returned to the room.

'It's Dodd. He wants you…Quickly, he says…'

She always called him Dodd when he wasn't there. It was her way of showing lack of respect for him. Her daughter, Dorothy, had worked in Dodd's office in Cambridge until six years ago. Then the pair of them had run away together. A terrible scandal, because Dodd had a wife and grown-up children.

The old woman turned her ear in the direction of the hall, trying to hear what was going on.

Dodd hadn't wanted his wife to divorce him, but the family had pushed it through. His son took over the business in which the bulk of his mother's money was invested. He made it pay better than his father did. Harry Dodd was a funny, lackadaisical sort, who liked knocking around in old clothes, free-and-easy, talking and drinking with common people. His family pushed him off in spite of their mother, and the price at which they bought out his shares in the firm was quite enough to keep him.

And then Dodd hadn't married Dorothy Nicholls at all. He'd bought *Mon Abri* in Brande, taken her and her mother to live with him, and started a *ménage á trois*. Dorothy called herself Mrs Dodd in the village. Dodd never objected, but he slept in his own room, a sort of cockloft over the bungalow, and treated his two women like relatives. Dorothy didn't seem to object. Dodd kept her well in funds and was polite to both of them. The old woman felt her presence there gave the union a kind of respectability…

'But you know I can't, yet…'

Dorothy sounded scared.

'All right then…If it's that important. I'll get it out…'

She hung up the receiver and almost ran into the room, her bosom heaving as if she were ready to have a good cry.

'He wants me to take the car and meet him in the village…'

'But…'

'He says he's ill and can't get up the hill. I'll have to try. He sounds bad. I could hardly hear him at the end.'

'But you'll smash it up. You never were any good at it. Didn't you stop learning because you hadn't confidence…?'

'I'll have to try. He might die. I don't know how I'm going to turn round, once we get there…'

'I'm coming with you.'

They hurried to the garage at the side of the house. In the

confusion it took them twice as long to get the door open and light up the drive.

'Where is he?'

'In the phone box at the bottom of the hill.'

Every night Dodd walked down the hill for a drink at the village pub; then he walked back. Sometimes he got in very late, but the women left his supper and went to bed if he wasn't in by eleven. Now it was just after ten.

'I've forgotten how to start it...'

The old woman never tired of talking about when her father had a carriage and pair, but she knew nothing of motor vehicles.

'I've forgotten the ignition key...'

She ran indoors, rummaged in a drawer, found the key, and this time got the engine turning over.

'Don't you have to put the lights on?'

She fumbled with the dashboard again and this time illuminated the whole of the car, inside and out. The head-lights shone full and fair into the road, with moths flitting about in the beams.

Dorothy went through the drill, like a child practising something. It was nearly two years since she had tried to learn to drive. Dodd used the car quite a lot himself and took the women with him now and then. Dorothy had once taken a fancy to driving, but could never pass the tests. Finally, she had abandoned it.

'What if you're caught? You haven't got a licence. It's not fair of Dodd...'

Clutch out, gear in, brake off, accelerate, clutch in...Dorothy ran through the routine and then tried it out.

'I say, it's not fair of Dodd. What if...?'

'Oh, shut up, mother. It's bad enough...'

The car leapt forward, down the drive and into the road with a wide sweep. It was a good job nothing was coming in the other direction. Dorothy was scared about changing gears. She decided to run downhill in bottom. They progressed uncertainly down to the village, Dorothy clinging tightly to the wheel, keeping unsteadily to the left.

The headlamps blinded oncoming traffic and cars began to signal frantically. Dorothy didn't know what it was all about...

Then, near the bottom of the hill, they saw Dodd. He was not a tall man, but now he looked like a little hunchback. His arms swung limply in front of him, his head was bowed, his shoulders sagging. He could hardly put one foot after the other.

Dorothy frenziedly tried to remember how to stop. But before she could act, Dodd had fallen on his face in the road, his arms spread out above his head, his hat in the dust. More by good luck than good management, Dorothy stalled the engine and found the brake in time.

It was only when they picked him up that the pair of them discovered that Dodd had been stabbed in the back. Whimpering, they struggled to get him to his feet, and then they found the blood. All they could think about was how to get him in the car. He was a heavy little man, and they tussled and dragged him between them and finally sat him on the floor. Not another vehicle passed, or else it might have been a different tale. As it was, Dorothy contrived to get the car home by taking a loop road instead of turning, and when they got Dodd to his own fireside, he was dead.

Although the Nicholls women drove Dodd home just before eleven, it wasn't until hours later that they finally did something about it. PC Wilberforce Buckley had long been in bed and was annoyed when they roused him. Dr Vinter, the police surgeon from Helstonbury, who had just retired after a rather hectic night at the Medical Ball, was even more annoyed.

'Why did you put it off till now, Mrs Nicholls?' asked Willie Buckley.

Willie was a young officer whose father had been in the force before him. He was a tall, heavy, red-faced constable, with the beginnings of quite a formidable moustache on his top lip, and heavy black eyebrows, which looked like little moustaches as well He had a comfortable wife and four children. The youngest had started to howl when the telephone rang, and Buckley had left him yelling his head off.

'We didn't realise he was dead…We didn't quite know what to do…It was so sudden, like…'

Frantically Mrs Nicholls tried to find excuses, whilst her daughter, alternately scared by the situation and anxious about the future, wandered from room to room, weeping now and then, with a wet handkerchief screwed tight in a ball in the palm of her hand.

At first, the women hadn't believed Dodd was dead. They had put him in his pyjamas, fixed up his wound with plaster and lint, and put him to bed. Then, they'd realised he had died quietly whilst in their hands. It troubled them, not so much out of affection, although, in a way, it was nice to have him about the place. What bothered them was what was going to happen to them now that supplies were cut off.

Harry Dodd had been a genial enough man, but very self-contained. He never mentioned his family, they never visited him, and the Nicholls pair didn't even know their address, except that it was somewhere in a suburb in Cambridge. He had an only brother, too, somebody well known in politics. Dodd had betrayed that once when Dorothy had found his brother's picture in the paper and had asked Dodd if he were any relation. He had been the image of the man in the paper; you would have said it was Dodd himself. Harry Dodd had grown annoyed and impatient whenever asked about his personal affairs, but Dorothy had looked it up in the reference books at the library, and as Harry and William Dodd were both from Cambridge and had both gone to the same school, she had put two and two together.

The Nicholls women were anxious to know if Harry had left a Will. If he hadn't, it meant they would soon be out of *Mon Abri* without a cent.

'It's not good enough,' said the old woman. 'Here he's died and made no provision for you. And you as good as his wife, and more good to him than his beastly family...'

They started to turn the place upside down to find any documents Dodd might have left behind. He seemed to have had no private papers. A cheque-book—all stubs and no forms—a lot of old sweepstake and lottery tickets, some seed catalogues and a few paid bills were all they could find in his desk, and when they forced open the only locked drawer, they found it full of home-made dry-flies for Dodd's fishing trips. In the loft it was the same, except that there they found a locked trunk which resisted all efforts to open it.

'He's done it on us proper, the rogue,' panted Mrs Nicholls after their fruitless exertions.

'He was good to us while he was with us, mother...'

'Good to us! I like that. Do you know you'll have to find a job again...'

And she started to pace the room muttering, 'I can't believe it', until finally her voice rose to a hysterical shriek and she began to beat the walls in temper.

To tell the truth, Dorothy was standing it better than her mother. At first, taking a man from his wife and family had seemed quite a conquest, especially when he was rich and decent. Somehow she had imagined in those days a life of elegant ease, servants at her beck and call, cruises and the Riviera...All the stuff she read about in the novelettes she gobbled up. But it hadn't turned out that way. How was she to know that Dodd's business really ran on his wife's money? Or that Dodd still loved his wife after his lapse, in spite of the fact that his family wanted to get rid of him and pushed through a divorce? And then Dodd had said nothing about marriage, but taken her on as a kind of housekeeper at *Mon Abri*, where he retired from the world. He'd even suggested she bring her mother along for company!

Dorothy had long been fed-up with it. Dodd had never been

her idea of a romantic lover, but after the divorce, he'd behaved like someone who had done wrong and was anxious to make amends to his former wife. He'd started to treat Dorothy, too, as if he'd wronged *her*! He'd given her all she needed in the way of money, never put anything in the way of her enjoying herself, but had retired with his personal secrets to his bed in the cockloft. It had suffocated Dorothy sitting at *Mon Abri* with her mother when Dodd was out in the evening with his vulgar pals at the local pub, or away for a day or two, fishing somewhere with nobody knew whom. Dorothy was still under forty, romantic, passionate and comely. She wanted a taste of life before she grew like her mother, bitter, querulous and parsimonious. Sooner or later she wouldn't be able to stand the hot-house imprisonment of *Mon Abri,* and Dodd and her mother...She'd kick over the traces and go...Now she was free again, although the way she'd secured her release made her weep for poor Harry Dodd.

'What are we going to do? There's only ten pounds in his wallet. He must have put his remittance in the bank. We can't get that out...'

'Oh, shut up, mother. We can work. I can get a job. I'm not too old...'

'Well, I'm not taking any more lodgers in to please you or anybody else. It's a dirty, mean trick life's played...'

'What are we going to do?'

'What do you mean...?'

'With him...With Harry...?'

They had been too busy wondering how the affair was going to affect them to get in a panic. Now they faced each other in fear.

'He's been stabbed by somebody. Likely as not by one of them Dodds, his family. They always hated him. And here we are, holding the body. It's not fair.'

'We'd better get a doctor, mother.'

'What's the use? He's dead. It's a police job, my girl. But before we get the police in here messing about, we've got to think things out.'

'Police!'

Dorothy hadn't thought of that. She started to cry noisily, tears like glass peas running down her cheeks.

'Shut up! I've got to think.'

The old woman's face was as hard as a rock. She'd had plenty of troubles of her own in her time, and it needed a lot to put her out. Dorothy had inherited her father's amorous propensities. He'd had two girls in the family way on his hands at the same time, and then drowned himself in the canal. There wasn't much Mrs Nicholls didn't know after Nicholls had finished with her.

They turned the house upside down again, looking for the Will, but nothing more came to light except a little diary with a list of investments from which Dodd seemed to derive his income. And they were in the hands of a firm of London solicitors! Mrs Nicholls solemnly took the photograph of Dodd which stood in a silver frame, beaming on Dorothy's bed, flung it across the room, and then followed it and ground it under her heel.

'The swine!'

'We ought to do something...The police ought to know...'

It was three in the morning, Dodd was lying dead in the old woman's bed, and they weren't a bit nearer getting his money.

'Has it dawned on you, my girl, the police might think we did it?'

Dorothy's mouth opened wide and she emitted a loud, high-pitched scream.

'No...No...They know we wouldn't...Besides, why should we?'

'You never know, when the police get about, what they find out, and if they don't find out, they make up. However, there doesn't seem any way out. If we bury him in the garden and keep on drawing his income, it'll mean getting round the bank and them solicitors. It just wouldn't work. And if we ran off, they'd find us, you being too dumb to drive even the car. No, better get in the police. We've done nothin' wrong. They can't say we did it. Who's goin' to do it, you or me? What shall we tell Buckley when he gets here? He'll want to know what we've been doin' all this time with the body.'

'I can't think…'

'You never could. I'd better ring them, and we'll say we didn't know he was dead or the formalities in cases like this. We'll just act dumb. And that won't be difficult for you, my girl. You're never any help…'

But Dorothy didn't seem to hear. She was actually smiling a kind of smug, feline smile at her own thoughts. Freedom and adventure again…

'Well…? What are you smilin' at? Go and phone Buckley at the police station. Just tell him Mr Dodd died suddenly and will he come up. Don't say any more. You hear me? Not another word. Now get goin'…'

Dorothy undulated to the hall. There was a new provocative swing of her hips and her lethargy was gone. Mrs Nicholls suddenly changed her mind and took up the phone before her daughter could get to it. She never knew what Dorothy would say with a man at the other end! She dialled a number, after looking it up in the book. At the police house in Brande the bell began to ring, the dog barked, PC Buckley turned and grunted, and Charles Buckley, aged ten months, awoke and started to howl.

Join the

GEORGE BELLAIRS READERS' CLUB

And get your next George Bellairs Mystery free!

When you sign up, you'll receive:

1. A free classic Bellairs mystery, *Corpses in Enderby*;

2. Details of Bellairs' new publications and the opportunity to get copies in advance of publication; and,

3. The chance to win exclusive prizes in regular competitions.

Interested?

It takes less than a minute to join. Just go to

www.georgebellairs.com

to sign up, and your free eBook will be sent to you.

Made in the USA
Middletown, DE
26 June 2019